George Valentine is a Greek author, actor and musician, as well as the founder of the Millenniumpunk Fiction subgenre.

Born in 1994 and raised in Athens, he was involved with theatrical and music studies from a very young age, graduating from the National Conservatory at the age of 18 as an accordion musician.

Having signed for his first novel in 2019, it came out in 2021 in Greece, titled *Three Dimensions*, marking the beginnings of his career as an author.

In 2022, he graduated from the Culinary Academy of Le Monde as a certified chef, having previously worked for a long time in various positions in different kitchens.

Being in love with discipline and teamwork, he was educated as a reserve army officer, where he expanded his knowledge of war tactics and procedures, something that inspired his later works.

In 2023, the official Millenniumpunk Fiction website was established by George Valentine, after having dedicated the previous years searching for what made nostalgia an important factor in peoples' lives, having himself been affected by nostalgia for the late 1990s and early 2000s.

To my friend and role model, Chrysiida Dimoulidou, who has continued to amaze me with her work and her fighting spirit.

George Valentine

LIGHTS OF THE SHADOWS

AUSTIN MACAULEY PUBLISHERS
LONDON * CAMBRIDGE * NEW YORK * SHARJAH

Copyright © George Valentine 2025

The right of George Valentine to be identified as author of this work has been asserted by the author in accordance with sections 77 and 78 of the Copyright, Designs and Patents Act 1988.

All rights reserved. No part of this publication may be reproduced, stored in a retrieval system, or transmitted in any form or by any means, electronic, mechanical, photocopying, recording, or otherwise, without the prior permission of the publishers.

Any person who commits any unauthorized act in relation to this publication may be liable to criminal prosecution and civil claims for damages.

This is a work of fiction. Names, characters, businesses, places, events, locales, and incidents are either the products of the author's imagination or used in a fictitious manner. Any resemblance to actual persons, living or dead, or actual events is purely coincidental.

A CIP catalogue record for this title is available from the British Library.

ISBN 9781035893003 (Paperback)
ISBN 9781035893010 (ePub e-book)

www.austinmacauley.com

First Published 2025
Austin Macauley Publishers Ltd®
1 Canada Square
Canary Wharf
London
E14 5AA

To my mother, Emily and my father Dimitris: You were always there, supporting me in every step! Thank you for being there anytime I need your advice. Keep being original and, to follow the family moto, "Have faith!"

To author, Miss Chrysiida Dimoulidou: I would like to thank you for supporting me when I published my first book and I would also like to thank you for inspiring me with your own literary work.

If you put good apples into a bad situation, you'll get bad apples.
Philip G. Zimbardo

Prologue

He was walking through an empty square. The scarce light made it difficult for him to see very far, yet he was trying to find a way to leave that place. Buildings lined the streets around the square, and right in the middle, the stairs leading to the subway that remained abandoned and deserted.

It was dawn. At least five hours had passed since he had found himself there, and he could not, for the life of him, find his way back. It had all started with a wrong choice. Of course, everyone makes wrong choices, but his had cost him an entire night.

The decision to follow a scream and run to offer help. Within one night, he had run out of water and found himself wandering through empty streets with no sign of life. All this for a woman's scream that he had never heard since and had no chance of ever hearing again.

He felt exhausted. Perhaps it would be better to rest a little. He had walked quite far from the square and was heading into streets unknown to him. He could now discern more things in the landscape around him. A bit further on, behind apartment buildings and trees, the wheel of a theme park loomed majestically.

Below him, the cobblestone road was still in good condition, although like the rest of the city, it showed signs of abandonment. The streets were filled with cars he had never seen. Not because they were from the 70s, as their body suggested, but because he had never witnessed any such small European car.

The stores had weird letters on them, clearly not Latin alphabet letters but rather letters which he couldn't read. He continued his wandering through the deserted city that looked as if it had appeared out of nowhere inside the forest he was previously wandering in.

Somehow, he had to return to his campsite and find the other campers. Perhaps they were looking for him in case they had woken up and hadn't found him. He felt abandoned and forgotten like the city in which he found himself. A phone booth was a few meters away.

With quick steps, he approached and searched his pockets for coins. After pulling out the necessary amount from his jeans, he quickly turned the phone dial, forming one number. He would try to call the police for help. The dial was covered in moss and stuck from disuse, and several times, he had to exert extra force to turn it.

"Come on, you worthless piece of shit."

Beeep. Beeep. Beeep.

"Come on."

"East District Police Department of Tennessee, what is your emergency?" A woman's voice said.

"I'm in a remote city. I don't know exactly where; I think I'm lost."

"We will try to help you!" The woman replied reassuringly. "Can you describe how you ended up there?"

"I was camping a bit outside Beaverstale Village. In the morning, we were going to take the bus to Savannah."

"Are you still there?" She asked.

"No," he replied, "I heard a shrie—" He hesitated for a moment. Why hadn't she asked him his name at all? Wasn't this what they always did in the movies?

"Are you still there, Sir?"

"Yes! Yes, I strayed a little from the group while we were in the forest. Then, I got lost and found myself in a deserted city. I didn't know who to approach, and there was no one to help me."

"I understand. I will inform the sheriff immediately. Please stay where you are until a rescue team arrives."

"What do you mean? Wait a minute! Are you going to hang up on me?" He asked, feeling his entire body tremble. "Don't you dare hang up on me, you fucking bitch! Do you hear me?"

"Please, calm down!"

The last remark made the man temporarily lose control and start hitting the walls of the phone booth with repeated punches. He couldn't control his movements. It was as if some higher power had possessed him. Like he had suffered an epileptic shock.

Everything around him blurred, and he couldn't count the countless punches that made the phone booth shake with each hit as if an earthquake was happening.

"Sir, are you still there? Are you okay?" He heard just as he began to come to and realized what he had just done.

"Yes, I'm sorry."

He felt a strange presence near him. He turned in all directions. No one! And yet, he felt it. Someone or some people were there, watching his movements.

"I have begun the process for your rescue operation. Until then, please stay where you are, okay?"

He didn't reply.

"It would also be useful if you could find any clue that helps us locate you, such as a street name or even the welcome sign with the name of the city where you are, so you can call us and provide additional information," the woman continued to say.

The man continued to look around him. He was sure he was not alone and that he was not safe. Suddenly, he saw her. A glimmer from the reflection of glass on a roof. Snipers! He couldn't see clearly, and no silhouettes formed, but he was sure.

The glimmers were coming from scopes aimed directly at the phone booth. He quickly ran out and bolted away, leaving the receiver hanging and the woman trying to talk to him.

He ran toward the square. He would quickly enter the station and hide there. It was perhaps the best hiding spot he could imagine. He was casting furtive glances in all directions. There was no one anywhere. Yet, he felt their presence. He was out of breath and felt his mouth now numb and dry.

He was only a few steps away from the subway station, already having crossed most of the square running with all his strength. Suddenly, he felt something burning his eyes. A red flash. A red dot that had just fallen onto his eyes, momentarily blinding him.

He instinctively covered his face with his hands and stood still for a moment, unable to move. Once he regained his senses, he saw at least four similar small red dots moving on his light gray short-sleeved shirt. The dots multiplied. That was when everything around him darkened. His senses were deactivated, they disappeared. He now knew what was happening. He was no longer alive.

One

John Emmerson, Lieutenant Commander of the American Navy SEALS, was in a transport helicopter heading toward a small islet off the Libyan Sea. Early that morning, they had departed from the military base in Souda of Crete for a highly classified mission.

According to the information he and the other two team members had received from their superiors, they were to locate, photograph, and destroy a new secret weapon that was under construction at a base on an artificial island. The way they had identified and gathered information about the military base was somewhat mysterious, but they weren't in the habit of asking for information about things their superiors didn't tell them if it didn't concern them.

Normally, a team would consist of at least four men, but this task force had been more than hastily gathered. Things did not sound or look normal at all, but John was one of the people who knew there was always reason behind everything.

Besides, from the moment he had heard that they were not being backed by the Pentagon, he knew that he and his squad mates were being sent on a mission and their very existence would be denied by everyone should anything happen to them.

After smearing his white, angular face with special black camouflage paint, he covered his cropped black hair with a woolen beanie and checked his night vision goggles, placing them in front of his blue eyes to conceal them.

"Just like the old days, right John?" The muscular man with the large head who sat across from him asked.

"I'm glad to see you're still enjoying our job, Steve," he replied after taking off the goggles and securing them atop his beanie.

"America needs people like us to pull the trigger. You taught me that."

"Yeah, but I'm a bit too old to feel enthusiastic about saving the world, don't you think?"

"I don't know about you, but for me, every day in this job is a new day," he said, turning to the man on their left. "Andy, you'll provide us cover as a sniper."

"Let's hope he doesn't fall asleep again like last time," John muttered quietly.

"Shut up," Andy responded, stretching the words to sound more humorous.

"He wasn't sleeping; it's just that his eyes are so slanted that you can't tell when he's asleep and when he's awake," Steve joked to tease his friend.

"Ha-ha-ha!"

The signal for their jump from the helicopter was given. The large rear door of the Chinook opened, and they stood up from their seats after unbuckling their harnesses, checking their gear one last time.

"Alright, boys, this is where you paid the toll. I'm afraid you'll have to use the inflatable for the rest of the journey to the base," they heard the pilot say through the speakers.

"You heard him, let's go!" John said, securing his harness hook onto the descent line.

The inflatable was already in the water, still tethered to the helicopter's crane, battling the waves. With quick yet careful movements, all three descended, stepping onto the boat, releasing their ropes from their hooks and the inflatable from the crane's large hook.

"We're ready, you can leave!" John said, placing his left hand near the microphone of the earpiece he had put in his left ear to block the wind from falling onto the microphone, complicating their communication.

"Have fun, boys! The destroyer is on its way to pick you up at the rendezvous point once you're done," the pilot told them as the helicopter moved away.

The sun had not yet appeared on the horizon. Without wasting any time, they started the engine and began heading toward the base, John in front, Andy behind him, holding onto his round hat to keep it from being blown away by the wind, and finally, Steve managing the inflatable.

"We're almost there!" John announced. "Shut off the engine and let the boat approach quietly. Remember, we're technically not here."

Suddenly, the light from a spotlight passed over them in an instant. The guards conducted their usual check.

"Do you think they saw us?" Steve asked.

"Shhh! Shut up! Get down and stay still," John whispered in response.

The spotlight continued its path for a little while longer before returning to the spot they had just been, remaining there, illuminating the waves. Luckily for them, the boat had moved far enough ahead, so they could not be detected.

They reached the shore. After making sure the boat was tied up in a spot where the waves wouldn't sweep it away and no one would find it, they started heading toward the base.

They were well-trained. They could infiltrate any area, no matter how well guarded it was. Thus, without being noticed, they stealthily slipped into the camp like felines, searching for the weapon under construction. However, what no one had prepared or informed them about was what was to follow.

As they moved inside a building within the camp, they suddenly heard screams. They approached silently to see the lights flickering on and off due to a power surge. Someone was in the room being interrogated.

"Nobody move!" John ordered quietly, signaling for them to take cover.

Two almost dark-skinned men exited the room, laughing and speaking in a language John and the others could not understand. Probably Egyptian. They wore brown tunics and camouflage pants, red berets, and held Zestava M70 semi—automatic rifles.

They waited for them to move far enough, crossing the corridor in front of them and heading out into the yard through an archway, then proceeded into the room with great caution.

"Steve, check if he's still alive!" John whispered, his hoarse voice a very small sound within the silence of the waves crashing on the shore away from them, pointing to the man who was sitting tied to a wooden chair, his head leaning to one side as saliva dripped from his dried and bloodied lips.

He appeared to be around sixty years old, close to John's age. With short gray hair, almost white, brown eyes, not particularly tall and relatively muscular, the man looked battered. Dried blood covered his thin, fitted, white short-sleeved shirt and his black camouflage pants.

"Welcome!" He rasped with the little strength he had left, while his voice indicated he was a chronic smoker, having enjoyed his fair share of cigars.

"Who's this guy?" Steve asked, confused.

"Oh, great! They've brought me the scouts," the man responded.

"Who are you and what are you doing here?" John asked.

"Calm down, cowboy, I'm one of yours."

"One of ours?" Andy asked, puzzled. "We weren't informed that there would be someone else here, nor of a rescue operation."

"And how do you think you received the information about the existence of the weapon under construction, Einstein? Anyway, we don't have time. I advise you to follow me, and let's get this over with as soon as possible," he said and attempted to stand, but fell to his knees, unable to walk. "Damn it. Does anyone have something to drink?" He said, looking at them pleadingly.

John took out a water canteen and offered it to him.

"I figured as much, scouts," he said, pausing for a moment to look at their uniforms. "You're with the SEALS, right?"

"Yes. And you?" John asked, taking back his canteen after seeing the man was reluctant to drink.

"I'm from another *novel*," he replied. "If they deny your existence on the island once, then they'll deny mine ten times if something goes wrong. Come with me!"

"Okay, let's follow the old man," Steve said.

"The old man gets easily irritated, so if you don't want me to bury you alive, I'd advise you to keep quiet and follow me," he replied.

"What's your name?" John asked.

"Alex, though between us, I'm sure you don't care, just as I don't care about your names. Shut up and follow me."

It took them a little time to reach the underground facilities where the weapon was located, mainly due to Alex, who, because of his condition, couldn't move quickly and was slowing them down, his body badly beaten up. Just before they arrived, Alex collapsed, falling to the floor and groaning, trying to suppress his pain and exhaustion.

"Come on, get up!" John urged him.

"Don't give me orders, kid! Here, take this," he said, handing him a computer diskette he had pulled out from his pants. "The idiots didn't check to see if I'd hidden something in my underwear," he said, laughing.

John hesitantly took the diskette, feeling nauseated, and then helped Alex to his feet.

"We'll finish this together!" He told him.

"Or you could just take the diskette and leave. You have all the data you came for."

"If I'm not being indiscreet, how did you learn about the weapon?" Andy asked.

"Governments in the east and south are becoming dangerous for the rest of the world, especially since the Soviet Union collapsed. From having just one major enemy that we knew and who knew us, we now have dozens, armed with weapons they received from the Soviets while they were in power and thirsty for power. We've been tracking various political leaders' movements for a long time. At least this is what history will be teaching kids in the near future. This is where my story begins."

"Spy?"

"No, but I was sent here along with a team of men, to accompany a spy who had quite a bit of information and needed to be evacuated as soon as possible. The life of a spy isn't as fun as they show in Bond movies."

"So, we need to find one more person before we leave here," John muttered, pensive.

Alex began to laugh.

"He's already got us all out of the trouble," he said. "He's not alive anymore. He was shot just before we reached the point where they were going to pick us up with a helicopter. The western side of the island wasn't well guarded, and it was easy for someone from our side to reach there."

"Security measures have increased dramatically now," John announced to him.

"Yeah, thanks to that idiot. At least he managed to tell me about the diskette."

"How long have you been here?" He asked.

"Days? Hours? I don't even know. That's usually how it goes with interrogations. Hey, did you know that if you start feeling like you can't take it anymore, it's better to just hold your breath and die?"

The four of them stopped talking. The man had clearly lost his mind. Had the island taken its toll on him or was he like that because of his time on the field? John was not a gambler but he could easily put all of his money on the second guess. The man had clearly been interrogated time and again in the past, so much that his eyes could whisper, *I'm enjoying this hell,* to whoever looked at them.

They had now arrived at the area housing the new weapon. Some sort of amphibious tank that could enter the water and move like a ship. It had a light brown to beige color and was huge, like a large destroyer. Two fully equipped

Hind helicopters were tied to it, ready to unleash destruction if deemed necessary.

The behemoth was directly in front of them and below, as they stood on the metal walkway that traversed the sides of the building, connecting one side of the building to the other. A personnel elevator, right in front of them, led to the vehicle and the lower levels of the building, where maintenance of the engine was performed.

"Follow me," Alex said quietly, scaling the small railings of the metal ramp to grab onto the support columns.

"You heard him! We don't have time," John said and followed.

They began descending. Soon, they found themselves on the metal bridge leading to the vehicle's hatch. Two guards were on the vehicle, walking slowly and leisurely. With two shots, Andy pinned them to the ground.

"Don't waste time trying to hide them," Alex said, seeing them lifting the bodies of the guards. "Tell me, how much explosive you have with you?"

"Is this enough for you?" Steve replied, pulling out seven brick-shaped objects covered with film and a mechanism that looked like a calculator stuck to each one from his bag.

"Are you kidding me? With this much C-4, I can demolish an entire block. You three will take care of putting some of this on the tank's treads and fuel tanks. Just give me one of these to place inside, so we don't waste time."

"Wait!" John told him, giving his handgun at him. "Take this. You'll need it."

"Thanks for the thought," Alex replied, moving toward the hatch to enter the vehicle. "Set the timer for six minutes!"

It was left to the three of them. With quick and methodical movements and avoiding the three guards on the lower floor, they placed the rest of the explosives and headed back toward the spot they had left Alex, using the support columns to climb up without using the elevator and making noise.

"Fortunately, you didn't delay me," he told them as he started climbing one of the columns.

The others followed him. Two minutes later, they had exited the building and were heading toward a hangar to take cover from the explosion. Alex began laughing.

"What's wrong?" Steve asked, confused.

"They're so stupid! That's what's wrong."

Steve didn't reply.

"They failed to find the explosives I had already placed in the engine room before they caught me. Now, all that's left is—"

The explosion was so loud that it shook the entire camp, and for a moment, the lights flickered. The vehicle had surely been blown to bits, judging by the sight of the building it was housed in, as well as the neighboring buildings.

"That's called professional sabotage!" He said loudly.

Within minutes, the guards had surrounded the destroyed building while some of them searched for the intruders as the four of them ran toward the inflatable boat. It wasn't long before gunfire erupted, a moment after one of the guards shouted something loudly that the four of them didn't understand, and the others drew closer, starting to shoot wildly.

"Fire a few shots for cover!" John ordered, beginning to return fire.

Steve grabbed his machine gun and started shooting non-stop at the guards.

"I'll call for reinforcements on the radio," Andy said.

They ran toward the boat, trying to avoid slipping on the rocks while attempting to take cover and occasionally return fire. Andy yelled into the radio, trying to call for reinforcements while Steve shot at the enemies. The guards retaliated with gunfire and wayward grenades, but it was enough to cause confusion and force the four of them to stay in constant vigilance before each move.

"Hurry up with the boat, before I run out of ammo!"

The others did as fast as they could to untie the boat, launch it into the water, and let Steve know to run and get on. Seconds after they had boarded the boat and moved away, two planes flew overhead, engulfing the island in flames after unleashing a series of air-to-ground bombs that obliterated everything in their path.

"Wolf to Den, we have completed our mission and are heading to the rendezvous point. Ensure the birds cover us while we float. Over!" Andy said, looking at the others with a satisfied smile forming on his face.

"Den to Wolf. We're waiting for you. Over!"

"We're bringing you an old friend."

"That's good news, Wolf! We look forward to your arrival. Over and out!"

The four of them floated away, leaving the island and everything on it engulfed in flames. Returning to their homeland, they would have to avoid mentioning the slightest detail to their families. This was one of the strictest rules to which they were forced to comply.

Even though no one would ever believe them if they mentioned everything they witnessed whenever they were on the battlefield. Those were the little everyday moments they kept to themselves, and only they had the right to know and remember.

All memories within the brain, like film inside an old VHS tape that would always play, no matter the noise it would end up adding to the image during the years, due to its age.

Two

"Mom, there's no way I'm taking that ugly sweater with me where we're going! Don't insist."

"Leah, my dear, please! Your dad's mom will be so happy to see you wearing the sweater she made for you."

"Great, a runway in Grandma's exotic living room and an after-party in the kitchen drinking orange juice and eating cherry pie. On the decks, Uncle Melvin. What a blast!"

"Leah!"

Leah Emerson, daughter of John Emerson, was in her room on the second floor of a small typical wooden house in Columbia, South Carolina. The room was a large square space with wooden walls, where the light blue color had almost faded from the countless posters of bands and artists, such as Aerosmith, Nirvana, Green Day, the Prodigy, and a very old giant poster of the Rolling Stones that covered every part of the walls, giving a more youthful and rebellious tone to the room.

The wooden floor, which was usually covered with a thin white carpet in winter (for the past two years, Leah Tracy Emerson had replaced it with a red one to match her tastes) was now bare due to summer, with some rock and punk culture magazines having escaped from their hiding place under her bed at the back of the room, opposite and to the left of the white door and below shelves full of cassette tapes she had bought with her pocket money from her grades over the past two years and some small records that she had paid dearly for although they had become cheaper in recent years.

Initially, when they first came out, and a friend of hers wanted to get a CD player, as she'd put it, she thought it was some kind of doll that would make sounds and behave somewhat humanly and that it was named Cindy, like the Barbie doll she hated. So, arriving at the store and seeing the CDs for the first time, she felt grateful that sometimes, she kept her constant thoughts to herself.

Next to her bed was her desk. A small wooden desk, somewhat worn from the years, with schoolbooks neatly stacked in fives, and in the middle, two pens, so she could keep writing in case one of the two ran out of ink. Directly opposite was a large dark brown wooden wardrobe full of clothes and of course, it was also Leah's hiding place for the bulky television and an Atari console that she had bought just a year ago.

On the bed lay a jet-black suitcase full of clothes, shoes, and cosmetics, and right beside it, her grandmother's sweater. A bulky gray wool cardigan with colorful patterns reminiscent of children's woolen clothes from the 50s, sewn with special care and passion—something that Leah obviously ignored since she believed that for a simple trip to the countryside, it was unnecessary.

"I'm not dressing like a clown," Leah said defiantly.

Her mother sighed and looked at her daughter, who had changed far too much in recent years. The little girl with long hair and a calm, chubby child's face had now been replaced by an angry teen with black hair, glued back with limitless gel in large threatening spikes that resembled a porcupine's quills.

"Please, sweetie, try to understand. Your grandmother would be so happy to see you wearing something she made for you. I know you don't like it because you don't think it fits your style, but you won't be there for many days."

"Fine, fine!" She said reluctantly and headed out of her room.

"Where are you off to?" Her mother asked, puzzled.

"We leave in the morning, right? I'm going to Clara's for a movie."

A movie at Clara's house. Clara was her neighbor and classmate and hung out with her best friend, Victoria, who would not be with them that night as she was several miles away on vacation.

However, other people would definitely come to Clara's house, like Mike, known as the class heartthrob, as his straight hair with bangs and a middle part, his bright blue eyes, and his perfect white smile were ways for him to easily become number one on every classmate's list in high school.

A way, because other ways he caught attention were the fact that he played on the school rugby team and had that shiny red Honda CBR. Leah, of course, hated Mike, as she considered him a jock, but Clara liked him, so there was nothing she could do but tolerate him.

Then, there was Mary, the class know-it-all, but particularly likable to everyone, and despite studying constantly, she made sure to take care of herself, leaving no room for the others to call her a nerd, although she still called herself that for self-mockery.

If she showed up, Jim, her boyfriend, would surely come too. Strangely, Jim wasn't very good at studying but preferred skipping class, all-nighters, and of course, he was the one who brought the forbidden substances to the parties, and of course, not alcohol, which they could find anywhere. She sighed just at the thought of the possible combinations of who might be at Clara's house and headed to the bathroom.

The art for a successful makeup was a ritual before any outing. Usually, it involved placing emphasis on the pencil around the eyes to highlight their intense brown color and some dark lipstick, creating symmetry with the eyes and forming a triangle. Little secrets she didn't share with anyone.

After she was done, she returned to her room to choose her clothes. The choices she had were countless, but after some thoughts and combinations she made in her head, she chose a black very short skirt with chains and a bullet belt all around, and a silver animal skull at the waist, a fitted short-sleeved red shirt with a syringe with some green liquid printed in the center, with the syringe being deliberately drawn clumsily, like those in cartoons, so that it looked funny, and right below it written in black letters haphazardly, making them look like they were written with some dripping liquid: 'Shall I treat you to a shot?'

And just above the shirt, she put on a black denim vest, white and red striped knee-high socks that emphasized her tall stature. Exiting her room, she grabbed her favorite red All Stars and after tying their laces, she quickly descended the wooden stairs that led down to the living room.

Her father was sitting on the couch, watching the news from television with interest, sipping a beer.

"The television of Saudi Arabia posted photos from Kuwait today, filming the aftermath of Iraq's invasion of that country," said the woman presenting the news bulletin.

"Anything interesting?" John asked as she approached the couch. "They'll probably need me soon," he replied in his deep, raspy voice.

"That's bad," Leah stated.

"Um," he replied absently and took another sip from the bottle. "At least we'll have money for the house and the bills since I'll have a job, other than being retired and only training self-defense techniques to people for peanuts as most of them are living on their pension," he said, looking her in the eye.

He kept staring at her like that for a moment.

"Let me guess, you want money?" He asked, and his straight smile barely showed beneath his thin lips as he half-closed his blue eyes with an examining look and raised his left eyebrow.

"You guessed it!" She replied, giving him a thumbs-up with her left hand and winking at him.

"You're going to be late."

"Since when you care?"

"I just asked because Lisa won't be coming with us on the trip, due to her job."

"Dad, I'll see Mom, don't worry! Besides, I was just with her a moment ago."

"Okay, okay! You're the boss," he told her and handed her the money that had been resting on the table.

"Thank you so much, Daddy!" She said enthusiastically and kissed him on the cheek.

"We leave at eleven in the morning!" He told her in a stern tone, just as she reached the door.

"Yes, sir, Sergeant!" She said, saluting him military-style and hurrying out of the house, calling him a *sergeant* as she could never truly memorize his rank.

"Kids." He sighed thoughtfully, hunched over on the couch, no longer paying attention to the EEN news.

Clara's house was a few blocks away from hers, so she had to cross a straight line of identical one or two-story houses until she reached her friend's home. Upon arriving, she knocked on the door and waited until they opened it. Clara, a medium-height blonde girl with perpetually flushed cheeks, opened the door and pulled her inside.

"I'm so glad you finally decided to come! Ever since Victoria left, you don't usually go out much."

"Columbia isn't the same without my best friend," she replied. "But I do have other friends, and I'm grateful for that."

She stared at her intensely for a moment, trying with her look to ask, 'Hey, psst, who's inside?' But Clara didn't understand and began walking toward the living room, talking non-stop and telling her about everything that had happened throughout the week.

She felt awful. Only with Victoria could she communicate silently and completely understand each other. Just before they entered the living room, Clara took off her huge round glasses, and her green eyes, which a moment earlier had been like little dots behind the glasses, appeared. Mike was definitely inside; otherwise, she wouldn't bother to hide her glasses.

She always hid them whenever he was around, to look pretty. She sighed just at the thought of Mike being with them, and swallowing this thought, she walked into the living room with her head held high, greeting everyone. They were all there. Mike, Mary, Jim, and finally, Sean and Jennifer, who was glued to Sean, even if he hadn't realized it yet.

"Hi!" She managed to say.

They greeted her with a smile. She sat down next to Jennifer, whose coppery red hair had grown quite a bit, reaching her waist. Jennifer looked at her with her unnaturally bright green eyes piercing through her as if trying to see into her soul. That always made her feel uncomfortable, and combined with her dark skin tone, it was a frightening sight, but to a large extent, she had gotten used to it.

"Are you coming with me to be cheerleaders next year?" She asked her.

"Cheerleader. Yeah, look Jennifer. I don't think that's a good idea," Leah replied.

"Of course, it is; you meet all the standards. Okay, maybe your hair needs a little improvement, and you'll be all set."

"What's wrong with my hair?" She asked, puzzled, touching one of the spikes with her left hand.

"Well, we'll talk about it when the time comes," Jennifer said, leaning on Sean's shoulder who was next to her.

He looked shocked and stared at her awkwardly. Leah watched them, smiling. She thought they suited each other and visually made a perfect contrast as he had dark skin, and she looked white as a sheet.

"I rented some tapes for us to watch, since none of you felt like going to the theater to see *Robocop*," Clara told them, showing them the boxes of the tapes.

"Obviously, we're all saving our cash and appetite to go watch the *Predator 2* when it hits theaters," Jim replied.

"Ugh!" Clara said, turning her back to him.

"*Predator* is okay," Leah said quietly.

"Whatever you say, it's a quality movies night! I brought *Batman, Indiana Jones*, and *Karate Kid*. Which one will we watch first?"

***

She returned home around three in the morning. Her parents were asleep. In the fridge, there was chicken with fries, but she had already eaten enough pizza at Clara's house, surpassing her previous record, having devoured two whole spicy pizzas with twelve slices each and leaving everyone wondering how such a skinny person could consume so much food.

She went to her room and grabbed the black phone sitting on her desk, stretching the cord enough to lie on her back in bed without needing to sit up or on the desk chair.

With an irritated grunt, she got up again to find the paper with the number Victoria had given her on the phone, so she could call her while on vacation. After dialing the number, she lay back down and waited. On the other end, a continuous screeching sounded, like a compressor.

"Yo, who's this?" A heavy, youthful voice came through.

"Can you get Victoria for me, please?" She said insistently, not in the mood to start a conversation with a stranger.

"Ah, yeah," he replied with a tone of boredom. "Vic, your mom is on the phone. You all lower the music, you dimwits, she'll figure out you didn't go to her aunt's house."

Her laughter came spontaneously and effortlessly, but she tried not to let them hear it.

"Yeah?" Victoria said hesitantly on the other end.

"It's me, this idiot mistook me for your mother."

They both laughed.

"Where are you, who's this guy, and what the hell is all this noise?"

"Ah, it's a guy. I'm at home in Beverly Hills. We were listening to music with his group, and from what I gathered from the introductions, it's his whole school that he invited over, and we were chilling."

"It sounds like the guy has been drinking like a fish," Leah said, laughing.

"No wonder he keeps going to the bartender to have him mix drinks. I get the feeling the bartender would very much like to splash him with vodka and set him on fire judging by the look on his face."

"Yeah. I still can't understand how you convinced your parents that your aunt changed her number and invited you."

"The first part was easy. Plus, since Mom is on bad terms with her sister, it was easy for her to believe that whenever Aunt calls, she's not home, which she interprets as her avoiding speaking to her, even just politely. As for the second part, let's just say I'm glad I'm good at forging letters. How do you think I escape all these years with all the school letters for my absences that my parents have to sign?" She said proudly.

"Sometimes, you're unbelievable," she remarked, astonished.

"And you haven't heard the best part yet!" She replied with enthusiasm, "Thanks to my ability to persuade people, I landed a role in a movie. When the producer finds out that the director kicked out all the other candidates and gave the role to me, he's going to start chewing on his clothes, but it will pass once he sees I'm a born actress."

A shrill laugh escaped Leah's mouth.

"Incredible! Within a week of vacation, you've turned Los Angeles upside down."

"No way, I'm serious!"

"Do you still have the phone number of my grandmother's house?" She suddenly asked.

"Supposedly? Not that I remember. I'll check my planner tomorrow."

"Okay, I'll take the paper with the number with me, so I can call you from there, just in case."

"Convenient."

Suddenly, a horrible crash was heard from the other line.

"What was that? Are you okay?" Leah asked, alarmed.

"Oh, nothing! One of the guests passed out from too much drinking and fell onto the glass coffee table. Dude, this house is massive!"

"Look, I better get going. I have a trip in the morning," she told her, thinking that perhaps she would ruin the fun.

"Call me as soon as you arrive! I hope I wake up."

"Agreed."

She lay staring at the ceiling for a while. As a child, she used to stare at it for hours until she fell asleep, but this habit had started to become increasingly rare. Eventually, she sat up, took off her shoes and clothes, putting on a long yellow shirt with the figure of Super Mario printed on it and comfortable gray shorts, and fell on the bed to almost immediately drift off to sleep. She woke up several hours later, exhausted, feeling as if she hadn't slept at all, to prepare and start her journey.

Three

They were in her father's car, a well-polished dark blue Buick Regal Coupe that he had bought the same year, just a few days after its release. She was wearing a black short-sleeve blouse beneath a denim vest adorned with rips, a few spiked bracelets, a comfortable pair of torn jeans, and tall boots, which were not at all convenient for the length of time she was in the car.

She was constantly trying to adjust herself in the seat without ruining the spikes in her hair, which she had painstakingly secured with gel. Her father preferred more comfortable clothes, wearing a black short-sleeve shirt with the buttons of his chest open and a classic pair of jeans, which he had perfectly matched with a pair of black suede shoes with bright white soles. They had started their journey an hour earlier, although traffic was unbearable and holding them back.

They were headed toward Sorterville, Alabama, a small town with very few residents, where her grandmother and uncles from her father's side lived. John had been looking forward to this moment for a while, as he couldn't wait to arrive in the town and go fishing with his siblings and their families at the river.

Leah wasn't particularly excited about the family gathering idea, but after nothing else, a few days' escape to nature would do her good. They were following Interstate 20, trailing an endless line of vehicles moving along it like a giant centipede.

"What is that we're listening to?" He asked, puzzled about the music she had chosen from her cassette tapes, which she had carried along in a special case with slots.

"Trance!" Leah replied enthusiastically.

"Trance? Like the grease from those cool snacks, you eat at parties?" He asked, bewildered.

"Trance, like the state of ecstasy," she answered, laughing. "It's a new kind of music that's part of an expression movement."

"I've never heard that before! I feel a bit old at times," he told her. "Have you been listening to this genre for long?"

"A month ago, a guy from Holland brought us some cassettes."

"Us?"

"Me and Victoria. We met him randomly in a bar."

"I used to meet people in a similar way, randomly," he said, as if reminiscing about his younger years.

"Do you want me to change it?" She asked him, wondering if he didn't like it.

"No, it sounds good. Trance."

A few miles later, and after they had made a half-hour stop at a rest area to refuel the car and grab a snack at McDonald's, one of the cassette tapes Leah had brought had stopped, and it was John's turn to choose the music. She handed him her cassette case for him to select.

"What will you choose, I wonder?"

"You know me. I may not be particularly aware of these new music trends you listen to, but I'm the one who taught you to listen to good music," he told her as he placed a rock music cassette from the 70s into the deck.

Traffic was still heavy, meaning they hadn't covered much distance since leaving Columbia behind. Occasionally, John managed to pass the cars in front of him, but most of the time, he was forced to follow the vast mass of cars ahead. The sky hinted at a storm, as the sun hadn't shown itself much since morning.

For about half an hour, they continued moving slowly, traversing the highway and literally stuck behind a red GMC jeep, and to their left, a truck carrying a long shiny oil tanker trailer. The median that had been filled with trees a few miles back was now giving way to metal barriers, while vast fields fenced off with tractors or cows appeared sporadically on the left and right of the road.

Behind them, three vehicles were constantly vying to get ahead, passing each other all the time. A motorhome, a silver Subaru Legacy, and a pitch-black Eagle Talon with a pair of college kids, a slim and well-built boy with white skin, light eyes, and straight hair split in the middle, dressed in a gray tank top and constantly had his arm hanging out the window, next to him a smiling blonde girl who was nestled against his shoulder as he drove.

She wondered when she would also get her driver's license, so she could go on vacations wherever and whenever she wanted. Maybe next year, she could persuade John to take her to a driving school and teach her some basics himself.

Eventually, she might end up with a spacious station wagon, probably a Ford Taurus, traveling all over the United States with her friends, loading it with tents, food, a grill, and sleeping bags, camping wherever they found a place. Perhaps these would be the dream vacations she had been envisioning for years.

The cassette player continued to play music. Now, they were listening to *Gimme Shelter* by the Rolling Stones, as the clouds thickened above them.

"At the next stop, let's call your mom, so she won't worry," he said, showing her his watch. They were about an hour behind schedule.

"It's a shame she couldn't come," she replied.

"Next Christmas, on her leave, we'll go on vacation together. I was thinking Las Vegas. I don't know if it's a good choice though."

"No, that's fine. Las Vegas is okay."

They continued for a little while longer until the traffic became increasingly slow. The sky darkened even more as the clouds now covered almost every part of the horizon.

They stopped. No cars were moving in front of them. It wasn't long before the angry horns of vehicles were heard, with drivers exchanging curses and threats, while some had gotten out of their cars to see what was happening.

"An accident must have happened. There's no other explanation," John muttered.

"Great. That's just what we needed."

They waited for a few minutes until the tension made her father unable to stay cooped up in the car any longer. He looked in the mirror to make sure no motorcycle was passing by and opened the door slightly.

"Wait here!" He told her.

He remained still, staring at the spectacle as soon as he stepped out of the car, while at the same moment, the truck to their left had just started to turn around to move, probably from a smaller road, as the opposite lane was completely empty, something they couldn't notice before.

Time suddenly slowed down. Like a scene of suspense from an action movie, where all sounds, even the music, became distant and almost hollow, and the only thing that could be heard loudly was the thud of his heart, which grew louder and faster.

A breeze made her father's shirt begin to flutter like a sail from a ship in the storm. The cars behind them wasted no time and rushed with screeching tires to close the gap that had formed. His face turned pale as he caught sight of the spectacle happening some distance away.

It was at least two to three miles away, but he could see it clearly. A massive tornado from their left was rapidly approaching the road, moving north. That was the reason the traffic had stopped. Voices rose from various directions.

"Oh my God!"

"Quick, get Lacey out of the car, and let's go!"

"Calm down! The tornado is far away and not heading toward us."

"Dear God, what is that?"

Time began to take on its normal proportions again, and suddenly, everything was as it had been before. The sky flashed several times, and then thunder was heard, but no drops fell. Not where they were, at least. That was when Leah realized that time was moving normally and that in her anxiousness, she had forgotten to breathe all this time, resulting in her now breathing quickly and heavily.

"We're leaving here," her father said, hastily getting back into the car and slamming the door shut.

"No objections," she replied with her eyes still wide open.

They started to turn around, following the lead of the truck driver. Some drivers mimicked their example and started their engines to follow them. She watched, glued to the window, as the tornado now crossed the road and headed north.

A large passenger Boeing 747 flew dangerously close to the tornado, causing its left engines to fail and it began losing altitude, leaving a trail of smoke until it crashed to the ground, and the field where it crashed was engulfed in flames. Screams and cries erupted, followed by deafening booms from the explosions in vehicles that were swept up by the aircraft and from the engines of its right wing.

She turned toward him, her breathless state making it feel as if her voice had gone lost. Her throat felt dry and scratchy, and her breath was rapid, just like her pulse.

"Did you see that? I didn't imagine it. You saw it, right?" She began anxiously.

"Yeah, I saw it," he replied as calmly as he could.

"Oh damn! Oh damn! I can't believe it, it's impossible!"

"I'm sorry, Leah, but it happened."

They remained silent for a moment. Behind them, she could make out in the mirror some drivers following them, believing that if they turned around and looked for another road, they might still be able to reach their destination, or simply fearing the tornado might cause more accidents. Only when they had moved far enough, did she decide to speak to him.

"Where exactly are we going?"

"There's an intersection about a mile from where we are. I don't know the road, but with a bit of luck and help from the locals, we might reach our destination without further surprises," he told her.

"Hopefully!" She exclaimed.

She was still in shock from what had happened and seemed uncomfortable. She was thinking how lucky they were to not be at the plane's crash site. Silence prevailed in the car, and neither dared to utter a word. What had happened was definitely horrifying, and the mere thought that they could have been in those people's shoes sent chills down their spines.

About twenty minutes of silence passed, during which she stared out the window while he drove silently. Finally, he decided to speak to her. He would tell her about something that had happened to him on one of his missions. The truth was that he encountered such scenes daily at work.

People—enemies or allies, armed or civilian—being torn apart, mothers engulfed in flames in their attempt to rescue their child from a house that had caught fire from a bomb that had fallen on a nearby building filled with armed soldiers, friends dying in his arms, and children getting shot for holding a weapon, fighting a war of someone superior who had forced them, giving them drugs and indoctrinating them to recruit them for his camp.

It was hard to remember every night in his sleep the harsh scenes of all he had lived through, yet he had learned to face it with composure. He sacrificed himself so that his daughter and so many other children in his country and allied countries could live freely without the fear of death.

"You know, once I happened to be on a plane that crashed. It's been at least four years since then, but it was a very terrifying experience."

"You never told us that," she replied, looking at him suspiciously.

"There's a lot you don't know about my job, and you shouldn't learn," he replied, pretending to sound stern. "Well. Previous job, since I've been off duty after they decided I was too old to be involved with the special ops."

"Or that's the official story you keep telling us for the last four years, each time they put you off duty for reasons you can't share with us."

She laughed, seeing him trying to maintain the serious expression that had formed on his face, and he followed suit, playfully shoving her. Although he actually had things that he needed to keep secret from his family, it seemed funny to him that when they figured out or suspected certain things, he pretended—not at all convincingly, since he couldn't hide it from his own family—that they didn't know anything.

"You're not going to tell Mom, right?"

"Let me think," she said, looking at the ceiling of the car, placing her right-hand index finger on her cheek as if contemplating and letting out a grunt to dramatize the situation. "If you buy me a Game Boy for Christmas, then it's a deal!" She said with a smile.

He looked at her with a look that meant he didn't quite understand what she was asking for, as his eyes had widened, his eyebrows raised, and his lips slightly drawn down, making him look like a frog.

"Wouldn't it be better to ask your boyfriend for that if you plan to use weird gadgets? Romantic that you're waiting until Christmas though. Sounds sweet."

"Dad," she said in a serious and calm tone of voice, trying not to laugh. "It's not what you think. It's a gaming console. Like the one I have in the closet, but smaller, portable."

"Portable Tetris. The second time today that this kid makes me feel like a grandpa."

She settled comfortably into the beige leather seat of the car with a triumphant smile on her face. The cassette had now stopped, but neither of them had realized it. They were heading south, following a small side road. As far as John knew, there was some highway around there, possibly parallel to their route. He hoped to find a local to ask which way they should head if they wanted to reach Sorterville.

They stopped in a field for five minutes. Leah, thirsty, decided to drink some water from the bottle that was in her backpack on the back seat. John returned shortly after, wearing a childish, almost triumphant smile on his face.

"You found the way!" She said confidently.

"No, but I stretched my legs."

"Ah," she replied, sulking.

"I'll look at the map," he told her and opened the trunk to take out a backpack. He quickly unbuttoned the protective cover and pulled out a large folded shiny paper, which he unfolded to reveal the map.

He stared at it for a long time, but he couldn't figure out where they were. From time to time, he glanced to his left and right, hoping to see a sign with the road number they were on. Nothing. They were two travelers lost on a narrow, poorly maintained road filled with potholes and cracks.

"It would help if there was at least one sign around here. Did you notice any while we were coming?"

"Not a single one," she replied.

"Damn."

They decided to continue on their way. Turning back was pointless. The road was certainly closed due to the accident, and even if it weren't, they would need at least another hour to get back to Interstate 20. For quite a while, they moved between scattered vast fields with no signs of life, save for a few wooden houses, one in each field that seemed too far away to approach.

The road remained narrow. Cracks appeared intermittently, indicating that the road hadn't been repaired in a long time. At least the traffic was minimal to nonexistent at that point, as they hadn't encountered nearly any car on the entire trip.

Arriving at a gas and water stop, they learned from the locals that the only road that could lead them to their destination was several miles further south, and that the road they had chosen wasn't the shortest one.

Four

Leah and John were heading south to reach the nearest crossroads, from where they could ultimately continue west toward Sorterville. On the radio, for the past few minutes, a report about the plane crash and the tornado that was now heading north-west was playing.

It was raining. Not too heavily. The dull, almost straight, narrow, and poorly maintained road had now given way to an equally narrow but relatively well-maintained road with freshly paved asphalt, with yellow lines running through a forest, many times resembling a snake zigzagging to avoid the fir trees.

At certain sections of the road, they could discern fields and several scattered houses to their right as they crossed the edge of a cliff. There were many times when the road ended on the left or the right in a steep drop, with warning barriers appearing, trying to prevent a possible accident.

Then, the forest thickened and rose higher and higher until it reached about a foot and a half above the road they were crossing, nearly covering the sky. The rain had stopped now, except for a few drops still falling, while the wet asphalt glistened. Fallen leaves from oaks, firs, and other trees had fallen onto the road and had stuck due to the rain.

Unable to bear listening to the journalists' necrologies, who were trying to be as dramatic as possible to make the listeners unwittingly cling to their radios, anxiously listening to the chilling details describing the accident site, John decided to change the station, but he couldn't find anything worthwhile.

After a few failed attempts, he turned off the radio completely. Leah decided to take out her cassette player from her pocket, connect it to the headphones she had in her bag, and listen to one of her favorite cassettes.

The landscape around them was certainly beautiful. There wasn't a part of the forest, apart from the point where the road passed, that wasn't covered with dense vegetation. Squirrels, hedgehogs, raccoons, and other small animals often appeared, running between the trees or hastily crossing the road.

Both of them had begun to relax and try to forget what had happened earlier. No other cars were on the road, allowing them to drive a little faster than the speed limit. The road they were on was not new, according to the information they had received from the man with the big gray beard at the gas station when they had stopped there earlier.

Usually, no one chose it, as it was one of the most time-consuming roads, resulting in it being nicknamed the road of isolation by the locals. A rather melancholic title for a road. From there, they would cross a small, almost unknown settlement, the name of which they had never heard before: Beaverstale Village.

Just by hearing the name of the settlement, John believed that the guy giving him directions was making up everything he was telling him, truly not knowing how they would soon reach their destination, not even the surrounding area. Yet, everything he said was delivered with excessive confidence. In fact, he advised him to try fishing sometime at Casey Lake, a few meters south of the village, or to swim in its healing waters.

A deafening noise suddenly disrupted their peace as the car began to move uncontrollably. John gripped the steering wheel with all his strength, trying to keep the car moving straight, and abruptly pulled the handbrake. They had stopped, and more importantly, they were safe and unharmed.

"Damn it!" John shouted irritably and got out of the car. She mimicked him and after unbuckling her seatbelt, she exited the car to follow him.

The back left tire had burst. They had probably run over a sharp object that had caused the tire damage. He moved toward the trunk to open it. After taking out some luggage and placing it aside, he found what he was looking for; a spare tire and a jack to temporarily change the damaged tire.

"We're lucky I've never taken it out of the car," he said to her as he moved toward the driver's seat. "Stay to the side. I'll move the vehicle to avoid any accidents."

She climbed up a little hill on the right side of the road and waited for him. After a while, he brought the car close to her and got out to change the tire. She offered to help him, but he refused, wanting to handle it himself, having gotten annoyed with himself for not noticing the sharp object on the road. With quick motions, he lifted the back left side of the car with the help of the jack and took a wrench in his hands, starting to nervously unscrew the bolts.

"I won't be long," he told her hurriedly.

Suddenly, she felt discomfort. Several hours had passed, and she could no longer hold it. She looked back toward the forest. Beyond a few small animals that occasionally showed up, running between trees or from tree to tree, she saw nothing else. Hoping that no giant bear or wolf would come and tear her apart, she took a deep breath and released it a few seconds later.

"I'm going to pee," she announced to him.

"Be careful!" He told her, just like he would tell her anytime she would announce she was leaving his side to go someplace he didn't know, such as in the forest.

She hurriedly ran a few feet away, enough to ensure that no passerby would see her, even though the only car on this road for quite some time had been theirs. She found some bushes about ten to fifteen meters from the car. Smiling and rubbing her hands in satisfaction, she ran behind the bush.

Just as she finished, she made sure to take a look around her. She started approaching the car slowly and calmly. Her father hadn't finished yet and was on the right side of the car, taking a short break, resting all his weight on the car, which was now lowered.

He still had to gather the damaged wheel and the tools and place them with the luggage in the trunk of the car. In his right hand, he held a nearly full water bottle.

Something moved on him. On his shirt. Was it an insect? No. It glowed, like the lights at the disco she used to frequent with her friends. A small red dot on his right shoulder. She squinted her eyes to see better. The dot wasn't completely still. It was moving slightly, and so, the movement wasn't easily noticeable.

Suddenly, the dot began to move downward, until it reached his back, ending up on the left side of his back. It was a laser sight. She was sure of it because when she was younger, her father had taken her to the shooting range to train her with a .45 pistol that had such a red sight attached to the lower front of the weapon.

She quickly turned to locate the shooter. Maybe it was a hunter looking for game and she needed to alert him. There was no one, nowhere. She searched everywhere with her gaze. If anyone was there, they would see the reflection from the scope.

She turned back to discover that the red dot had vanished. Probably whoever was aiming at her father had realized he wasn't any wild animal and had left to find whatever he was searching for. It wouldn't surprise her if she soon heard gunshots in the clearing.

She returned to the car. John was sipping slowly from his bottle, unaware that he had almost been shot, mistaken for some wild bear. She looked up and shook her head, thinking that sometimes, ignorance truly was bliss.

"This tire won't last long. Once we reach the town that guy told us about, we'll visit the garage," he said to her.

"Wonderful," Leah replied reluctantly.

They continued on their way to Beaverstale Village without any surprises, the two of them discussing various topics that weren't directly related to one another. About her father's childhood experiences, Leah's concern for her best friend who was quite far away, her future goals, and music.

About an hour later, they had nearly arrived at the small town they didn't even know existed. Having left the forest behind, they were now heading into a less wooded area, with small buildings.

On the road, an arch rose about a kilometer from the town, saying: Welcome to Beaverstale Village, with a painted beaver appearing behind the last letter and waving cheerfully. The clouds hadn't yet moved away from above, which predicted more rain and soon.

They reached the interior of the town. The first thing that caught their attention was the lamp posts, the phone booths, the mailboxes, and the walls of public buildings in the town. There was an unusually high number of papers announcing missing persons on each one.

The townspeople looked anxious, almost fearful of their arrival. At least a significant percentage of them, if not all, as their eyes had not left their car for a single moment.

The town, although small compared to theirs, was quite large, including a large hospital unit, a police department, a school, five video rental stores, a cinema, and at least two theaters. These buildings were all they had seen on the main street of the town, so they suspected that there would definitely be even more.

Stopping at the traffic light, they saw a black vehicle pass through the perpendicular road of the intersection, heading south at a slow speed. Behind it followed a crowd of people in black clothing, many of whom were crying heavily. It was a funeral.

A man in black from the crowd stood in front of a pole to look at one of the dozens of missing persons announcements. Full of irritation, he tore down one of the announcements, probably of the person for whom the funeral was taking place, and then crumpled it up and threw it away angrily. Then, he followed the rest of the silent crowd.

They continued their journey through the town until they found a garage, which, luckily, was open. The mechanics welcomed them with smiles and warmth, a tall, hefty man, around sixty years old, who had not stopped smoking his pipe since they had arrived at the garage, and an equally tall but skinny guy, clearly younger, who was running all over the garage doing whatever the hefty man asked him, who seemed to enjoy piling his partner with chores.

"We had a flat tire just before entering the town. Is there a chance it can be changed immediately?" John asked.

"Of course. Tony, bring me a jack, a wrench, and measure the diameter of the rim, so you can bring me a tire!"

"Okay, Derek!" The skinny redhead said and began to run.

"That's my nephew. I'm teaching him the trade to take over when I retire," Derek explained, smiling emotionally. "I assume you have the rim."

"It's in the trunk of the car."

"Perfect! It won't take long. Tony, move! Bring the jack!"

"I'm coming, Derek, just a moment."

Tony arrived, bringing the jack and the wrench, and then started measuring the diameter of one of the other wheels to bring the right tire.

"Still measuring? Oh, you foolish boy! When I worked with your father, we repaired three cars in the same time! One day, I'll die, and you'll see that I was right to yell at you," he said, rising to look at them. "Deep down, he's excellent, but I never want him to become complacent and stop trying."

"Sure," John replied. "Your town is quiet."

"Yes, pretty much," the man replied reluctantly, awkwardly scratching his short curly black hair with his left, grease-covered hand.

"Do you have tourism?"

"Are you interested in staying?"

"It's quite late, and we have miles to cover. It might be better to find a hotel around here."

"You'll find something as long as you don't leave the city limits looking for lodging. Especially at the resort west of here," he replied.

"Does it relate to the disappearances in the area?" Leah asked.

He stopped unscrewing the wheel. He looked like he was trying to keep his composure. Then, he started unscrewing again, avoiding looking at them.

"I don't know what you're talking about, my dear."

"But you must have seen something. The town is filled with papers announcing missing persons," she continued.

"It's about the forest!" Tony exclaimed as he approached with the tire. "Those who have gone there in the last five months have mysteriously disappeared. Only a few have been found, and they weren't alive."

"Foolish boy," Derek muttered.

"Is it true?" John asked.

Derek exhaled.

"Yes, it's true. Our forest has caused us quite a few problems lately, to the point where we've begun to believe someone, or something is out there."

"We'll be on our guard then."

"Talk to Felix. He rents houses," he said, opening his hand in front of John. "It's twenty bucks."

Derek was a strange man. He seemed to know things that he couldn't tell anyone. At least he did a good job, quick and cheap. They were starving enough to stop at a traditional restaurant where a large portion of the town had gathered, along with a truck driver who had merely stopped there to drink his coffee.

The noise inside the restaurant was enough to give Leah a headache, who hadn't felt well for quite some time, but couldn't explain exactly how she felt. Nausea, perhaps a stomach ache—maybe because the sensation was distant, something she had never experienced before.

She wanted to vomit and at the same time sleep for hours. She tried to tell her father, but each time she attempted, the urge to vomit intensified. They arrived outside the house Derek had told them about.

The house where Felix and his family lived, a family of four consisting of him, an elderly man—or at least that's how he appeared, thin with shiny black straight hair styled like an old dandy from 1950s movies, his wife, Susan, a nice woman significantly shorter than her husband, clearly younger in appearance, and two little boys, Darrell and Tim, who looked to be about elementary school age and kept making noise.

After welcoming them and proposing they eat together, something that didn't happen since despite Felix's insistence, they did not want to feel obliged, he led them walking to a house a few blocks away that he owned and was available for rent. It didn't cost them much, which made John feel bad. Once they were alone, he dashed to the neighborhood grocery store to buy supplies. He would cook and invite him and his family over.

Leah was still dizzy. Entering the house, she threw her bag onto the couch and quickly took off her vest and the accessories she was wearing, feeling they were causing her discomfort.

"I'm going to get some food supplies, do you have any special preference?" He asked her.

She held back from spewing the vomit she now felt rising and burning her palate and nose, and to not show that she didn't feel well, managing thus to muster a very funny grimace that John interpreted as her playing coy because he was the best dad and he knew she wanted him to make one of her favorite meals, but she wouldn't tell him so as not to put him in an awkward position, quickly shaking her head left and right to express that she didn't mind what he cooked in the end.

"Okay, I got the message!" He replied to her, making her look up, grateful that he had understood she couldn't speak. "Penne à la crème with broccoli and red pepper. Damn my luck!"

Her cheeks puffed out as she could no longer hold it in. She nodded vigorously, and he smiled at her and left the house. Perfect! Now quickly, let's find the bathroom.

She ran upstairs, where there had always been a bathroom somewhere between the rooms in houses like this. She searched, opened each room on the upper floor one by one, and eventually found it. She rushed to the sink and bent over completely, emptying a disgusting, thick, brown-green liquid that flowed slowly over the pure white freshly washed porcelain.

After several seconds, she tried to lift her head. The smell of vomit reached her nostrils, causing her discomfort. Her mouth burned, and a bitterness made her want to drink water and brush her teeth.

She felt her stomach contract and expand abruptly like a sponge someone had squeezed, and without a second thought, she bent down again to unleash more of the chemical mush that apparently hadn't completely exited her body.

Her breath cut off momentarily, like after intense crying, and for quite a while, her vision was blurry as she felt her brain pressing against her skull as if it wanted to break and come out.

Each time she tried to rise and head toward a room to lie down and calm down, the urge to vomit returned, and she fell abruptly with her face back into the sink to prevent staining the floor and needing to clean that as well besides the sink, which was already quite messy.

After a long time, she felt quite a bit better. After thoroughly cleaning the area, pouring plenty of water and some sink cleaner she found in the bathroom, she headed downstairs to find her toothpaste and toothbrush to brush her teeth. She scrubbed for quite some time, creating excessive foam, until she was sure the taste of vomit had gone.

When her father returned home, she lay on the bed in the last room of the upstairs hallway, trying to calm down after having taken at least two painkillers to ease her headache.

Sleep wouldn't come. She felt numb and weak, but paradoxically, even though she felt like she was in the midst of some dream, she had a full sense of everything happening around her. Her father entered the room to greet her, throwing a bag of chips beside her with enthusiasm, saying, "I found these amazing chips! You have to try them, I ate some on the way."

Then, he left and shouted triumphantly in the hallway like a fan at a game, almost singing, "Chips!" Thunder struck, and curses came from the house across the street as the neighbors clearly weren't pleased at all with the fact that it would rain, and then the room darkened as the clouds had gathered right above the town, pouring incessantly; falling droplets of rain that could be heard and made her want to go to the bathroom, but she felt so weak that she ultimately never got up. At least not for the next hour and a half.

"Dad, maybe we should return to the car?"

She looked around her. It was now evening. For about half an hour, they had wandered through an empty town, certainly not the one they had been in earlier in the afternoon. This town looked foreign and out of place. As if they were in another country, likely some European nation if she could judge by the architecture of the buildings.

And the streets seemed to bear no relation whatsoever to the classic American roads she had been used to traveling for so many years, and it wasn't just part of her imagination. She had traveled with her parents to several cities in the United States to have a general picture.

The minimal lighting coming mainly from traffic lights on the sidewalks was insufficient for them to see far, and simultaneously, all the buildings were dark, without a hint of life. They had tried ringing some doorbells, but to no avail.

They tried in the center, in several apartment buildings with almost pre-war architecture, in a mansion near the center of the town called Valkyrie, with the letters carved into the wall next to the gigantic iron door that led to the estate's yard. Nothing.

The owner, someone Count James or George Princeton, something they couldn't make out from the now dull letters on the button of the doorbell, had either died or forsaken the mansion forever. When a traffic light momentarily flashed behind them, they could make out the plants that had covered much of the mansion with their green branches, as if the snakes were trying to strangle their prey.

She took a few steps back, frightened, but her father seemed unfazed. From there, they ended up in a massive skyscraper, entering inside to find that no one was present, no security personnel, nor anyone at the reception. The lights didn't work, nor did the elevators.

She tried to remember how they had ended up in that place. Impossible. Her mind had probably stopped at the point where she was having dinner with the family who had rented them the house to stay the night. After that, nothing! Blank.

"Let's go find the car," he finally responded, stopping her thoughts and her attempt to look back in time, leaving her stunned at the sight before them.

A park. An abandoned playground, quite large, with the strange green plants having made their presence felt here as well, covering the floor and certainly a good number of the playground's equipment.

The electric game with the colorful, now faded, horses and unicorns had succumbed to rust, and one of the horses had fallen into the muddy ground, devoured by the moss that had wrapped it, causing it to fall over time.

Although it was a playground, it was quite well equipped, with a small track for bumper cars making its appearance, making them wonder how big this town could be, as for a brief moment, when all the lights turned on together for a short while and then suddenly went out, with only a few remaining lit, like a sudden power surge, they had noticed a giant wheel from a theme park quite a distance from them.

The bumper cars were motionless. Stacked in a corner, probably with the area's staff having cleaned them the previous evening, waiting to return to their jobs the next day. A blue merry-go-round, which now showed signs of rust everywhere along its length, trying to cover the last hint of color, leaned over on its side, no longer able to serve as a suitable toy for children, with the muddy water beneath it making it look like a shipwreck.

The benches were no better. Ruined, some filthy, and others with their boards swollen and smelling sharply of mold. The swings, the seesaw, and a small slide had also succumbed to the ravages of time. Around the park, a road surrounded by apartment buildings and large, tall buildings.

Behind the now dilapidated wooden shooting range with air rifles, there was a message written on the wall in bright red spray paint, quite poorly written and not artistic at all.

NOBODY!

Their blood froze. Small red dots began to move around them, five in total. Occasionally, some moved on them too. *The hunters from earlier!* She thought. But how could they be there, in a town, free to use their weapons? Could they be responsible for the town's desolation? And the story of the disappearances began to appear interconnected. Were they planning to ravage other towns too?

"Don't move unless I tell you!" He whispered to her.

Before them now was a large red dot. A red circle. The only source of light. The lights had gone out, surrendering everything around them to darkness. It had appeared out of nowhere, and the sudden blackout was alarming. Something was definitely not right, but she couldn't clarify what. Everything felt distant yet simultaneously near.

She felt dizzy while hearing her father shout at her, "No Leah, don't follow it, be careful!"

She had momentarily lost her sight from the red glow, just as she had numbly stepped onto the red circle. She hovered in a black abyss. Her father was not there. Was he dying? Was this what it felt like to die? Why hadn't she felt the slightest pain, though?

The only sensation was fear, so immense that her heart was beating way too fast. She reached her hands up, trying to scream, but no one ever heard her calls.

Five

John was still cooking in the kitchen, while Leah had gone outside to play ball with the children of the people who had rented them the house, Darrell and Tim. It had stopped raining, although the clouds stubbornly remained above their heads.

The wet ground was not particularly safe for playing, yet the two boys seemed to do it often. Nonetheless, Leah decided it would be good to stay with them to keep an eye on them.

"Does it rain this much all year?" She had asked at one point.

"Sometimes," Tim replied. "It rains quite a bit, and there are often thunderstorms."

"Yeah, and at night, we can't easily sleep," Darrell complained.

Although she temporarily felt somewhat better, Leah still experienced fatigue overwhelming her at times—brief moments, but long enough to think that she might have been better off staying in bed.

Meanwhile, in the kitchen, John was excelling, feeling satisfied every time he looked at the results of each small detail he added to the food to enhance its flavor. He glanced out the window and saw Leah playing with the kids she was voluntarily keeping an eye on.

He was glad that at least she was not having a bad time, despite the unfortunate incident that had brought them to that place. Leaving the food on the table to cool down, he went outside to visit Felix and Susan's house. A bit later, he returned, holding four dozen cans of cold beer in his arms. As he approached Leah, he showed her the beers.

"You can't have good food without beer!" He told her. "Felix and his wife will come over soon to have dinner with us."

"Okay, sounds good to me," she replied and turned to the kids. "Last game, guys! We'll eat soon."

She did not sit with them at the table. Just before arriving at the house, she rushed to the bathroom, where she started making strange groans, causing her father to worry and enter to discover that she was vomiting, and to inform him that this was the second time that day.

Afterwards, she had locked herself in her room for quite a while. When Felix arrived, John explained to him why his daughter wouldn't be sitting with them to eat, causing both him and his wife to smile mischievously.

"Come with me!" Felix said.

They visited the store from which John had earlier taken the ingredients for the meal and then the beers that same afternoon. The employees must have gotten used to him by now. Felix led him down an aisle with medicinal products, gauze, bottles of alcohol, first aid kits, and even antidepressants.

John followed him silently. Perhaps there was some remedy for food poisoning if that was the issue, and maybe Felix knew more than he did. He picked up a box with a device that resembled a digital thermometer and held it in front of him.

DIGITAL PREGNANCY TEST

He looked at him, astonished, glancing between the box and Felix.
"What is this?" He asked.
"It's exactly what it says it is," he replied.
"No way! Leah would have told me. She tells me everything."
"Are you sure?"
"Of course I am," John replied, somewhat annoyed.
"Alright, alright! No need to get upset."
"Anyway, bring it here," he replied, irritated, and headed to the checkout. "How much does this thing cost?"
"Three dollars," the cashier answered him.

After paying, John and Felix headed back to the house.

"Look, I'm sorry if I said something I shouldn't have. I've just seen too much in my life and have a niece who probably hurried to grow up. I mean, Beaverstale is quite infamous for teenagers and their parties at the end of school year, turning into freaked out kids that don't know how to tell their parents they weren't careful enough."

"It's all good! It just seems odd to me that she would hide something like this from me. I know about all her relationships, from high school until now."

"Wow!" Felix exclaimed. "You two seem close."

"Yeah, everyone keeps telling us. So, what else is Beaverstale famous for?"

"Hmmm. Indian fairytales and stories about the war between the Apache and the Cheyenne tribes, a mixed cuisine from Alabama, Georgia and Tennessee, as our city was built right between the three states and great whiskey, I guess. There's no chance you haven't heard or even tasted the smooth and sweet taste of Wild Beaver at least once in your life."

"You mean the distillery that appears in almost every film?" John laughed. "Ah come on!"

"You don't believe me? It's eleven miles west of the city. The farm they use to get the grains is so big, I felt like I was exploring a city when I first saw it."

"And you mentioned the Fight of the White Eagle?"

"Someone knows history. Yes! Our ancestors helped the Apache defend themselves."

"You mean, they let them be slaughtered while watching from afar, smoking their pipes," Jack told Felix, looking at him with an expression on his face as if he was trying to tell him he was not dumb, "Yeah, history books tend to make things sound prettier than the way they actually happened."

"A philosopher?"

"Something like that."

They kept driving for a while. For a town he didn't know at all, it seemed truly odd that it looked appealing to him. There was something about Beaverstale that made him feel intrigued to explore every inch of it. Maybe the fact that everything seemed quiet and standing still in time.

"So, you mentioned the city exists between the three states, right?"

"Yes, of course."

"Which state does it belong to?"

Felix grinned, probably having been amused by the question.

"Well, it's hard to tell. We have a mayor but the town has never been officially registered with any of the three states. We once were part of Georgia when Beaverstale was county seat, but that's ancient history. For the time being, you could say that we are being influenced by all three states."

Arriving at the house, he left the box on a counter in the kitchen. He would give it to her in the morning, being very careful with his words so as not to make her feel bad or awkward. They sat down to eat, leaving Leah to rest, believing that at some point, she would come down to sit with them.

They ate in the dining room inside the house, talking about various topics: John's work—whatever he could say about that subject—the life in this small town, Felix's previous job, and interesting memories they had. Leah never appeared.

Finishing the first two plates of food, and still having enough for the rest of the evening (he was used to making large quantities after having spent quite some important time in the kitchen with his siblings, making food for the entire family and their parents friends' families on weekends), he decided to call Leah to eat with them, believing she had probably fallen asleep and if he didn't wake her up, she would miss out on the delicious food.

"Leah, my dear, you're going to miss the penne I made. Come on, we have beer too!" He said, entering the room.

He stood, bewildered. Leah was nowhere to be found, and simultaneously, the window of the room was closed, which meant she couldn't have left through the roof. He was stunned. Leah had vanished. For a moment, he thought she might be playing hide-and-seek and had hidden in the closet.

He was disappointed, though, as soon as he opened it. He searched all the rooms on the upper floor, even in the bathroom. Nothing! Feeling that something was wrong, he quickly went downstairs to find Felix, his wife, and their children unsuspecting of what was happening.

"Have you seen her come down?" He asked.

"No. We thought she was upstairs," Felix replied, almost indifferently.

"It's impossible!" John exclaimed. "Quickly, we need to find her!"

"What do you mean?" Felix asked, puzzled.

"I mean, she's not in her room or any other room. She's gone."

"Dad, did Leah's dad kill someone?" Darrell asked, as he was just returning from the downstairs bathroom, pointing at two parallel lines of bloody footsteps that stretched across the floor to the back door.

With a quick glance, the blood indicated that someone had been dragged violently to the front door. He ran over to realize that it was raining and that it would be very hard to find any trace with all this rain. Perhaps it would be better to go to the police station and ask them to search for his daughter with him.

They quickly left the house. It was still raining. Susan suggested that she would take the children to their house to put them to bed while John and Felix would go to the police station. They took John's car, which started with a loud sound from the tires squeaking on the wet asphalt.

He drove quickly and recklessly. He almost caused an accident at an intersection when a van heading perpendicular to his direction tried to cross the intersection, having the right of way at that moment. Fortunately, the driver of the van braked in time, and the accident was narrowly avoided. The driver didn't let it go easily, and with a wild burst of his horn and a string of curses, he crossed the intersection.

They arrived at the station. John rushed straight in, followed by Felix.

"I need to speak to the chief, please," he said as he reached the reception.

The blonde receptionist, who was reading a novel, looked quite engrossed and probably didn't hear him at all.

"You're not being paid to dawdle!" He said abruptly, seeing her jump from her chair.

"I'm sorry. I'll alert him right away!" She said, blushing with embarrassment as she picked up the phone next to her. "Mr. Palmer? Mr. Foster and another gentleman have come and are looking for you." She paused briefly and looked them in the eye. "He said you could come in."

The station was not particularly large, but it was big enough for a town of its size. Many rooms, one next to the other, all stacked on one floor. At the back on the right was the chief's office.

Palmer, a wrinkled old man with a broad back indicating that he was once quite fit, sat at his desk reading a newspaper with his thick eyebrows raised slightly, one more than the other, above his blue eyes, which were examining the article he seemed to be reading intently, his index finger of his left hand resting on his left cheek of his square face, tapping lightly in rhythm.

His uniform shirt, an almost beige to khaki well-pressed shirt, was enormous, with its wide, short sleeves almost hiding his arms, which had sagged with age, making him look quite old for the job. In front of his chair, on the desk, among papers and a half-eaten cheeseburger, there was a golden nameplate: Fred Palmer.

"Hi Felix!" The chief responded warmly.

"Freddy!" He replied, shaking his hand.

After exchanging some typical pleasantries like, "How's your wife? How are your kids? Heard anything about the wine festival?" Felix got straight to the point and immediately mentioned the incident.

"She went toward the woods, you said?" The chief asked.

"Yes. We found blood on the floor that leads toward the trees just beyond the back yard of the house."

The chief sighed and sat back in his chair, placing both hands on his face. After a loud exhale into his palms, he looked them in the eye.

"I'm sorry," he said finally.

"What do you mean?" John asked.

"I mean, if she went into the woods, then it's futile. She'll be gone or worse, killed, just like the kid a few days ago," he said, looking conspiratorially at Felix.

"He was found in terrible condition. He had fallen off a cliff and was found smashed against the hood of a car that was passing below that hill, this year was supposed to be his last before going to college," Felix explained to John. "Most, however, disappear and are never found. We've tried to warn people to avoid the woods, but they almost never listen to us."

"My daughter did not go there voluntarily, Felix. Something can be done."

"You heard him," Palmer said. "If she's in the woods, then it's a waste of time."

John felt his blood boiling and rushing through his body with speed. He walked toward Fred, who was still sitting in his office chair, and grabbed him by the collar of his shirt, pulling him violently from his chair, which slid back and fell over, pushing him against the wall on the left side of the room.

"Fucking irresponsible bastard!" He started yelling.

"Calm down!" Fred tried to tell him.

"I told you she was kidnapped. All you can do is sit here and read newspapers, isn't that right?"

Felix held him by the waist, trying to restrain him, shouting at both of them to stop.

"There's nothing we can do. I'm telling you the truth."

"Useless!" He said, throwing him down. "At least give me a gun, so I can go find her myself."

"No," Fred shouted. "Several people have gone missing this week, mainly tourists like you who don't listen to us and go into the woods. I won't let this continue. I'm warning you! Tomorrow morning, you will leave this place, or I will arrest you."

"Arrest me?" John shouted. "Do you see this?"

"If that's the case, then you can go to the woods and do what you want. Good luck killing something!" The chief replied irritably, after seeing John's black identification tag.

"Fred!" His friend shouted. "He's a good man. Understand that he's worried about his daughter just as you would be for your own kids. Let's help him."

He stood for a moment, looking down at the floor, doing absolutely nothing. He simply looked with eyes that betrayed him, thinking.

"Very well, then," he finally replied. "Two hours," he said and paused to look John in the eye. "If we don't find her in two hours, then we won't pursue this any further than a person should with something so dangerous."

He walked toward the exit of the room, and the other two followed him. He was shouting, giving orders to the officers in the station to arm themselves, prepare, and follow him. It would be a difficult night for the Beaverstale police department.

From the available men and women that were in the department, only about a quarter, or maybe less, remained behind to be on standby. Even the officers who were on patrol were asked to come along. Two fire trucks with rescue personnel and an ambulance arrived with them on the main road, blaring their sirens toward the place where Leah had disappeared earlier.

"It seems this forest scares a lot of people," John said as they drove down the wet road, with the rain having stopped now.

"We all fear the forest. If it's a kidnapping, which personally I can't understand the reason for, then let's hope they're not stupid enough to go into the woods."

"What exactly happens in the woods? I mean, besides the disappearances."

"I'd be lying to you," he replied, looking him in the eye to indicate that he was speaking honestly. "For about three, four, maybe even five months, whoever gets close, vanishes."

"I heard from the mechanic that those who were found weren't alive."

"Yes, that's true," Felix told him. "I assume he warned you about a resort just outside of town, right?"

"Yes, why?"

"It all started from there. Until then, we were a quiet town. Suddenly, the sheriff's office received a phone call from an employee returning from sick leave," he said, pausing to emphasize what he was about to say next. "All of them—guests, staff, even the lazy dog that lounged around—vanished magically."

"Only three people were found, who had died under very strange circumstances. One had his head crushed, as if it had been run over by a steamroller, another was burned alive. There was also a young girl among those three, she likely had the worst fate."

"Sheriff?"

"Ah yes, you couldn't possibly know. Palmer is actually the sheriff. Beaverstale and its surrounding villages and towns used to be Pinetree County until 1988, so the county would be overseen by the sheriff's office, now a small, abandoned building. Palmer was appointed chief of the police department."

"I suppose you never learned what happened to the resort," John replied, looking at him intently, making him feel nervous because he wasn't looking at the wet road and was driving fast to catch up with the fire and police vehicles in front of him.

"Not only that. A few days later, the group of five officers who had already been there for the investigation went again to continue their search and also disappeared. As for the employee, he committed suicide a few days later. In his last days of life, he was saying nonsensical things; we assumed it was the shock he experienced after seeing the staff vanish and then doing the identifications on the three dead."

Both paused. John was thinking of all the possibilities, unable to allow himself to consider that his daughter might be dead. He wouldn't let that happen.

"Thank you," he finally said.

"For what?"

"Back at the police station. You convinced the sheriff to help me."

"I'm a parent too. I know how you feel right now, so there's no need to thank me."

They were approaching the house. The first vehicles had already arrived outside, nearly blocking the road with their sirens on. People were coming out onto the street to see what was happening—some in their pajamas and others in their clothes.

Some even held newspapers, drinks, or food in their hands, having rushed out of their homes in a panic. They parked wherever they found space and approached the groups of police officers who were already lined up outside the house.

"Go home, Fel!" Palmer said.

"I want to help too," he complained.

"Look behind you!" He told him, motioning with his eyes toward his family standing a little further back on the stairs of a house, looking toward them. "Who will help them if something happens to you?"

Felix nodded and went toward his family. He then turned to the police officers with him.

"I want you to be particularly careful!" He said. "We don't know exactly what has happened, so we can't act recklessly and disorganized. The forest is dangerous, and you all know that well. I want us all to always stay close during the search."

"We'll need an item to see if the dog can track her scent," said one of the men, who firmly held the leash of a giant Doberman that remained still, waiting for orders.

"Yes, one moment," John said and quickly headed toward the house.

He climbed the stairs approaching Leah's room. Her vest was tossed on the bed. He sighed, feeling defeated and helpless for a moment. Then, he shook off that thought and grabbed the vest, coming down to find the police officers, reinvigorated and ready to do anything to find his daughter.

"Here!" He said, handing the vest to the sturdy young man with blonde hair, who was holding the dog.

"My name's Bob, Bob Fisher," he said, shaking his hand and smiling reassuringly.

"John Emerson," he replied awkwardly, reacting to the handshake by offering his hand in return.

"We'll find your daughter, don't worry!" He told him, trying to make him feel better.

John simply nodded in agreement.

In this way, they set off for the woods. A team of sixteen people—ten police officers, four firefighters, a doctor, and John. Leading the way was Bob with the dog, Lacey. They seemed to match. He was tall and quite muscular, like a football player, and the dog appeared strong and fierce. They definitely spent a lot of time together, as Bob talked to her all the time, and she seemed to obey anything he told her.

The somewhat dark, muscular young man next to him walked silently, indicating that he was anxious.

"What's your name, kid?" He asked him.

"Quill Johnson, sir," he replied.

"Thank you for your help, Quill," he said.

"I loved this forest a lot, you know," Quill began. "I'm half-Indian, and with the Indian minority that lives in the village, a few miles south of here, we used to visit often."

"I understand."

"Maybe the spirits hated us. Maybe we did something wrong. Quite a few people from the Indian community in the village have disappeared here in recent months."

"Why hasn't the state intervened?" He suddenly asked, puzzled, thinking that, since the spirits didn't exist, at least to him, then maybe someone or some people were responsible for the disappearances.

"They did!" Quill told him. "They even sent a helicopter, which couldn't find anything that suggested someone, or something was responsible for the disappearances. I'm sure the spirits are doing this to punish us!"

The forest appeared seemingly harmless. Tall trees emerged everywhere, casting shade over the ground. Small and large animals occasionally appeared, making Lacey abruptly turn her head toward them, letting out a growl, and Bob teasing her, laughing that the dog reacted to every sound that echoed in the forest and that they likely couldn't hear each time.

Quill still looked anxious. A few meters ahead, Fred was walking silently. The short man with straight black hair and a large mustache walking close to him seemed to believe it was pointless to search.

"Do you think we'll find her?" He whispered to him.

"I don't know, man. But let's say we find her. Have you ever seen many people we found to be alive?"

He thought for a moment about Palmer's words.

"You're right, man. I want to see the look on his face when he realizes the effort was in vain. I hope he at least apologizes to us because you warned him that he wouldn't find anything."

"That doesn't worry me, Jeff. In town, I suppose, they've gotten used to our inability to find a solution to this specific problem and have long stopped bothering us about searching for people we would never find. Just think about how they'll react now that they see us searching for this guy."

"We've fucked it up!" Jeff declared, shivering at the mere thought.

"Exactly. Felix will owe me a huge favor after this."

John listened in silence. He couldn't say anything anyway. Although he partially had a point in wanting to find his child, he understood that at the same time, it was selfish of him not to consider the other residents. Almost all of them had lost a loved one, as things seemed, and this forest had now become their worst nightmare.

How many parents, perhaps, stayed up all night until their child returned from sports or a friend's house? How many parents cried or worried every night knowing that their suddenly missing child might never return? How many women had been left widowed, and how many men had lost their wives because of this forest?

Families, individuals, and entire groups of people. This forest swallowed them and only spewed a few corpses to the surface, warning about how dangerous it was.

Time passed quickly, and they found nothing. Even Lacey seemed to be having a hard time finding the scent. They reached a dead end at least twice. It wasn't Lacey's fault, as Leah seemed to have passed through there, judging by the footprints in the mud.

What annoyed them, however, was that at certain points, the tracks disappeared completely. It also didn't help that the cover from the trees wasn't enough for the rainwater that had fallen earlier to be unable to cover them, but it complicated their orientation as they didn't ultimately know which tracks to follow.

She seemed to be circling around and probably returning to a path to choose another one when there were available paths; she wasn't just walking between trees. Therefore, they would probably need to check all paths, which would take hours.

At certain points, footprints from other shoes appeared to be imprinted over hers or to the right and left of them. Were they from the kidnappers? They were starting to get tired. The search was leading nowhere, and most had begun to visibly fidget. Leah was probably lost forever, and that was something he would have to come to terms with.

"Lacey found something!" Bob said, drawing everyone's attention to him.

The dog was literally going wild. She was barking and growling toward the direction the tracks were leading. Bob struggled with all his might to keep her from the leash without letting her escape, but he couldn't succeed.

Lacey, after struggling for a few more seconds, managed to slip from Bob's hands, running toward the spot the tracks were leading. The others followed her running without losing time.

"Quick, don't lose her from sight!" Fred yelled.

The ground was uneven. Branches and potholes were everywhere, making the situation more difficult as they tried to follow Lacey, who was running non-stop. Hope had returned within him. Maybe he would find his daughter and save her.

As the night progressed, the forest appeared more and more unwelcoming to visitors, with strange noises echoing around them as they ran, as if someone were following them, and with the constant feeling that someone or something was out there, watching their every move.

Six

"No, Liz, don't worry, everything's fine," John had said, holding the receiver of the white wall-mounted phone in his house kitchen. "It'll just be like a bad dream in a few hours."

"I'm really worried."

"I know, but everything will be okay," he told her. "I love you."

"I love you too."

***

A few hours later, he would be in a forest with a crowd of strangers who had come to help find his daughter, not knowing why all this had happened or what the outcome might be.

"What happened? Did you find her?" A firefighter asked to Jeffrey, who was emerging from the woods alongside the doctor, one of the other firefighters, and a few police officers.

"No, but they're still searching. They asked the rest of us to go back, so the entire team wouldn't be put at risk."

"Did the sheriff stay with the rest of the team?"

"Yes. Until then, I'm in charge," Jeffrey said, turning to the others. "Alright, listen up! We're going back to our duties."

"Pickens, can I get a statement from you?" A thin blonde woman who quickly approached said, holding a notepad and a pen.

"Sorry, sweetheart, I can't give you anything," he replied as he headed toward the sheriff's car, or police chief, as he was called ever since things had changed for his career in Beaverstale. "Stay on alert and keep an eye on the radios," Officer Jeffrey Pickens told the other officers before getting into the car.

He turned to the others. They all looked exhausted and were now trying to calm down a bit before getting into their vehicles to head back. One of the officers was gulping down water from a bottle someone had given him, while another had just grabbed a cigarette from the pack he pulled out of his pocket and was nervously trying to light it. He saw one of the firefighters take off his shirt, revealing his sculpted, muscular body.

"Where are you off to?" Jeffrey called out as he saw him running toward the woods.

"My cousin is out there with the others. In that forest, with the spirits lurking and waiting for the right time to get him," the man replied.

Some in the crowd that remained there began to mock him.

"Spirits are to blame for everything," one said.

"Bet they're probably responsible for the disappearances and using their superstitions as cover," another said, staring at the man who clearly seemed different than the others.

"Etu, please don't act recklessly. Come with us," began Jeffrey, and after getting close enough, he continued to speak in a whisper, "Let's grab a burger and Coke at Nancy's burger joint."

"Jeffrey, I have to do this. Quill is still a kid."

"Quill chose to be a cop. He should know the dangers of his job just as you know the dangers of yours."

"I thought you would understand," he said, pulling away and running off.

"You need to hear this!" One of the men standing near one of the vehicles called after him.

He walked over to him, visibly annoyed. Etu was always stubborn and unpredictable when it came to his family. He never calculated the risk and always stood by them. That was what he had chosen to do now, even though he knew the other men out in the forest had little hope of survival, let alone him going to find them alone.

"What's going on?" He asked the man who had called him.

"Listen!"

"Unknown female spotted in the center, I repeat, unknown female spotted in the center. She's wearing a white hoodie, torn jeans, obviously from a fall, and has a sling bag. She's likely under the influence of drugs and doesn't seem to hear us or have a clear perception of her surroundings. Awaiting orders. Over!"

"Look at that; we might have found our friend's daughter, he must be so proud to be raising such a gem," Jeffrey muttered.

"Hope she hasn't shared her stash with other kids in town," the other man said.

"Stop her and wait for us, we're coming immediately, I repeat, wait for us. Over!"

They all jumped into their cars, speeding toward the location where the girl had been found, the sirens wailing furiously into the night, disrupting the quiet of this small town. In less than three minutes, they arrived in the center. There were almost no other cars around to slow them down.

The girl was there, her face pressed harshly against the hood of a police car, with her hood still covering her head. The two officers who had stopped her were right behind her, one of them pressing down on her head with force.

"Is this the one we're looking for?" Jeffrey asked the officers.

"We don't know. She was a total wildcat. Refused to comply and started attacking us as soon as we touched her to restrain her."

"Great. If our friend comes back from the woods, I'll make sure to lock them both up until they rot. Screw what Palmer might say. I hate tourists, especially those who think they own the place they visit."

"Shouldn't the sheriff decide this?" One of the officers asked, bewildered.

"Do you see him here?" He asked, giving him a cold glare. "Until Palmer gets back, I'm the one making the decisions!"

"What about the judge?"

"You're speaking too much, kid. They've disrupted our town because he didn't make sure to send his daughter to a rehab center. They deserve it," he said, yanking the girl's hood back, lifting her from the hood.

"This isn't the missing girl," one of the officers said, staring at her in shock.

She turned to Jeffrey and gave him a rude gesture with her middle finger.

"Chloe? What the hell are you doing out at this hour?"

She pulled off the big headphones that had been hiding under her hood and placed them around her neck.

"Whatever I want. You're gonna see my dad when he finds out you touched me, and your transfer to Alaska is a sure thing, idiots!" The girl replied, angrily pushing her long brown ponytail that had been on her left shoulder back, clearly annoyed.

"Be careful, kid, because your daddy's money won't save you if I arrest you," he replied sarcastically.

"Can I go now or am I under arrest for just walking and listening to music?" She asked, pouting her tiny lips and glancing sideways at the hand still holding her by the arm.

"Go on, we're looking for someone else," he told her with a sigh.

She left in silence, her steps quick and nervous. The others exchanged glances, remaining speechless for a moment. Chloe was the daughter of Jacob Dawson, owner of Jay Dawson's Co Wild Beaver brand. The entire family had moved to Tennessee after 1975, although they would still visit Beaverstale every summer and stay there.

Jacob Dawson was a man of influence. His whiskey brand was on every magazine. In 1976, Forbes had claimed he was the most well-known American, second only to the president. The officers looked at Jeffrey in horror, as if they wanted to say: 'Are we going to be in trouble?'

He met their gaze with a fierce look, as if trying to say: 'None of you speak'.

"What are you all standing around like a bunch of fools for?" He asked. "Get back to searching!"

He got into the patrol car and drove a bit outside of town, up on the old highway, somewhere south, to a large gas station that housed a restaurant and a mini market. The ground was wet, and the trucks and cars passing by on the old highway sounded as if someone were tearing paper with their tires.

After leaving the car with the gas station attendants to refuel, he headed toward the mini market to buy cigarettes. He came out a few minutes later to park the patrol car in the lot, right outside the restaurant.

He sat beside one of the large windows of the retro restaurant that was still furnished and decorated according to the style of the 50s, allowing him to look out onto the street. He grabbed a newspaper from the little shelf next to the entrance door.

A petite, slender blonde girl with striking blue eyes and a somewhat large nose approached him. It was Nancy. She offered him a coffee pot and a cup.

"What can I get you?" She asked, trying not to be as cold as she wanted to be.

"I'll start with a quadruple burger, a side of fries, and a large Coke. It's been a long day today," he replied, winking at her.

"It'll be ready in a few minutes," she said awkwardly and started heading toward the kitchen staff.

"Etu couldn't come," he told her.

She tensed. She had been waiting all day for him to come and pick her up to go to the house they shared, but instead, she found Jeffrey, whom Nancy called slippery.

"When will he be here?" She asked him, trying to sound friendly to get what she wanted.

"In an hour? Two? Maybe not at all? It depends," he replied, waving his hands.

"Has he been stuck on shift?"

"Call it that."

"Please." She leaned closer and said, "You're high-ranking in the department, and they listen to you. Talk to someone from the fire department and let him leave earlier. I haven't seen him for three days now, with fire season and all. Besides, isn't the chief of the fire department of Beaverstale your cousin?"

"I don't think."

"Three whole days, Jeffrey!" She spoke more forcefully. "Three fucking days, he comes home late, eats, takes a shower, changes clothes, and leaves again. He works like a dog while other colleagues have more flexible schedules. Does it bother you that he's half-Indian? Or are you planning to let him burn out as a disposable member of the force, or push him to start using amphetamines, so you have a reason to later propagate against the Indian minority?"

"What? You think I don't know what you and your cousin chat about when you grill on Sundays? You hate them, just as your parents did. But labeling yourselves as liberals, it suits you whenever he is next to your cousin in photos for newspapers, right?"

"Sweetheart, it's not my fault your boyfriend is an idiot," he said, looking at her seriously. "He's out in the woods."

He saw her face go pale, her body freezing at the news.

"What's he doing out there? How is that possible?"

"His cousin and a team from the department went out to the woods with the chief to find a tourist's daughter and he thought it was smart to tag along."

"That can't be."

"I'm sorry, Nancy. I tried to reason with him."

She left in silence. A satisfied grin spread across his face. He had always wanted to make her feel weak. To make her feel humiliated. It had been a sore spot for him since the time he had tried to touch her without her consent behind the restaurant, where he had called her over, claiming to show her something she needed to report to her superiors.

Luckily for her, Etu had come out of the place, and he had stopped just in time before Etu arrived, so he wouldn't suspect anything. He had threatened her. Blackmailed her, and he certainly reminded her regularly that she should never tell Etu anything since they were friends. Without feeling any remorse for his actions, he opened the newspaper in front of him and started flipping through it.

"Hello, handsome!" A woman said to him, holding a tray with his order.

"Welcome, Lucy Ball," he said jokingly about her appearance, which maximized the look and makeup of the famous actress from the beloved show.

"You know you deep down like me, but won't admit it," she told him as she served him.

She also placed a dish on his table that he hadn't ordered. Lemon meringue pie.

"Compliments of me," she said, winking at him.

"You're making me indebted."

"When are you going to come fix my antenna at home? I hardly pick up any channels."

"Soon, sweetheart. Very soon," he replied. "Where's Nancy?"

"Back and crying," she said. "Between us, I think she's had a fight with her boyfriend. I haven't seen him come to pick her up."

He smiled at her.

"Maybe, who knows?"

He sat there for quite a while in the restaurant that night. Lethargic, as he always was whenever he was in that place, reading his newspaper, occasionally eating from the food that had been served to him, and sipping from the chilled Coke that was on the right side of the table.

Inside the kitchen, Nancy was curled up in a fetal position, leaning against the side of the fryer's counter, trying to recover. She was sobbing uncontrollably. That night, her life had been utterly ruined.

Four years entangled, as a teenager, with one of the most bloodthirsty gangs in Los Angeles, having fallen for the wrong person, a thirty-something neo-Nazi with tattoos covering his entire body, she had arrived in this city distressed, falling upon Etu, in whom all those years, she pretended to be a tourist who had come for a vacation and ended up staying forever because she liked the place.

The truth was, she found everything she was looking for in Etu. A partner, a friend, and a rope to pull her out of the swamp she was in. He treated her well, and she loved him. He was the one who made her find her joy again.

Now, he was out there; God knows where, with no one able to guarantee her that he would come back. That night, her soul died. She felt everything inside her go numb, and time suddenly stopped. The end had come.

Seven

He ran without a stop to rest or catch his breath. He needed to find the others and keep his cousin in sight. Naked from the waist up and slick with sweat, every detail of his muscular dark body was visible under the generous light of the moon when it fell on him.

Etu had no weapons like the team's police officers, except for a survival knife that swung back and forth in the right pocket of his pants. He crossed the entire path they had taken up to the point where they had separated. Fortunately, he knew the forest very well, having visited it frequently before the disappearances started.

He had tried to speak to them on the radio. Seeing they were unwilling and did not want him to follow for his safety, he had decided not to respond at all and let the radio hang closed on his belt.

He paused. He had reached a dead end. Large rocks and a massive fallen tree trunk had created a barrier from a potential landslide on the adjacent hill, blocking the path ahead. If the others had already passed that way, they would have likely chosen to go through the trees, following a different trail.

What surprised him, however, was that their tracks had disappeared just a few steps back. It wasn't raining, so he couldn't assume the water had washed away their footprints, and he didn't want to conclude that they had vanished. Keeping his flashlight on, he continued forward, calling the names of the others, but there was no response.

Silence reigned everywhere, making Etu shiver. He felt uneasy, as if someone or something was lurking in the clearing, watching him; yet, he could see no one.

"Is anyone there? Quill? Fred? Bob?"

No one answered. Silence engulfed everything. Even the animals that had previously made small noises, climbing trees, jumping from branch to branch, running over leaves or eating berries, had now stopped. Not even a rustle could be heard. Only his footsteps, his breath, and his voice calling their names echoed in the stillness.

He pressed on toward the small pond he knew was a few meters south of his current location. There was an old, small cabin right at that spot. A structure that had been built many years ago by a fisherman to store his belongings—some fishing rods, bait, a wooden table for gutting fish and preparing lines, which had rotted over the years, with the blood from the large fish he had skinned dried upon it, two or three hunting shotguns, food, and various tools.

The last time he had visited was two years ago with Nancy when they spent about three days camping by the lake. It had seemed useful at the time, as he had borrowed some tools and used one of the shotguns to catch a deer. The owner of the cabin had died long ago, so he wouldn't mind them borrowing his weapon for food.

He had told his cousin about this place and had even shown it to him a few months later, so he assumed they might have passed that way, likely to rest, as according to the digital watch on his wrist, it was almost three in the morning.

As he ran toward the cabin, he encountered a small young deer that had become trapped under a fallen tree trunk and was struggling to escape. He stopped for a moment and looked at it. It looked back at him, making him see the terror in its eyes.

Did the deer he had killed back then feel that same fear as the bullet approached its skull? He felt guilty for that moment and decided to help this deer escape from the trunk that would make it a meal for wolves or keep it trapped until it starved to death.

He approached close enough that the deer began to flail with fear. He tried to make his movements slow and soothing to calm it down and not torment it any more than it had already been.

"I want you to be patient for just a few more seconds. Everything will be alright!" He told it, using his large hands to grab the trunk, trying to lift it, exposing his bulging biceps beneath his skin as soon as he grasped the trunk.

The animal continued to struggle to free itself, making Etu's task harder, and he felt his entire body stretch from end to end like it did whenever he engaged in intense exercise or did some strenuous work.

"It hurts, doesn't it? I understand. I'm in pain too right now," he said and let one of his hands point behind him. "I have a sensitive back from birth. I'm normally prohibited from lifting weights, even from doing this job, but pain is meant to be ignored, as a friend once taught me."

He poured all his strength into it, giving rise to a pain that started from his lower back and quickly spread to his head through his spine. He grunted from the pain but had no intention of giving up. With even more force, he pushed the trunk until he finally lifted it and let it fall to the other side, finally freeing the deer, which had now calmed down.

Once it realized it was finally free, it stood on its feet and looked at him, initially frightened. It sniffed the air around it for a moment, and after assuring itself that it was safe, it slowly and hesitantly approached Etu. He watched it silently and motionless.

The deer nudged his hand gently with its head as if wanting to thank him for his good deed. Then, it limped away until it disappeared into the forest. He felt his bladder swelling. He urgently needed to relieve himself, so he quickly lowered his pants and felt the warmth of his urine rushing forcefully to the ground, rising up to warm him as steam formed from the sudden temperature change of the liquid.

Full of relief, he looked up and sighed in satisfaction. Then, he pulled up his pants again and, after fastening it, remained for a few seconds in a daze, feeling the blood in his body now flowing more slowly.

A bright red dot appeared on his body. It started from his neck and moved toward his chest. He hadn't noticed it yet. Quickly, the dots multiplied to three and moved across different parts of his body. He saw them as soon as he opened his eyes and looked down at himself, making a jerky movement as if trying to avoid or brush them off.

He looked toward the clearing and immediately understood that someone was marking him with a laser. It was definitely not from his team. None of them had a laser on their weapon.

"Person! Person! Don't shoot!" He shouted.

For several seconds, the beams wandered over his body. He looked more closely and distinguished figures of men holding rifles. He couldn't easily make out their features, as they were cloaked in shadows provided by the trees, but it was clear they were calm and working together, as they had strategically positioned themselves, as if lying in wait for someone, likely whatever was in the forest.

Without saying a word, the men faded into the shadows, taking the red dots off him. He grabbed the radio in his hands and called out to the others.

"Hunters in the forest. They are likely here to rid the town of whatever haunts the woods. Do not engage if you come across them."

"Etu, what the hell are you still doing in the woods?" He heard Palmer shout.

"I told you, I won't leave Quill alone," he replied calmly. "Tell me exactly where you are, so we don't waste time."

"Get home, Etu. Nancy will have died from worry. Don't you care?"

He sighed. Of course, he cared.

"Don't try to manipulate me with such tricks. I'm heading to the cabin, tell Quill. Once I grab a few tools, I'll come find you."

"No, I won't tell him anything, do you hear me? Go home now. Nancy is—"

A deafening noise from a gunshot and the shattering of plastic sounded as a bullet hit the radio, shattering it into hundreds of tiny pieces. He turned toward where the bullet had come from. It was definitely the men he had encountered a few moments earlier, and they certainly knew how to aim well.

So well that they had managed to shoot the radio he was holding in his hands so high that the debris hadn't somehow managed to hit his hand. He knew from stories his brother had told him that any bullet could create some sort of debris and possibly injure human flesh should it be within its radius, even if the bullet wouldn't hit the flesh itself.

He began to run with all his might toward the cabin to hide from the men, who seemed to be nowhere, but he felt they were close, watching him. His head pounded, likely from the stress, and he felt his throat had dried. Everything around him was blurry as he ran, and his eyes couldn't adjust quickly enough to the images appearing before them. Only the path ahead of him remained clear, although the image shook from the jostling as he sped along.

A few more meters to the cabin, which he could now see on the horizon, next to the lake, as the trees slowly thinned out. He hoped the weapons would still be there, and that the others might be close by, so he could meet them and face the mysterious men together, whom he now began to believe were more than five, as he had initially counted, with three of them marked on him and the other two waiting for orders. However, many there were, they threatened his life without any reason. Perhaps they were responsible for all those deaths.

He slammed the door shut and bolted it, leaning the heavy wooden beam against it to hinder anyone attempting to enter the small cabin. He looked carefully out the small window, the glass of which had now shattered. He saw them lining up, finding cover behind the trees a few meters away from the cabin.

He was right; there were more than five. He counted at least eight, but he couldn't be sure. They didn't seem eager to approach, waiting for him to make the first move, so they could fall into their ambush and shoot him all at once.

He couldn't waste time. Without losing a second, he ran to the shelf with the shotguns and rifles and grabbed a Winchester 1300, which he threw over his shoulder. He snatched a few boxes of shells and quickly stuffed them into his pants pockets, a box of bandages, a canteen he planned to fill with water at the first opportunity, a flashlight, and a survival knife.

The red dots were now moving over the walls of the cabin. They were trying to locate him to kill him, but fortunately, this shack provided pretty good protection, as everything was shadowy, and the little light coming through the small window wasn't enough for them to make him visible to his enemies.

What remained was to find a good plan to get out of there without being seen and have them open fire on him. He turned his gaze back to the shelves. Without wasting time, he grabbed a metal canteen he found and a box of ammunition and emptied all of his powder into the container.

He added a few drops from a bottle of whiskey that was lying around and soaked a towel with it, then poured in a little lighter fluid, knowing it could be found on one of the shelves.

He poured the rest of the oil into the whiskey bottle and, with quick moves, cut the large damp cloth in half, shaped one piece into a small ball, and placed it inside the canteen, which he closed tightly, using the remainder as a fuse for the bottle.

He tied the two containers together and lit the fuse. It had to work. Years ago, he had read about making a Molotov cocktail when he was still training as a firefighter, so as to deal with such a bomb should the need arise, and now, he found himself creating one to create a distraction.

He figured that after the explosion, smoke would form that would allow him to run to the back of the cabin and escape from the men trying to kill him. That way, he would have a few minutes to run as far away as possible and search for the rest of the team.

He opened the door and hurled the bomb a moderate distance, hearing the glass shatter and the sound of fire starting to rage through the grass resonate. Then came the explosion from the metal container, and smoke appeared a few meters away from the cabin.

This was the chance he'd been waiting for. He dashed out of the entrance and headed for the back of the cabin, running away without looking behind him. Gunshots rang out, but there were no voices. He ran non-stop, now feeling the fatigue creeping in as his legs began to grow heavy.

The gunshots had now started to fade, as if the men had lost him and were just shooting at random in hopes of hitting him. After a few minutes, they completely stopped. He felt relief and began to slow down, panting. And that's when he saw it ahead of him.

The red light. A large red dot appeared from the trees and blinded him. Surely someone was there, shining the beam directly into his eyes. Holding one of the two shotguns in his hands, he shouted at the top of his lungs, "What do you want from me?"

No one answered. He began to nervously twirl around to make his enemies think he could still see and was searching for them. His vision slowly returned. He could now see silhouettes all around him in the clearing. More than eight, based on the new count.

Yet, he couldn't quite make them out enough to see their faces. They remained still, waiting for him to make a move. Calm, motionless, and silent. He blinked rapidly, trying to improve his sight. Their faces. Did they wear masks, or were they just expressionless and almost faceless?

He couldn't tell. Perhaps he was too tired, combined with the low light making it hard for him to distinguish their faces no matter how hard he tried. He fired a shot and saw them scatter. He ran too toward the only section from which none of them had emerged.

The ground there was quite uneven, and he constantly attempted not to trip and fall. He was nearly out of breath and would soon be incapable of running any longer as his strength was failing him. By the time he realized the mistake he had made, he had already reached the highway, but he had no choice but to end up there since the men chasing him had left him little room for options.

He took a few steps until he realized where he was. The asphalt beneath his feet was still wet. He cursed and looked back toward the forest, which was split in two by the road. It was pointless to go back. They would find him.

He decided to take the road back, walking to the store where Nancy worked, always keeping an eye around him in case someone appeared to kill him. His cousin would have to survive on his own without his help. He kicked at the asphalt and began to walk. In the end, he hadn't made it.

Eight

They had no time to waste. Dawn was breaking, and they were still in the forest. Up ahead, John was running, followed closely by Palmer and the others. They hadn't stopped running since the time they had entered the forest. Exhausted and constantly on high alert, they looked around everywhere for Leah and Etu.

What had initially started as a simple mission to rescue one person—as simple as it could be considering the dangers of the forest that these townsmen were talking about—had ultimately turned into a search and rescue mission for two people.

Despite the fact that Beaverstale seemed like a small, peaceful town, if one didn't know about the forest, John could be nothing short of impressed after watching the MP5's the police officers had with them.

As Palmer had explained to John, after John had asked, a shipment of 27 MP5's had been issued to them after city's benefactor, Jacob Dawson had donated a significant amount of money to upgrade the arsenal and vehicles used by the police force, firefighters and had even donated enough money for the clinic to be able to buy seven more ambulance trucks and build extra rooms for patients.

The previous night had been difficult. The tension was high, and fatigue was overwhelming. Seconds after the gunshot that echoed both over the radio and deep in the forest, a bullet had fatally struck a member of the rescue team. One of the firefighters, Ian, lay dead on the ground, his uniform stained with blood at the point of his chest.

"One of us has been hit!" Donovan shouted, a relatively young policeman with a slight belly, as he rushed toward Ian.

There was a burst of fire followed by a sound like a pumpkin bursting on the ground, splattering its guts and seeds everywhere. The bullet pierced Donovan's forehead, exiting out the back. He collapsed onto the ground, his face in the dirt, his eyes opened as blood was now painting his blonde hair and the soil on the ground.

"Get down! Get down!" John shouted with all his might, dropping close to the two corpses to confuse the shooters, who wouldn't have a clear aim, as they wouldn't know which body was his, and to grab Donovan's pistol and the semi-automatic MP5 slung over his shoulder.

Everyone followed his example, falling to the ground where they could find the best possible cover. Some hid behind a big rock, others behind trees, and some behind bushes.

Bob crouched behind the trunks of two trees that provided fairly good cover, having muffled Lacey's mouth with one hand until he realized she hadn't sensed the shooters and wasn't moving, only showing some nervousness at seeing everyone else agitated.

Their opponents wasted no time and immediately began sweeping the area with laser beams, leaving bright red dots wherever they touched. Small lights coming straight from the shadows of the forest.

Two of the red dots passed near John's body, which he saw approaching threateningly, making quick yet sufficiently steady movements that revealed the shooters were well-trained and probably steady on their marks.

He remained motionless. The dots were now on his back. He tried to keep his breath steady. The opponents seemed to realize he wasn't dead, likely recognizing that his clothes were mismatched with those of the victims. Though the light under the trees was minimal, they could distinguish several details unlike him and his team members.

They were probably using night vision goggles or were accustomed to low-light areas if they were just ordinary criminals who had set up an ambush. His thoughts went straight to Leah. Had she encountered them? And if so, had she managed to escape?

The dots danced over his body for a few seconds, then moved to his head. They were trying to provoke him into moving, so they could shoot him. He felt as if someone was about to pull the trigger and shoot him. It might have been just an instinct, or even his imagination, but the feeling was very vivid, as if he could hear the characteristic sound of the trigger clicking as the finger pressed it back.

An explosion interrupted everything. Distant, but the noise was loud enough in the silent clearing for everyone to hear. Their enemies had fled, heading toward the site of the explosion.

"Quickly, don't lose them!" Palmer commanded, firing a shot in their direction with his pistol.

Having followed them to the cabin where Etu was supposed to be, had things not gone wrong, they had found the ground burning, and after wrestling with the flames to put them out, they hurriedly resupplied, taking the remaining rifles from the shelves, some cans, and other essentials, and continued to run as the bright dots frequently appeared, accompanied by the sound of gunfire or multiple bursts at once, forcing them to fire wildly and run, hoping to take out at least one of them.

Now, after so many hours of endless hunting, they were still in the forest, running and returning fire to their opponents. As soon as the bursts ceased echoing momentarily, gasping and exhausted, they took a brief inventory, always following John, who seemed anxious and pensive about the shooters.

"Stay close to each other and keep a lookout everywhere. Only then will we have any hope of getting out of here alive," he told them, his voice heavy and breathless.

"If they're responsible for all the disappearances and the deaths, then I want to know where they are and who they are," Palmer said angrily.

"They could be anyone—terrorists, sociopathic killers with sadistic tendencies, gang members, or even deranged former soldiers with PTSD who decided to go hunting to feel redemption and purify themselves from their mental disorder," John replied.

"Maybe you've worked too long in the Special Forces, Mister Emerson," Palmer said. "The most logical explanation is that they are just common criminals ambushing people in the forest and mugging unsuspecting passersby."

"Maybe you should quit and start a career as anything other than a cop," John responded. "No common criminal would have such steady aim, be so well synchronized with the rest of his team, not needing to even talk, and possess such equipment."

"In case you didn't notice, let me inform you that the sound from the automatics was that of M4 carbine military rifles, not to mention I'm sure they have sniper rifles too."

"And it sounds logical to you that some psychopaths formed a gang to kill people?"

"Let me remind you that some of the biggest successful dictators and warlords in history have been psychopaths," he replied. "The way they behaved seemed as if they were hunting for sport. Almost as if they were enjoying how we were scattered after they killed two of us."

A bullet grazed the sleeve of his shirt, making a small tear in the gray long-sleeved cotton shirt he had found in the cabin the night before, in a suitcase full of clothes that, as Quill had informed him, he and his cousin had placed in there during their outings to the countryside on their days off when they visited the cabin. By just a few millimeters, the bullet would have pierced his skin, creating a large scar on his left arm.

He was startled. The lights were coming from across the way, and now in daylight, having reached a small clearing and getting closer to a knoll, they saw no one ahead of them. Just the lights dancing above them. Those small red dots.

"Fire at will," he shouted, and for a few seconds, all that could be heard was bursts from their semi-automatics, pistols, and shotguns.

Apparently, they hit nothing, as the dots remained above them. They fell to the ground and rolled down the hill, now about a meter away from them, hoping it would reduce their enemies' visibility.

"Don't move!" He commanded in a whisper. "Who among you has binoculars?"

He looked toward the sheriff, who had a brand-new pair on his belt.

"You're coming with me!" He said. "The rest stay here!"

They crawled to the top of the small hill and found cover behind a small bush, between two tree trunks. They had to be careful with the lenses of the binoculars not to make any reflections, giving away their position. Right in front of them, within a radius of almost a mile and a half, was dense underbrush.

Palmer began sweeping the area with his binoculars. The beams of light danced nervously, searching for a target, but he saw no shooters anywhere. Just the beams, as if they were coming from nowhere, falling on trees and the ground, searching for something to shoot. He blinked and tried again. Nothing.

"This is impossible!" He said softly. "You try too; I think I might be having vision problems."

John took the binoculars from his hands and looked around. No one! This put him deep in thought. And the night before, their enemy had been invisible.

Though Etu had talked to them over the radio about some hunters, they hadn't seen anything.

Maybe one or two silhouettes running, shortly after the explosion, but they vanished suddenly, and the only thing they could see were those threatening beams that accompanied them everywhere, making them feel quite nervous. The sheriff was right. This was impossible.

"Those bastards," he murmured.

"What? Don't tell me they are aliens that escaped from Area 51!" Palmer mocked him, as skeptical as ever.

"No, but if it is what I think, then things have gotten serious," John said, returning the binoculars to him. "A month ago, the army invested a huge amount into experiments to create a real invisible suit. This suit would contain many small cameras and a handheld computer system that could reproduce images they saw, providing complete adaptive camouflage. It would be as if the suit was made of hundreds of mirrors ready to project illusions for the enemy."

Palmer fell silent. Even when they crawled back to the others, and John began giving instructions on how to avoid their opponents, moving westward through the dense foliage where, up until that point, no one had appeared, Palmer remained silent. Only when they began to run again, did he decide to speak.

"If you're right and these are government camouflage suits, wouldn't it be better to claim we're innocent and surrender? None of us would get hurt."

"That could be the case if so many people hadn't disappeared and they weren't shooting at us madly at every opportunity. There's a great risk that the suits have fallen into the wrong hands, like Russian spies, or that the government itself is trying to cover up any existence of the suit by ensuring nobody who has seen even a little of it escapes alive."

"For a member of the Special Forces, you seem a bit skeptical about the government, Mister Emmerson."

"Sheriff, unofficially I am out of duty, but trust me. When any government around the world wants to cover something, they won't hesitate to make an unknown city like yours disappear from the map, bury dead bodies and train cars of a train wreck with concrete for no one to find after an accident involving the government or even create an excuse for war just to remain in the office and prevent elections that might lead them to prison after they no longer are leaders."

"Damn. Why is all this happening in my town?" The sheriff sighed. "Hey, Quill, do you have any idea where we are?"

"I have no idea; I've never been here before, and it feels strange. I thought I had traveled almost the entire forest."

"Damn, maybe Lacey can help us."

"I doubt it, Fred; she's been acting as if she can't smell the bastards who are targeting us for a while now."

"Strange. Even if the suit contains traces of substances that can confuse an animal's sense of smell, she should be able to smell the gunpowder from the weapons, which, of course, is not the best solution as this could confuse her as we also have shot our guns more than a few times."

"Then again, Lacy should have been able to be able to at least smell of their sweat. Special deodorant substances have been used in the Special Forces to cover odors since the 80s but it's not natural for a trained dog to be unable to spot them after a while as even these special substances prevent the dogs spotting the trails of the enemy only for a little while," John said.

The dots had now disappeared. Temporarily, they had escaped, and unfortunately, as everything suggested, they had gotten lost in the forest, in a section Quill was unfamiliar with.

"They sound very well-trained," Palmer mused.

"Yeah, Fred, if what this guy tells us is true, then they are probably professionals. But how does he know all this?"

"He was in the Special Forces, Bob," Quill replied.

"Special Forces," Palmer repeated as if he was spelling the name of Satan.

"So, we have Rambo with us, huh? Tell us, is it always like this for you, or do you ever live a normal life? Because so far, everything seems to be unfolding like a movie," one of the men with a deep voice began, his partner next to him laughing hysterically, both from the way his colleague expressed himself and his incredulity that John actually worked in the Special Forces.

Palmer suddenly stopped and turned to John, pointing his pistol at him. They all were stunned.

"Fred, have you lost your mind?"

"What's going on, Fred? Tell us."

He looked at him for a few seconds, long enough to see that John hadn't made any expression at all, nor did he seem afraid.

"John, I'm going to ask you something, and I want you to be completely honest with me. Okay?" He continued when John nodded slightly. "Do you think you have enemies, that someone is tracking you down to kidnap your daughter and seek revenge on you in the forest, or that the people you work for might have staged everything, so we would end up here today, risking our lives?"

He looked at him for a moment and then answered, "When did you say the disappearances started?"

"John, you're not giving me an answer, and that doesn't help me much."

"Had I shown up here or had you heard of me from then until now?"

"Just one answer, damn it! Are you involved in all this or not?" Palmer began shouting.

"Does it seem logical to you that I have any connection to a place I didn't even know existed?" He replied loudly.

"Speak clearly, or I'll shoot you! I want the truth!"

"Would I endanger my very own daughter?"

"Who's to say she's really your daughter and not some agent? Who can prove to me that you're not one of them?"

"Then shoot me! Come on, do it! Show us how right your theory is."

The sheriff hesitated. He looked at him for a moment and immediately lowered his weapon.

"I'm sorry. I'm starting to lose it here."

"All I want is to find my daughter," John said. Everyone looked at him. Was it a tear coming from his left eye?

"You're right; I trust you."

"I don't," said one of the police officers, Thatcher, aiming the shotgun he held at John.

Everyone turned to him.

"Thatcher?" Palmer said. "Calm down, everything's fine!"

"Are you in on this too, Freddy?" He asked, redirecting the shotgun toward him.

"What are you talking about? Have you lost your mind?"

"I haven't lost my mind. Not at all! Which of you knew?" He said, nervously swinging the shotgun back and forth, aiming at everyone.

"Thatcher, settle down; none of us knows anything; we're in the same situation as you."

"Shut it, Johnson! You and your tribe have worried us all along with this story about the spirits. How much are they paying you to make a fool of us?"

"Kid, once we get back, know that you'll be put on leave," threatened Palmer.

Thatcher laughed hysterically.

"You think I care, old man? You've been clinging to the chief's position for years. You think I haven't noticed you're a politician's lapdog? There's no way you became police chief right after there was no need for you to be a sheriff anymore. Enough with the lies! Hands up, all of you, clowns," he said, turning to the fat man with the deep voice.

"And you too, Pierce. Just because we grew up together doesn't make you less guilty, nor does the fact that you're playing all dumb and lost in your movies make you potentially innocent."

John saw the moment he needed to disarm Thatcher as he turned his gaze toward his childhood friend. He lunged at him with a stride and grabbed the end of the rifle, pushing it upward.

A burst was heard as the gun misfired in Thatcher's attempt to resist. Then, Palmer grabbed him by the waist and arms, immobilizing him, while John took the shotgun from his hands as he struggled desperately to break free.

"Enough!" Palmer shouted. "This isn't the time to fight. That's exactly what they expect. For us to split up, making it easier for them to kill us. Don't you get it?"

John looked at him, signaling him to go on. Finally, he said something right, at least for the time he had been with John, enough to finally move up in his estimation.

"Thatcher, as long as I judge it appropriate for you to wield a weapon, you will remain unarmed," he said, grabbing the pistol from his belt.

Thatcher began cursing them angrily. Still skeptical about whether they knew more or not, he aimed his finger at them and threatened them. The red dots quickly reappeared. This time, without wasting any time, their enemies shot the last remaining firefighter in the neck, causing him to collapse on the ground, writhing in a pool of blood.

"Damn it!" Palmer shouted.

"Watch out!" John yelled, literally pushing Thatcher at the last second before the bullet flew over their heads as they fell to the ground.

"Colby, stay with us!" Pierce shouted, who had bent over the firefighter's body, his hands bloodied in trying to help the unfortunate man. "Can any of you do something?"

"Cover me!" John said, starting to crawl toward the firefighter.

They began firing for cover. The shots were not continuous as they tried to conserve their ammunition. Their opponents had the upper hand in equipment, and this meant they shouldn't waste all their bullets without managing to kill at least one to learn more about who they were, what they wanted, and who supplied them with such equipment.

After a few missed shots by Palmer and the others, their opponents stopped shooting and probably retreated further into the forest toward the north. John was now applying a piece of his torn shirt to the spot where the man had been injured to stop the bleeding, knowing it was already too late.

He knew he wouldn't achieve anything even though something within him urged him to try. A few seconds later, the man's eyes were vacant. Dead. He gently pushed the firefighter's eyelids with his fingers and slipped back into the cotton long-sleeve shirt, this time without the ragged undershirt beneath. For a moment, none of them said anything. Finally, someone spoke, and from his voice, everyone realized it was Pierce.

"It was Colby. Kid was only twenty-two. He was supposed to get engaged next week," he said almost coldly, staring in shock at the dead man's body.

They all looked stunned. Everyone except John. It wasn't his first time seeing someone die, let alone someone he knew. Only five of them remained now, including John—six, if they counted Lacey. After sitting for a few minutes to rest, they decided together to find the nearest exit.

"We'll return with enough men this time," Palmer promised John, who was tortured by the thought that his daughter might have fallen prey to the invisible enemies hunting them.

His head felt like it was about to explode. He felt nauseated and overly exhausted. So much so, that for a moment, he began to see blurry. He quickly drank a few gulps from the canteen that had been given to him before entering the forest with the rescue team and tried to regain his composure.

"Thank you for earlier," he heard Thatcher saying next to him.

"Don't mention it," he replied.

"I'm sorry for my behavior. I honestly don't know what got into me."

"Probably a panic attack. I've seen soldiers have them on the battlefield, so I understand. Stress can completely incapacitate a person in critical situations."

"Kid, are we far still?" Palmer exclaimed loudly so Quill could hear, who was now leading the group since he knew the forest better.

"Not particularly, Sheriff. Just a little further is the road that leads to the old ranch."

"Oh, perfect! You're taking us right to our dump," Palmer complained.

"I'm sorry, Sheriff; I thought it would be safer to be on the road than in the forest. At least there, some of our vehicles might come by and take us back to town. Besides, it's not too far away."

"He's right, Fred," Bob said in a calm, soothing tone. "Good idea, Quill!"

They called on the radio for a patrol car to come and retrieve all five of them. A young girl, Edna, who was on patrol at the time, replied.

"Of course! We'll be right there with the jeep," she answered, and then they heard her whispering, "Ronnie, hey! Wake up, we have work to do!"

"Guys, you don't know how thankful we are," Thatcher replied on the radio, ready to burst into tears.

Palmer took the radio from his hands to avoid leaking information before they returned to town or before someone suspected that the rescue operation had ultimately ended in a fiasco.

"Thank you very much! We'll arrive at the meeting point and wait for you there," he said.

"Of course. You weren't more than a pe—" came the voice from the other end before Palmer hung up the radio and returned it to Thatcher.

"We all have radios except for John and Pierce, whose fell while we were running through the forest earlier," Palmer began to say. "Stay close together. I can't afford to lose anyone else today."

"Sir?" Quill tried to say.

"As soon as we get to town, go home. I'll return with John, and let me tell you, if I get denied reinforcements this time, I'll threaten to resign."

"Sir?"

"John, I'm sorry for everything again. The truth is that I've feared this forest with all that's been said lately. I still fear it. But we have to act, don't we?"

"Sir?"

"I'm talking! What's so important that I must—" he started, and his speech was abruptly cut off when he saw them all stop and fix their gaze to the left, behind the foliage, where several meters away, appeared the buildings of a city.

A city they had never seen before. A city disjointed and quite different from a typical American city architecturally. As if they had traveled to another country. The dirt path on their left led to a highway that reached the town and disappeared among its buildings. He had never been in that place before. Apparently, neither had any of them.

"Interrupt," he managed to say, almost stuttering as he turned to face the city, frozen in awe at the sight. "What the hell," he murmured.

They were lost. They were somewhere from which they didn't know how to escape, and suddenly, they realized they were slowly forgetting the way back. What could this strange place be? And how had they arrived at that point? Did it have anything to do with the murderers?

Did the forest itself perhaps play tricks on them? Time stood still. They would remain for quite a while, staring at the sight. Staring, lost and powerless to do anything. They were lost.

Nine

Eda Walter, a rookie police officer who had just been transferred to the town of Beaverstale, was sitting next to Ronnie Robinson as they headed to the meeting point in a police jeep. She was driving since Ronnie, with whom she often patrolled, avoided driving.

She appeared pensive and suspicious. She was sure there weren't just five colleagues in the woods but many more; however, the sheriff had only mentioned those five for some reason. Had they gotten lost too, like everyone else who entered that forest? What would she face when she finally encountered them?

"Wow! Eda, I never thought I'd see you speeding," she heard Ronnie say, realizing she was going too fast.

"Sorry, I was thinking about something."

"You miss your city, right? I feel you! I don't tell this to many people, but I'll reveal it to you for solidarity," he began. "Before this, I was in New York. Great times. A woman, two kids, and a beautiful apartment on Victor Street waiting for me every day. I had friends, a very successful career in the force, and I was the local gym legend," he said, flexing his huge biceps.

"But everything stopped when I shot that guy in the car. Andrew Cross, his name was. A former convict with four murders under his belt. That day, he was going home to hide his son's Christmas gift under the tree. He was clean from drugs and had cut ties with the gang he belonged to."

"Seven times," he murmured with trembling hands. "I shot him seven times. He was just trying calmly and friendly to open his car trunk to help me with my investigation."

She was in shock. She didn't know what to say. No, she didn't miss her city; on the contrary, her life here was quite nice, and everyone treated her well. She was preoccupied for another reason, but at that moment, she couldn't tell him anything. She understood that her colleague wasn't mentally in a good place to hear what was troubling her, even if it was related to their job.

"I didn't know you had a family," she managed to say.

"It was a wonderful family."

"What happened? If you don't mind me asking."

"I drank heavily for two months, stayed out late and drove to forget. Eventually, I decided I couldn't stay in that house and that neighborhood anymore. I requested a transfer. My wife and I never separated; she just couldn't follow me. She visits whenever her job allows."

"I understand," she managed to reply with difficulty.

"Is everything okay?" He asked her.

"Yeah, I guess," she lied.

"If you don't mind, I'll crack the window open a bit," he said to see her shrug.

"I'll turn here for a detour, okay?"

"On the dirt road?"

"We're saving a whole turn," Eda complained.

"Damn, it's only been a couple of days since we washed the car."

"Okay, I promise that as soon as we get back to town, I'll wash it myself, to spare you the trouble."

The dark-skinned man next to her laughed, and his bright white teeth contrasted sharply.

"Deal!" He replied.

After a muddy descent among towering trees, they managed to climb a little and get back onto the road. They had saved at least ten minutes from a long uphill stretch that suddenly led to a very steep slope that turned sharply left, having previously caused several accidents, making drivers turn at incredibly low speeds.

Her head hurt, and she believed it was from the conversation she had just had with Ronnie. Meanwhile, she tried to shake off a disturbing image that had lodged deep in her subconscious for the past few minutes.

As they drove along the dirt road, she thought she saw a silhouette slowly moving toward them between the trees. It had perhaps brown or amber-colored eyes, close to caramel. With quick and almost spasmodic movements, the creature with a human body, dangling like a broken marionette, began heading their way, letting out a grotesque howl while holding a bloody chainsaw in its hands.

At that exact moment, she turned to check if Ronnie noticed anything, but he appeared not to have seen anything as he looked around calmly. He hadn't heard it either. Strange. She glanced into the rearview mirror. The figure in the red striped jacket, black shirt, green tie, pale face suggesting anemia and hypotension, the slick back hair glistening from pomade—except for the thin lines made by the comb as it had been styled back—and the enormous sharp teeth that had been exposed when he started running after them, had vanished.

She looked toward the forest, which would now be far from them for quite a while due to the cliff until they reached the next descent. No, there were no such creatures as the one she had seen. It was just her imagination running wild. It was definitely a figment of her imagination.

"Everything okay?" Ronnie asked her at some point.

"I think I'm a bit tired."

That was the truth. She hadn't been sleeping well for the past few days. Anyone could see that in her face, which had been quite pale lately with dark circles under her glossy blue eyes.

"Do you want to stop for a bit? I can drive."

"No, it's fine!" She replied and loosened her straight red hair.

She grabbed the radio in her hands and tried to communicate with the others but received no answer.

"Probably the signal isn't good here," Ronnie said disinterestedly.

She ignored him and continued trying. She knew her colleague might be right, but she was always meticulous about her work.

They arrived at the meeting point. They pulled in close enough to park the jeep on their left, at the entrance to the forest. If they followed the path, they would reach the old ranch. Normally, they should have shown up in a few minutes, but after ten minutes, no one had appeared.

"Do you think they got lost?" She asked him.

"I don't think so. They might just be delayed since they're walking."

"Okay. We'll wait for them."

"Exactly, we have nothing better to do."

A familiar noise made them both jump in their seats. The sound of a rifle shot. Judging by the strength of the sound, the bullet passed quite close to them.

"Are you okay?" She asked anxiously.

"Yeah. What the hell was that? Why would they shoot at us?"

"I don't know. Hey, what are you doing?"

"If it's our guys, we should let them know, so they don't waste more bullets; you know we'll pay for them out of our pockets later."

"No, Ronnie. Ronnie!" She whispered, trying to stop him as he got out of the jeep.

"Calm down! Besides, I always carry protection just in case," he said with a smile, lightly tapping the holster of his gun hanging at his waist as he moved in front of the jeep. "Nine shots," he muttered and then turned toward the forest.

He waved his hands for them to see him. His huge hands and back appeared as if they were about to tear his uniform shirt as he moved his arms quickly, like a bird trying to fly.

"Freddy? Kid? Bob? It's me and Eda! Come on," he began shouting in his powerful voice.

No response.

"Freddy? Guys? If you're coming closer, shout so we can hear you! We're waiting for you to leave!"

He turned to her, looking at her with an expression of disappointment. No one was listening. He shrugged and turned back in front of him.

"We heard a shot. Are you okay?" He shouted again, receiving no response.

Eda half-closed her eyes to pay attention to something on him. Small bright red dots were moving on his hands, which were now lowered. Maybe even on his chest, but she couldn't know that from where she was. Some dots appeared on the jeep's dashboard. Others started moving on the passenger seat.

Someone was aiming at them. That was the only certainty. They couldn't aim at her because Ronnie's massive muscular body was blocking the beams from reaching her. Time began to slow down. She was getting ready to shout at him to warn him if he hadn't noticed—and by the way things looked, he hadn't noticed.

She turned toward him to get back into the passenger seat. Everything was happening so slowly that she felt as though she were witnessing some scene of agony in a movie from a first-person perspective. Her heart was about to leap out of her chest, and she felt her pulse rising dramatically.

She opened her mouth, and her voice sounded hoarse as it began to take shape to become a loud and clear scream, wanting to yell at him, "Ronnie, look out!" He hadn't paid attention as he wasn't looking her way.

Gunshots echoed again, this time more than one. Time resumed its real speed as Ronnie instinctively ducked to cover behind the jeep's door while Eda pulled the gear lever to select reverse.

"Oh damn! Start it, Eda! Let's go!" She heard him shout as he emptied an entire magazine from his nine-millimeter pistol.

She jumped into the vehicle, which had already started moving, just before the enemy's bullets literally riddled the jeep, blowing the tires and making the engine start to emit smoke.

"Damn! It won't start, the damn thing!" Eda complained, trying to get the vehicle moving to escape.

She was so shocked that she hadn't noticed that a bullet hole had formed on the windshield, having struck Ronnie's chest. Only when she turned toward him to tell him to abandon the vehicle and continue on foot, did she realize that Ronnie was holding his chest with his hand, which was covered in blood.

"Oh my God! Ronnie, are you okay? Ronnie!"

"Luckily, they just grazed me!" He managed to say, showing her his wound and the hole in the passenger seat from the bullet that had continued its path. "But it hurts like hell! It stings!"

"I understand, but we need to get out of here. They're going to—Get down, get down!" She screamed at the sound of more gunfire and breaking glass.

Whoever was aiming at them wanted them dead. Suddenly, her thoughts began to rush through her mind like a wave. What if the radio wasn't working because their colleagues were dead at the hands of those criminals? What if the gunshot came from one of their colleagues in danger?

The forest really was dangerous after all. Who knew what was really hidden in there? And if they did know, then why hadn't any attempts been made to apprehend those causing fear in their quiet town? She remembered hearing about a helicopter flight attempted to find the causes of the disappearances and deaths. But nothing had been found. Would they die there? Had the time for their mysterious disappearance come?

She wouldn't get to make her family proud after all, as her career was likely about to end. She looked at Ronnie, who was loading his gun and emptying it rapidly, shouting and cursing at their assailants. He had only two magazines left. That was it. Their end was near. The sheriff and his men would never show up.

Ten

They all stood in awe in front of the city that lay just a few miles away. None of them uttered a word as they stood frozen in place. The sheriff, John, Thatcher, all of them. Only Lacey remained untouched by the spectacle, as if she hadn't seen anything in front of her.

Surely, a dog couldn't naturally comprehend that a strange city resembling a small town from a former Eastern Bloc country had sprung up out of nowhere in the middle of a forest, just a few miles outside a quaint little American town, yet she didn't seem to feel any curiosity to move forward.

She acted as if there was nothing in front of her, focusing solely on a frog that stared back at her with its big eyes, perched on a stone in a small marsh a few meters away.

"We're not at the farm," Palmer began to mutter. "Right, Quill?"

"Uh, sorry, Sheriff. I have no idea what—"

"Don't apologize, kid! I just wanted you to confirm that I'm not seeing some vision," he replied and turned to the others. "Do you see this too?"

"Yes, Sheriff!" Thatcher answered. "You see it too, right, Pierce?"

Pierce was frozen, staring blankly ahead with his mouth agape. He had no connection to the world around him.

"Pierce!" Thatcher shouted.

"What is this place?" Pierce asked, almost dazed.

"I don't know. None of us knows. Bob, make Lacey shut up already!"

"John, I think we're going to need your knowledge. Any idea what this city could be?" Palmer said, turning to look at him.

"Do you have an army base nearby?"

"Not a single one, why?"

"You have never seen or even heard an explosion in the forest, right?"

"No. Should we have?"

"And the size of the city is too large," John muttered, deep in thought.

"For what?"

"I was thinking it might be some abandoned missile testing site or a training ground for soldiers," John explained. "But from where we are, the city looks far too big for that to be the case. And if it was a testing site, then it is too close to the actual city and it's built inside a forest so that would not make any sense, especially since from what I've gathered, Beaverstale exists since—well—the beginning of the United States as a nation, if not earlier, before the Civil War."

"What if the Russians built a city within our country and are preparing to invade us?" Pierce asked.

"Pierce, we're not in one of those movies you watch," Palmer replied, trying not to laugh.

"It could be!" John said. "That would explain why those guys are chasing us. Would you ever shoot a cop if you were an American soldier? Because I doubt anyone else has access to a suit of adaptive camouflage that makes them invisible, other than our soldiers or their soldiers."

"Alright! Let's say that's true. How did they build the city without anyone noticing?" Thatcher asked, filled with skepticism.

"Have you noticed a sudden influx of people in your town recently, or even seen any construction trucks passing through?"

"No. Just the usual expected visitor rates, as always," Palmer said.

"Then, things are getting pretty complicated," John replied, gazing toward the city.

"Are they still following us?"

"No Sheriff, I don't see anything," Thatcher answered.

"Here's some good news. Quill, is there any chance we can find our way back to the farm so we can meet up with Eda and Ronny? They should have arrived, and I hope they haven't walked into an ambush."

"It's tough, Sheriff. I've never been in this area before."

"Can I ask what you're thinking?" John asked him.

"Unfortunately, only the military can handle something like this, right? All that remains is for them to believe us."

"That'll be difficult."

"Eda, do you read me? Over! Eda? Damn your radios and their goddamn inventor."

"Thatcher, calm down! We'll try with mine, alright?" Palmer suggested.

"That's not the problem, Freddy. They're listening, but not responding."

They all looked at one another for a moment. Maybe their enemies had reached the meeting point before them, and now, Eda and Ronny were dead.

"Don't even think about sending someone to check. If we split up, we're doomed, more than we already are," John advised. "Let's find a way to get to the main road and head back on foot if necessary to the city."

"I agree. Let's see if Lacey can lead us out of here."

"If she stops looking at the frog like it's Ramon the alligator," he said, pointing at her still engaged with the poor frog instead of noticing the city or the people who were chasing them.

"I think after this adventure, she should be relieved of her duties. She's starting to age," Palmer declared. "We can't rely on a dog that doesn't recognize danger to warn us."

"Shh, wait a minute!" John said quietly.

He looked around. The frog appeared anxious, but not because of them or the snipers, but because of Lacey. However, even the birds flying above didn't seem disturbed. It was as if nature didn't perceive the danger.

"Is something happening?" Palmer asked, breaking his train of thought.

"I'm not sure. Give me your radio."

He remembered an emergency frequency. A frequency they could reach out on in situations like this, created specifically for Task Force Scorpion, a small unit that had been established for black operations during the 80s to communicate in case the inevitable happened, like a Russian or North Korean invasion, or Escobar and Noriega releasing nuclear bombs, in case they truly had at least one in their possession.

Although the unit had been disbanded, John and everyone involved with it had kept that frequency open for emergency reasons, after being tasked with joining one of the three next-generation experimental task forces that would be trained to be deployed in future scenarios.

John knew about the Pentagon trying to create invisible suits and constantly failing, simply because he was one of the very few to test them, or more likely shoot down dummies wearing the suit in case he found one. After having riddled tens of them, John was confident that the suits were all another Hollywood fever dream. And yet, now, he was witnessing them in action, working as if they had been perfected years ago.

Of course, John could never talk about his work to his wife or his daughter. Colleagues of his, like Victor, he could talk to and share his thoughts about things he saw, because they were all deeply involved. There was no harm telling a fellow unit member or former fellow unit member whose nose was covered by the mud that was top-secret programs, about another top-secret program.

After all, the real reason John was now officially off duty was because he had been chosen to test tactics and form a new Special Forces unit, or more likely, a basis on which the next generation of Special Forces would operate, which included hand signals, movements, ways a soldier should hold a weapon for greater efficiency, accuracy and safety and even workout programs for them to remain fit and combat ready for the most demanding of situations.

He tried to reach out to anyone he could on that frequency. For a moment, he hoped it would be Sam responding, though he quickly remembered he had been deployed to Afghanistan recently, far away from his wife and daughter.

He heard a noise from the other end. Like someone was trying to communicate. The signal was weak, but they could definitely communicate. At that moment, he felt a bit calmer.

"Tail in the field, repeat, tail in the field. Over!"

He received no response for several seconds. Then, he tried again.

"Tail in the field, is anyone receiving? The tail is in the field. Over!"

"The Nest is receiving. Over!" A female voice replied. It was the Pentagon.

He turned to look at the others for a moment.

"Nest, please hold for coordinates," he said.

"Status?"

"Code Blue!"

"Hold on a moment."

He turned to face them as they looked at him, confusion written across their faces.

"Here is Scorpion King!" A deep male voice from the other end of the line said. "State your call signs!"

"Alpha Echo thirty-five, forty-eight."

"State your coordinates!"

He turned to them.

"Do we have a map?" He whispered.

They shook their heads negatively.

"Great," he muttered. "Scorpion King, do you read me?"

"Loud and clear!" The man with the deep voice confirmed.

"Check the map for the city of Beaverstale." He remembered the city was between three states, something that would not be easy to explain. "It's between the states of Georgia, Tennessee and Alabama. There's a forest by the same name as the city, surrounding it and I'm inside it."

He heard murmurs from the other line.

"Are we sure this isn't a prank?" The man with the deep voice asked the other men in the room.

"This is Lieutenant Commander Emerson, Sir, Special Forces? Former Seal? Operation Bleeding Sand?"

"You have got to be kidding me. Scorpion Unit Two?" The man said and returned to John. "Lieutenant Commander, Sir, we're going to need you to give us some additional information."

"They are highly trained and well-armed," he started to say.

He looked at Palmer for a moment. A red dot danced on his left knee. He hadn't noticed it. Pierce, who was checking their right side, had a similar dot marking his shoulder. Before long, he realized they all had at least one of these dots moving over them, ready to deliver an undignified end.

"Lieutenant Commander, do you read? Over!"

He ran to throw himself with all his strength onto Palmer, pushing him onto the others, so they all collapsed onto the floor like dominoes, while he started shooting into the air for distraction.

"Take cover!" He shouted.

They quickly got up and started firing in all directions until they realized they were likely about to be surrounded.

"We have no other choice!" John shouted. "Run toward the city, we'll hide in a building!"

Shooting at regular intervals and running as fast as they could, they managed to reach the outskirts of the city. It looked abandoned. Like a ghost town. Buildings resembling those of an Eastern Bloc city stood all around them. A little further off, an MI-24 helicopter lay crashed against a building, having smashed through the wall it struck, bricks scattered all over the road around it.

How that helicopter had made its way into American territory without anyone noticing was beyond John's imagination and he knew for sure that it couldn't be the Hind-D chopper that had been secured in Chad, almost three years ago.

"Open door, open door on the left!" Thatcher shouted, signaling them to follow him.

They entered the building and immediately headed for the upper floor. After they knocked over a shelf at the entrance to block the adversaries' entry and hastily sealed the windows with whatever they could find, they took defensive positions, waiting for them to arrive. Perhaps there was a way to set a trap for them. Perhaps they could manage to counterattack.

"John, call again and tell them where we are!" Palmer said.

"No."

"What do you mean no? That wasn't a question but an order! I don't care who the hell you are, but you're in my city. Call them now!"

"Listen to me!" John told him, staring down the street, waiting for one of their enemies to appear, or at least for some dot to show up in the space they had barricaded. "Everyone, turn off your radios!"

"Have you lost your mind?"

"No, I can't explain it to you yet, just do it!"

After exchanging skeptical looks for a few seconds, they decided to listen to him. After all, so far, he had saved their lives several times.

A good while passed, and no one showed up. Neither the terrifying bright dots made their appearance. They left Thatcher and Pierce on guard while the others reorganized right behind them to discuss. At one point, John and Quill went down two floors to search for anything that could be useful, returning with some water bottles, some cans, batteries, and a kitchen knife.

"We'll rest a bit and continue," John suggested.

"Aren't you going to call for reinforcements?"

"If what I'm thinking is true, then it's probably better not to call anyone."

"What do you mean?"

He straightened up and began to move toward the door.

"Stay here and cover me! I'm going to check the building across the street."

"Hey! Where are you taking the radio?" Palmer asked.

"You'll see. Everyone else, keep your radios off!"

He exited the building they had barricaded and moved across the street. He took a quick glance at the helicopter on his left, hoping its communication systems still worked, and then ran toward the building across from him, holding his pistol in hand.

Once he climbed high enough for them to see him from the other side, he purposely placed the open radio where the others could see it and then quickly began moving back down.

He ran toward the helicopter. His breath was heavy, and he felt exhausted. The abandoned MI-24 chopper in front of him looked like a gigantic bug waiting patiently to attack and tear him apart. He approached and opened the door, sealing it behind him to ensure no one else could enter while he was busy. By that time, his companions were still in their positions, watching curiously his movements.

He grabbed the radio and once he tuned into the frequency of the abandoned radio, began transmitting messages. It didn't take long for what he aimed for to occur.

The red dots appeared, simultaneously marking him and the location of the radio. He watched as a dot entered through the helicopter's window, making small jittery circles on his chest. Instinctively, he stood still for a moment, focusing all his strength in his legs to spring up and find cover behind the cockpit of the helicopter.

At the same time, he tried to listen for where the shooter might be, but to no avail. He was surely somewhere on the roof of the building next to the one they were in, but remained invisible, and an unseen sniper was just as dangerous as a sniper right behind him aiming straight at his head.

Where the hell are you, you bastard? He thought, and with his hand, tried to slightly tilt the helicopter's machine gun as close as possible to the point from which the dot was coming to create a distraction, discovering to his surprise that the helicopter's electrical systems as well as its weapons were in good condition and ready for use.

The sniper probably realized this and stopped aiming at him. The dot immediately disappeared from above him, and only then did John realize he hadn't been breathing this entire time. "Good boy," he muttered, watching the dot head toward the floor where the radio was.

He turned off the helicopter's radio and waited patiently. He took one last look toward the spot where he believed the sniper was but found nothing. A few seconds later, as the sniper turned back toward the helicopter, he discovered that its door was open, and John had vanished from his line of sight. That at least is what John realized when he heard a gunshot and the sound of glass breaking.

He climbed back up to the floor where the others were, taking advantage of the distraction. They looked at him, bewildered.

"How did you know?" Palmer asked.

"Most of the time, when a group of soldiers wants to find their target, they use different tactics, such as trained dogs or scouts. We haven't heard any dog barking, apart from Lacey until now, right?" He said, looking everyone in the eye.

"In case there's no dog, like in small Special Forces teams, they usually send the team's tracker forward, while the others follow after his signal, leaving behind him the sniper or snipers, who only move when given the order by the team leader to proceed. All of this in case they're exploring an area or trying to locate their target without falling into an ambush."

"That sounds time-consuming," Palmer commented.

"So, it would probably be a mistake to assume that they located us so quickly after we lost them back in the forest just because they happened to get lucky," John told them.

"Great," Thatcher muttered.

"Throw away your radios!" Palmer commanded. "From now on, we rely solely on our ability to communicate as a team."

They sat down to eat, taking turns on watch. Their invisible enemies did not appear, nor did the terrifying dots from their scopes. It would be getting dark soon, and they would have to sleep. Perhaps their enemy was waiting for that moment to set an ambush; after all, who could predict the movements of an entirely invisible enemy?

They would continue a little after midnight after they had regained their strength and had all slept for at least two hours. If they could voice their feelings at that moment, they would have said fear. That was what consumed them at that moment. Fear.

Eleven

After he returned to the town, he didn't speak to anyone. Not to those who looked at him in confusion, nor to those who approached to ask what had happened and if he had found the others.

He had hidden the weapons in an abandoned dumpster just outside the town, which firefighters had previously used to simulate fire situations, and continued toward the store where Nancy worked. She was the only thing he could think about at that very moment.

As he walked in, the customers suddenly turned to look at him as if they had seen a ghost. Without paying them any attention, he walked to find one of the waitresses to speak to her.

"Is Nancy here?"

"Etu? Yeah, she's back at the fryers, hurry!"

"Thanks!"

"You should be ashamed for making her worry!" He heard the waitress's voice echo behind him.

The moment Nancy caught sight of him, her breath nearly caught in her throat.

"I'm sorry," was all he could respond, knowing that he had upset her.

She ran to him and hugged him with all her might. She couldn't believe he was real; yet, here he was.

"You look terrible!"

"Sorry!"

"No, it's okay! I'm just glad you came back alive."

As soon as they got home, he rushed to the bathroom to shower. After a while, he emerged naked, with Nancy admiring his toned body. He hadn't told her anything about Quill, nor that he planned to return the following morning. He felt he needed to go back and find his cousin, as leaving him alone might not bode well.

Hours passed quickly, and afternoon arrived. By this time, Etu hadn't gotten out of bed. Nancy hadn't complained. He had returned alive. It would have been unfair for her to be angry because he hadn't really spent any time with her.

"Baby?" He heard a familiar, melodic voice say. "Honey?"

He felt someone nudging him. With great effort, he managed to open his eyelids, unable to move his body. Everything in front of him was blurry. Someone approached to see him better, and then came into focus.

"Are you okay?" She asked.

He tried to respond but felt completely powerless. His mouth and throat were dry. He attempted to nod and wave his hand affirmatively, feeling exhaustion throughout his body. Even such a simple gesture seemed difficult for him. He made it down to the kitchen, where he drank an entire bottle of water.

After that, he returned to their room, trying to hold himself steady as he climbed the stairs. He struggled to walk to the bed, where he collapsed like a lifeless mass, seeing Nancy watching him anxiously.

"I'm so glad to be back with you," he replied hoarsely, his voice still weak from fatigue, caressing her.

"You're burning up!" She exclaimed. "Etu, you're on fire!"

She was right. His skin was hot as if it had come straight from a furnace, but he couldn't easily perceive it. His pulse was elevated, which combined with the exhaustion he felt, likely meant he was beginning to show symptoms of a fever. Perhaps the dampness of the forest and the fact that he had been naked for a long time, exhausting himself while running through it, to blame. That had to be it! Nothing serious. He would rest a little, and the next day, he'd feel great again.

"Don't worry; it's probably just exhaustion," he replied and leaned in to kiss her.

She couldn't resist. She had been waiting for him all night and had been worried. Now that he was near her, she would do anything to prolong the moment as much as possible. They began kissing softly, their hands resting on the mattress. Calm and wet kisses echoed in the room.

He grabbed her hands to bring them to the back of her neck, and he pulled her closer, starting to caress her while kissing her more passionately now. She began to explore his toned, muscular body with her hands, which was as hard as a rock. They continued for several seconds without taking a breath until he pushed her down to lie back and continued kissing her while lying down.

A queasiness stirred in his stomach. His pupils instantly constricted as he felt his stomach churning and ready to explode, as if someone had poured a large amount of grease inside him, turning his stomach into a viscous mush. He fought to avoid vomiting on her and pushed her away, so he could get up from the bed.

"Etu, what's wrong?" She asked, bewildered by his strange behavior.

He looked at her for a fleeting moment and then ran to the bathroom. She followed him and found him with his head in the toilet, making sounds as he vomited uncontrollably, leaning against the wall with his left hand for balance.

"Do you want me to bring you something? A glass of water, anything?"

He fell again with his head into the toilet and started to vomit again. He seemed to be suffering. Sweat began to pour all over his body, as if he had gotten drunk and was now reaching the point where all alcoholics were embarrassed about and disgusted by when they came to their senses and remembered their actions during their drunken state.

"Did you drink or eat something? Could it have upset your stomach?"

"Burgers," he tried to respond.

"The burgers I made?"

"Yeah," he answered in a hoarse, wet voice. "I don't know what upset me."

He reached out with his right hand to flush, but at that moment, his stomach lurched again, forcing a wave of chemical mush of chewed food and gastric fluids to spew from his mouth, along with blood.

"Damn it, damn it," he muttered almost silently, now unable to speak loudly, as saliva dripped from his lips.

He continued this way for a little longer. Each time he thought it was over, his stomach would start to torment him again. His throat was now burning, and he had a taste of spoiled cheese in his mouth. Alongside this, a severe headache began to stab at his head.

He gripped his head with both hands, instinctively trying to ease the pain, disregarding at that moment that holding his head was doing absolutely nothing. She grabbed him, trying to lift him after many attempts, and eventually managed to lift him and lead him back to their bed with great effort.

"Don't move, I'll go get the doctor," she said, flustered.

He was left alone in bed, waiting for her. Unable to move, he lay on his back gazing around the room. It was getting dark, as he could tell it was late afternoon. And then he saw the beams from the scopes of snipers entering the space, searching for him.

Instantly, he closed his eyes, as he had no strength for anything else, and when he opened them again, he saw Doctor Lazlo, that kind bald man with the long beard who, when not at the town hospital, one would find walking the streets smoking his aromatic pipe. Nancy stood next to him. The room was even darker now, and the beams had vanished.

"Etu, good evening. How are you?" The doctor asked.

"Where's Harold?"

"Harold wasn't feeling well, as he was out with you yesterday until late with that crazy situation, so he went home. Two hours ago, when we spoke on the phone, he was fine; now, he's likely just sitting and watching the Lakers score."

He chuckled quietly at the doctor's comment, exerting the little strength he had left.

"When he was still new to town, he would come to the camp, supposedly to watch the Lakers with a friend from the locals. But the real reason he came was for his sister."

"He's still young. As far as I know, young people tend to fall in love."

"Yeah, but her brother didn't agree with this, and once he discovered the real reason for his visits, he never called him again."

"Well, Etu!" The doctor said. "Your girl was worried about your health and came to me, begging me to examine you. She said you were in very bad shape to walk here."

"That's an exaggeration," he said. "I'm fine, see?" He continued, trying to prop himself up and walk, but before he could finish his sentence, his legs betrayed him, and he collapsed to the floor. "I'm fine, I'm fine! I'm fine, I'm fine," he began to nervously repeat, trying bewildered to hold onto the bed to stand up again.

Nancy rushed to help him, but he raised his hand to stop her, continuing to murmur, "I'm fine! I'm fine, I'm fine, I'm fine," with his eyes betraying that he was starting to lose touch with his surroundings.

"Etu, please, what's going on?" Nancy asked anxiously.

"I'm fine."

"Etu, buddy, I'm afraid I'm going to have to check you. Nancy, please give me a hand."

They grabbed him against his will and laid him back on the bed. He was beginning to calm down and come to his senses now.

"Look at this!" The doctor muttered, "This guy is burning up like he just came out of a volcano. How do you feel, boy?"

"Not so good. I'm burning and my head, my head hurts, it hurts."

Unable to hold it back, he started to vomit, soiling the bed and himself. Blood came from his mouth again, along with gastric fluids and pieces of food.

"He did it again, huh?"

"Yes, Doctor, he was throwing up blood and couldn't stop."

"I'm sorry, Nancy," Etu managed to say, saddened that he had soiled the freshly washed sheets.

"No, my love! It's okay, we'll change the sheets together, and everything will be fine, alright? Go take a shower to clean up, and we'll talk later. Can you walk, or do you want us to help you?"

He nodded affirmatively and managed, though with difficulty, to get up and eventually walk slowly toward the door as he grabbed onto anything nearby to steady himself.

"You did well to tell him to go take a bath," he said.

"How bad is it?" She asked, pulling the dirty sheets to replace them with fresh ones.

"I can't say. What's for sure is he has caught a cold. What concerns me, though, is that he's showing such extreme symptoms. I worry that he didn't have sufficient antibodies, or that he might have exhausted his body, to put it colloquially, so that the microorganism managed to multiply so quickly and get him to this point."

"Oh my God!"

"If it's a cold, then the only thing he'll need is to eat solid foods if you both want to avoid the entire vomiting situation and hot foods at the same time for the fever. Of course, if the vomiting stops, I'd suggest soups. It's not too professional of me to say this but a goulash soup can work miracles! Anyway, try to give him some Snapples, you know, from the supermarket. The vitamins will do him good."

"So, I shouldn't worry?" She asked, just finishing up changing the sheets.

"I don't think there's a need. I believe that in two or three days, he'll feel better."

She accompanied the doctor to the entrance. Outside, it was getting dark, as another day had come to an end. She would start her shift in an hour. She sighed and looked at the doctor.

"Thank you! Really, thank you."

"When I left Miami six years ago, I knew I wanted to go somewhere where I could really be useful to people and not just see lawyers with bloody noses begging and bribing us so that no one would find out they had been in the hospital. I'm glad to be here and glad to help," he said and then walked away.

She returned to the room to take the soiled sheets and put them in the washer, discovering with great surprise that they had disappeared.

"How much time do we have?" He asked her, and Nancy startled as he approached from behind without her noticing.

"Etu? Are you okay?"

"Of course, I'm okay," he said, pulling her into his arms and starting to kiss her.

Twelve

She felt dizzy and exhausted. Maybe, in the end, her choice hadn't been a good one. Perhaps all her choices up to that moment had been wrong. That was it! Her choice to become a police officer was a big mistake, one that found its own special place among a series of ongoing errors.

Maybe it would have been better if she had stayed home with her family in Crystal Pine. Perhaps she should have chosen a different career, like being a supermarket employee, for example. What was so wrong with that?

Okay, she admitted it might not sound as interesting or dynamic, and it didn't carry the same prestige as being a police officer, but it was still a job, and maybe if she did well, she could make decent money from it since she would be saving money on the side and make sure she would keep her job.

She missed home. Her grandmother's cookies, the chocolate milkshake her parents used to make for her, the comics she bought with her pocket money every Friday, her small but warm and protective bed in a room full of memories, some well-preserved and others weathered with time, and of course, she missed Lex, the superhero boy with the perfect abs, the square glasses he wore with the yellow frame that he put on deliberately to give him style, and his gorgeous straight shiny red hair, which was cut and styled in a way that definitely reminded her of Japanese influences, which suited him even though he was American.

He was the person every boy wanted to be like and nearly every girl fantasized about. Eda looked forward to each Sunday. She would sit patiently waiting for the cartoon show to end, and then she would snuggle in her bed to watch the new episode of *The Punishers*, the series starring this Lex guy, the epitome of obsession for every modern teenager of the past decade.

The Punishers had their likenesses in action figures, T-shirts, bags, pencil cases, notebooks, books, cassette tapes for game consoles, and even deodorants. She reminisced about home and thought that maybe the best thing she could have done was never to leave.

Her parents would have been proud in other ways that carried less danger for her life. If she had died, would they have found out, and if so, how would they react?

She opened her eyes as she was coming to. At first, everything in front of her was blurry, but after blinking a few times, everything began to come into focus, and a beautiful forest, bright and filled with lovely colors, appeared before her. In front of her feet lay a blanket, a picnic set, food, and drinks.

She was sitting cross-legged while bunnies with almost human proportions, looking like they had jumped straight out of a comic book, drank tea and laughed. Some were eating from a cake that sat on the main platter. She wondered where she could possibly be.

She had almost forgotten everything that had happened before. Or had she completely forgotten now? She couldn't remember how she had ended up there, what had come before, not even the thoughts that had been swirling in her mind just moments ago.

Then, someone appeared before her, walking slowly and elegantly toward her. He was wearing the white body armor and the white plastic helmet they used in battles for protection, just like the other members of *The Punishers* wore armor and full-face helmets in different colors.

She felt somewhat strange. Was it real? Was she really in the universe of her favorite show? How was that possible? She was paralyzed while trying to give herself a logical explanation. She couldn't find one. Maybe there wasn't one.

He approached further, nearing her more and more, and with each step, he seemed clearer. He smiled at her, and although his protective visor was almost blue, she could make out his shining eyes the color of caramel. They didn't talk, and the awkward silence made the scenery seem even more serene.

She felt safety and calm inside. She thought about whether there was anything she could say to him, but nothing came to mind; perhaps that was for the best. The moment was beautiful enough even without talking. She felt the strong sun warming her and lulling her. Everything was wonderful. Or maybe it wasn't wonderful. It was terrible and horrifying, she thought, as she saw everything change.

Bright red dots appeared, dancing on Lex's armor. He seemed to ignore them, as he continued to move toward her, smiling, as if nothing was happening. His eyes gleamed, and then, there was an explosion of blood and flesh that splattered his armor and helmet, as one of the cartoonish bunnies was shredded by bullets that rained down on it.

She hadn't even realized that the blood from the bunny had splattered on her when suddenly, Lex grabbed one of the other bunnies and smiling at her, slit its throat, sending its blood splattering onto both of them.

This was not Lex. He was not the member of *The Punishers* who hunted ruthless criminals and terrorists to save the world with the robots and dozens of vehicles and weapons at their disposal. He was some monster who was now conspiring with the shooters threatening to kill her. Yes!

She had started to remember again. The shooters were trying to kill her. They had shot Ronnie, who wasn't there. And now, this boy in front of her was acting strangely. Still, inside, she didn't exactly feel fear, anger, or horror. She didn't know exactly how she felt.

As the shooters killed the other bunnies, Lex sat across from her, calm and smiling as always, and picked up her cup to pour her some tea. He filled the cup and offered it to her. When he realized she wasn't going to move, he gently set it in front of her and began crawling toward her across the tablecloth.

He took off his helmet and moved close enough that she could smell his scent. He was even more handsome up close. His lips were now getting closer to hers. Just a bit more, and he would kiss her, fulfilling her dream. At that very moment, she realized how she felt.

She felt that she was enjoying it. And yet, it wasn't natural, considering that the person she admired had just done something terrible. Yet at that moment, she was savoring it. She heard the sound of gunfire and felt a pain in her chest. She looked at him, baffled, while he still smiled at her. He hadn't come closer to kiss her but to execute her. In his right hand, he held his gun, which he had just used.

She slowly blinked her eyes. She was no longer in the strange landscape she had found herself in moments before but inside her police jeep, which was hanging from a tree trunk that had sprouted on the side of a cliff. It took her a few seconds to realize what was happening.

She hadn't dreamed of the place she had just been. It was too real to be a dream, and the pain in her chest still existed, though a quick check revealed that thankfully, she hadn't been shot but only hurt. She turned to her right. Ronnie was not there, which made her start to wonder where he could possibly be at that moment.

She needed to be very careful with her movements. If she moved too suddenly, there was a great chance the trunk could break and the vehicle would continue its path to the ground, killing her.

She heard a sound of breaking wood, and her adrenaline shot up. She had only a few seconds—if any—to get out of the jeep and grab onto something to avoid falling to her death. She tried several times to unbuckle her seatbelt, which had jammed from the weight that had shifted forward and was pulling on her.

Her mind began racing incredibly fast to try and free herself from the seatbelt and save her life. With much effort, she managed to push against the floor of the vehicle with her feet, lifting herself slightly and allowing space for the seatbelt to loosen.

This, of course, meant that the weight of the vehicle shifted, causing the horrific sound of wood breaking to echo again, freezing her in fear and making her feel her blood come to a complete stop. She tried to press the button on her belt to release herself.

"Come on, please," she murmured.

After several attempts, she finally managed to free herself and grab onto the ceiling of the car to prevent herself from fully falling onto it and shifting the weight of the vehicle even more. Carefully, she opened the door, trying not to do so too suddenly, and slowly began to walk onto the door to step outside the car.

"Please, God, I'm only fifty-five kilos; let the door not break like in the movies."

She heard the signature sound of wood still breaking. She realized she didn't have much time. The vehicle was already starting to fall as the trunk leaned and broke. She took a deep breath as quickly as she could, just as the trunk had finally been severed, and the jeep began its descent toward the ground.

At that exact moment, literally in the last fractions of a second, those crucial fractions needed for her reflexes to kick in, she jumped, grabbing the back side of the jeep and without wasting a second, like a cat escaping its cage, she leaped again and momentarily clung to the cliff as the jeep fell away from her.

The cliff didn't have any rocks or even a ledge to grasp onto, so she began to fall as well, trying to hold onto something. She pushed with her feet and hands against the uneven ground, trying to get as close as she could to the remaining part of the severed trunk until she finally managed to grab hold.

She looked down. The jeep was almost to the ground. There was a loud crash of metal hitting the ground violently and shattering glass. For a moment, she felt the urge to burst into laughter. She had the impression the jeep would catch fire and explode in a dazzling flash of flames, just like in action movies. But in the end, the vehicle merely lay there, still and lifeless, crushed. With great effort, she managed to climb up the slope of the cliff. She looked down once more, and her vehicle was still in its place.

It began to rain. That complicated everything, as she didn't know where in the forest she was now, and she had no means of transportation to return to town. Soon, it would be dark, and she needed to find shelter for the night. She attempted to call the others on the radio, but she realized she had lost it.

"Damn it!" She muttered.

She sat for quite some time under a tree, shaking with anxiety and frustration. What would happen next? The shooters who had attacked them were still in the forest, and she knew that well. She was alone and unarmed, as she never carried her gun with her while in the vehicle. She grabbed a piece of wood and a rock. She would sharpen it and continue to search for an exit in the woods.

Thirteen

The residents of Beaverstale had grown accustomed to the phenomenon of disappearances over the last few months. Nevertheless, they still couldn't digest the disappearance of the sheriff and so many police officers. A day had already passed, and the sheriff and his men were nowhere to be found.

The second day was approaching noon, almost halfway through. Nancy woke up, feeling exhausted. She looked beside her and saw Etu peacefully sleeping. Just the day before, she had been so worried about him that she thought she might have died from anxiety. Yet, here he was, right next to her, and she was watching him sleep.

Despite the fact that Doctor Lazlo had never made her feel like he was a professional, his advice that Etu would just rest seemed to have worked. No medication, no nothing. But then again, for however long she knew the good doctor, she could only tell a thing for sure: His advice never seemed to be professional, despite his posture, but he could treat any patient like a magician.

Even the people from the Indian village seemed to adore him, despite the fact that they hated doctors with a passion, ever since the early 50s when Doctor Gustav Meyer had tried to poison them deliberately, leading to the Indian tribe to feel disbelief toward anyone who was a doctor—Doctor Lazlo and Harold were the only exceptions since then and Harold was more likely tolerated by them due to the fact he never spoke about his profession, but rather his passion about the Lakers.

The phone rang, and she rushed downstairs to answer it. After managing to free herself from Etu's heavy, muscular arm that was holding her tightly, she quickly slipped on one of her slippers, trying to find the other one, but eventually tossed it aside and decided to proceed without her slippers.

"Hello?"

"Hi Nancy, how are you?" She heard a familiar voice say.

"Doctor! I'm fine; is something happening?"

"No, no, don't panic! I just wanted to ask if Etu is feeling better."

"You won't believe it," she told him. "Since you left the house, he got out of bed and acted like nothing ever happened; it was strange."

"That does sound strange. Hey, Harold, watch out!"

"Is everything okay?" Nancy asked, after she heard a glass shattering sound from the other side of the line.

"Yes, of course. It's just that Harold is a little too enthusiastic today, I'd say."

"I took care of the fat lady in the other room!" Harold declared loudly with a tone of joy.

"What the hell? Harold, do you think you could please go home and rest today? I think everything will be fine."

"Doctor, are you sure everything is okay?" She asked him again.

"Of course, Nancy! Listen, I'll come by later."

She felt someone standing right behind her, just a breath away. Like a shadow stalking her, or like the creatures in the room she and her classmates would often see at night when she was younger. She turned around, and her blood ran cold when she saw Etu looking at her almost expressionlessly. He snatched the receiver from her hands and forcefully placed it back in its cradle.

"He doesn't need to come," he told her in a steady, quiet voice.

"But my love—"

"Enough!" He shouted.

She looked at him, bewildered. This was not the Etu she loved. Something had changed in him. He really was acting strange. He grabbed her in his arms and began kissing her possessively. She pushed him away.

"He doesn't need to come because I'm perfectly fine, my love," he told her.

"Are you sure?"

"Sure."

She didn't believe him. His behavior had changed so much and so suddenly that she could no longer trust him, and she had no intention of letting him convince her with sweet words and caresses. Something strange was going on, and she could feel it.

Etu had never shouted at her. He was always sweet and caring. And now, he was acting cold and emotionless, his entire body hot, so much that she could feel the heat touch her skin, despite him not holding her hands or touching her.

"I'll cook," he said, heading toward the kitchen.

She didn't waste a second. She quickly rushed up to their room and got dressed in record time. She was going to meet the doctor. Her gaze happened to fall on her nightstand, where there was a photo of them. In an instant, her eyes teared up as she thought about how everything had changed so suddenly.

She slowly made her way down the stairs, feeling her heart ready to break with every step. She was worried that Etu would realize she was leaving the house and try to stop her. Downstairs, she heard the methodical sound of a knife hitting a cutting board with force.

She managed to crawl from one side of the open kitchen to the other without him noticing her. Etu was busy cutting, or rather destroying, a piece of meat with nervous, almost robotic movements. The sight was terrifying and clearly made her realize that Etu was no longer himself.

She headed toward the main entrance of the house. After reaching it, she tried to open the front door.

"Damn it!" She muttered.

Etu had locked the door, probably knowing she would try to leave the house sooner or later. She looked around desperately, hoping to find keys, but there was nothing. That was when she heard the sound of the knife abruptly stop, followed by footsteps coming from the kitchen.

She ducked behind the couch to hide just as Etu stepped out of the kitchen and moved toward the front door. She remained there, motionless, staring at the door without daring to blink, and she could swear he was barely breathing. In his hand, he still held the large kitchen knife.

Nancy tried to move slowly and crawl toward the basement of the house, a small space they used for storage, knowing there might be a way to escape through the small window. When she was almost at the stairs, she accidentally bumped into a metal magazine holder that produced a faint creaking sound on the wooden floor—so low that anyone could have easily missed it.

Yet, Etu immediately turned his head back and then his body, starting to walk briskly toward the point where he had heard the sound, just behind two armchairs that were a little before the stairs leading to the basement, where they kept magazines and photo albums.

The phone rang, causing him to momentarily stop walking nervously and glance at the wall where the phone's base was mounted. He picked it up to hear who it was. This was her chance. Without wasting time, she got up and ran toward the basement as Etu sliced through the cord of the receiver, just a few steps behind her, not paying her any attention.

She reached the basement. Once she climbed among some boxes and old items that had been left there, she managed to reach the opposite side of the room. Nervously and now clearly having lost her composure, she tried to open the window, which had become stuck over time and could barely open.

She put all her strength into it to force it open and attempted to jump to get up and out. It ended up being much harder than she had imagined, but it was her only escape, and she had to get away from Etu, who appeared to be completely unhinged, judging by his actions.

"It was that baldie, old, fat piece of shit, Lomaz," Etu shouted as he was now trying to find where she was. "That cartel supporting fat fuck might have fooled everyone that he's a doctor with his forged papers and shit but he won't fool me! Did you know his papers were forged? You're not talking, are you?"

She pushed with her hands to free herself from the window as her legs dangled in the air. Fear overtook her. She pushed again. Then again and again.

"Why did you defend him yesterday when he told me I had to stay in bed? Are you hiding something from me?" He said while he started kicking and punching things, the sound of the hits coming right into her ears, getting closer and closer as Etu was approaching her, oblivious to where she was.

When Etu finally reached the basement, realizing she was there, Nancy had escaped from the house.

Fourteen

He didn't know how it was possible, but it was. John was far from the rest of the group. One moment, they were together in the same room, taking shifts as they thought of a plan to escape from their enemies, and now, he found himself wandering the streets of a ruined city. A strange city. Very strange.

The buildings reminded him mostly of a country from the Eastern Bloc—or, as he should have gotten used to saying by now, the former Eastern Bloc—while other parts of it appeared as though they had been uprooted from some Western European metropolis or one of the cities in his own country, having been placed there from someone or something.

All of the city was abandoned, forgotten, and unmaintained, especially some structures that were almost being swallowed up by the ground. After spending the entire night wandering the city, he was now trying to gather his thoughts and finally find Leah.

He felt odd. It was as if he had visited this place recently. But he wasn't sure about that. He felt at once as if he had been to this place again and, at the same time, as if he were seeing it for the first time. With these thoughts in mind, he entered a building to rest for a few minutes before continuing his search for his daughter.

A man holding an automatic rifle, probably a soldier if he could read the state of his uniform, pointed it at him while sitting in a corner of the building, almost unable to get up.

"Bang!" He said. "You're not with the others."

"The others?" John asked, puzzled. "Have you seen them? Do you know where they are?"

The man burst into laughter.

"No one knows where they are and when they show up."

He realized the man was referring to the snipers. He seemed to have completely lost his sanity. How long had he been there?

"Do you know anything about them?" He asked.

"Absolutely nothing. Thirty. We were thirty people on maneuvers. They decimated us! None of us remained. Vehicles, weapons, even a barrel of water had vanished, and we ended up here, trying to escape them."

"Have you been here for several days?"

"Yes. The last ones left is me, the sergeant, and a maggot named Tim. I've lost track of them for a few days, so they're probably dead."

He paused for a moment. Perhaps he had seen Leah somewhere. Maybe there were other people there. He had nothing to lose by asking him.

"Have you found anyone else here?" He asked.

"Now and then, I come across strangers. After that, I never see them again. No one escapes this place."

"A teenage girl, tall, black-haired with a punk haircut?"

"Punk haircut?" The man with the old uniform and automatic rifle said. "Anyone might have passed through. Sorry, but I've lost track of everything by now."

He looked out the window for a moment to think about his next moves, as the soldier chuckled quietly, saying, "No one escapes from here, chief." He turned toward the door he had entered and began to walk outside. "I'm bored," he heard the soldier say calmly.

There was a sound from the soldier's rifle safety, then a loud crack from a shot. John turned toward the soldier, aiming his pistol, as he momentarily thought the soldier had shot to prevent him from leaving. He faced the lifeless body of the soldier, his head flooded with blood pouring out abundantly. He had placed the weapon in his mouth to commit suicide.

He didn't know him, but John was one of those people who always followed the code of ethics they had learned. He stepped closer and searched the soldier's pockets for a handkerchief but couldn't find anything. Finally, he tore a piece from the soldier's shirt he wore under his camouflage tunic and buttoned it back up.

He covered the soldier's head with it and then placed the soldier's dog tags on top, keeping one of the two plates to return to the soldier's family. That was all he could do at that moment.

He moved toward the door through which he had previously entered. In the corner building across the street, there was a commotion. And music! He moved slowly, keeping his pistol in hand, and peered stealthily through the window to see what was happening inside. Nothing.

The smoke in the room kept him from understanding much, other than the fact that there were people inside, probably having a good time, with the sounds of broken dishes, bottles of drinks slamming violently against tables, whistling from people dancing, and of course, music. There was something strange about this music. It reminded him of older times.

He suddenly burst through the door, aiming in all directions. The smoke from the cigarettes began to pour out through the door where John stood, and the area inside the establishment became clearer. At least thirty people were inside, indifferent to his presence.

Old music from the 1930s played on a phonograph. The patrons looked strange. As if they had just stepped out of some black-and-white movie. Dressed in old clothes, neatly groomed, and the men had styled their hair with pomade—while the women had curled theirs. He lowered his gun and hid it.

After approaching a group of men smoking their pipes, he stood for a moment to grasp what he was just seeing, and then he spoke to them.

"Have you seen a girl walk into this bar?" He said loudly to be heard.

"Other than the employees? Of course not! They don't belong here," one of the patrons replied seriously, his voice deep and resonant.

He was puzzled for a moment by what he had just heard. He literally felt as if he had been transported to another era.

"Hello sweetie, come with me!" He heard a woman's voice say as the woman behind him pulled him by the elbow.

She led him to the bar, sat him down, and signaled the bartender to bring them two beers. Then, she sat down next to him.

"I heard you're looking for a girl. You're in the right place," she said, winking, slightly turning her head and making her platinum curls sway.

"Look, I don't want you to take it the wrong way, but I'm married," he told her, showing her his wedding ring.

She burst into giggles.

"First time here, huh? It's okay, drink your drink to relax, and everything will come in time," she said, caressing his leg before getting up to approach another group.

"Wait!" He said, holding her hand, feeling awkward.

"Changed your mind, sweetie?" She asked, bored.

"I'm looking for my daughter, a teenager, she has black hair all, you know what? Forget it! Did you see any girl other than you walk into this place?"

"No. What would she be doing in a place like this?"

He repeated her words, muttering, as she walked away from him. He stayed for a while, observing the patrons, trying to better grasp what he was seeing. He decided to approach another group and talk to them.

"What about those outside? The killers?" He asked a man with a thick mustache, who was calmly sipping his whiskey.

"We're winning!" He replied.

"We winning?"

"Come on, what world do you live in, kid? The Nazis have nowhere to hide."

He must have flipped, he thought.

"Damn the Nazis!" Someone shouted, and everyone in the bar echoed him, raising their glasses high.

"I think it's time to have some fun," the woman who had spoken to him earlier said, pulling him toward her and starting to dance with him, against his will.

She held his hands and spun him around, making him feel dizzy. He tried to stop her, but she was too strong. He couldn't give any logical explanation. The music now got louder, and he felt himself spinning more and more. Suddenly, the record on the phonograph stuck, and the melody repeated, becoming monotonous and annoying.

He began to see everything as fragmented scenes with small intervals of black background. As if he were closing his eyes for a period and then, the next moment, the landscape around him had changed, becoming more sordid, more horrific than before.

The patrons, one by one, suddenly found themselves dead in their seats, their blood covering themselves, the furniture, and the floor. Those who remained alive, until they died too, did not seem to realize what was happening. They continued to laugh, drink, and have a good time.

Then, just as John came to again, he found them dead as well, as he spun mercilessly in the very center of the establishment, driven by that woman. She smiled at him with her pearly white teeth, and her blue eyes shone. Perhaps she too didn't realize what was happening.

Blood began to flow from her nose. Then from her eyes. She remained calm and smiling, as if she felt no pain. Her body began to fill everywhere with deep stab wounds, and every time John came to and looked at her, she had more. Finally, having lost her strength, she released him, and he fell onto a table, shattering it as he spun.

The music stopped, and he lifted himself up. Everyone in the bar was dead. He didn't know who had killed them or how, until small memories sprang up in his mind like flashes. He saw himself grabbing anything sharp he found in front of him and stabbing the patrons, sometimes knives, sometimes bottles, breaking them before he would slit someone's throat, and other times dragging them to impale them on screws that protruded from the beams of the establishment.

He took a few steps back, trying to comprehend what had just happened. There was no way he could have caused this. At that moment, the dead stood up, tall and proud. They began to dance and have fun again, without paying him any mind, as now the music had started echoing in the bar again, this time faster than before.

With quick steps, he approached the exit. Just before opening the door, a hand grabbed him, forcing him to stop. It was her. Her eyes were covered in blood. They were gone. They had been removed, and blood dripped abundantly.

"Come back and visit us!" She told him in an eerie, shaking voice.

He had never felt such intense fear in his life. He felt like he was about to explode in a panic attack. He recoiled and quickly left the bar. He was out of breath and felt his throat go numb and completely dry. His heart was beating excessively hard, and despite being scared, he also felt a strong sense of confidence.

An inexplicable contrast struggling within him, as he walked down the street, aiming in all directions, trying to identify any hostile targets. A significant amount of time had passed since he entered that bar, yet it felt like just a few minutes.

Meanwhile, the deeper he went into the strange city, the more he felt he was losing his sense of direction. The instincts that made him capable as a soldier were now on standby.

John continued walking through the deserted city. No one was visible anywhere. As if the invisible snipers had simply abandoned them or, better yet, imprisoned them inside that strange city, and now had left in search of more victims who would become prisoners.

Or perhaps they were somewhere, on some rooftop or high vantage point they used as an observation post, watching every desperate move they made to survive? They were watching him. They were all watching him that was for sure. He may have felt lost as he couldn't find the way to the forest that would lead to Beaverstale, but he sensed their presence. He felt their eyes fixed on him.

They might not have been aiming at him with their rifles anymore, as the horrible red dots hadn't appeared for a while, but they were certainly ready to shoot him if they decided the show no longer entertained them. Silent, unseen, and armed. Perhaps for the first time in his life, the thought danced in his mind like fire that continuing forward might ultimately be pointless.

He fell to the ground and swiftly crawled over to the car that was on his right. A few meters away, two soldiers with respiratory masks and automatic rifles walked as if patrolling. Their gear was definitely not American. He could easily tell that.

But it didn't seem like it was from any nation he knew either, as the uniforms looked like those he had seen in science fiction comics when he was a kid, black, bulky, tailored with some really heavy cotton, polyester and canvas fabrics that made them look rugged, just like in the comics.

They hadn't spotted him yet, although he needed to decide whether to kill them to steal their weapons and perhaps search their clothes and bags for any clue that would help him understand who they were, if they had anything to do with the snipers, and if they knew where his daughter was, or if he should avoid them and continue wandering in the ghostly city.

The men seemed to be unaware of his presence, making it easy for him to slip by them and reach the opposite block, using the cars as cover. He sighed with relief as he finally reached a safe spot. So, the city wasn't truly abandoned after all.

As he continued onward, a patrolling man suddenly jumped out from an alley. John didn't lose his composure and immediately grabbed the man's rifle, pushing him toward him and striking the gas mask-covered forehead with all the strength of his head.

He then hit him with the edge of his pistol in the chest, causing him to let his weapon hang as his hands instinctively tried to cradle the spot that hurt. He doubled over in pain and seemed defenseless. John wasted no time. He grabbed him by the collar and shoved him against one of the two walls that created the very narrow alley.

"Who do you work for? Who are you?" He hissed in a low voice.

The man started cursing, or rather making strange sounds, as John couldn't understand the language he spoke. It certainly was not Russian, Colombian, or Arabic, or John would have been able to tell. He hit him with his left hand on the neck to make him stop shouting.

"A teenage girl with spiky black hair. Where is she?"

The man continued to speak incoherently as he struggled to get away from John. He shoved him against the opposite wall, kicked him in the waist just before he crashed against the bricks and collapsed on the ground. He violently lifted him and continued the interrogation.

"Listen, jerk. You've kidnapped my daughter. Tell me where she is, and I'll let you live."

After realizing that the man was unwilling to help him, John aimed his pistol at him and, holding him, began to push him along.

"Take me to the others, so I can explain the dream, shithead," he told him as they walked, stepping over a wet patch that had soaked part of the wall. "If you don't want it to be your last piss, you better take me to the others. Do you understand my language?"

The man abruptly turned, slipping from John's grasp, and grabbed the knife from his person to attack him. John quickly stashed his pistol in the back of his pants and seized both hands on the knife, closing it within his flat palms. He swiftly turned the knife to the left, causing his opponent's hand to hurt.

After holding his opponent's hand firmly with one hand, he delivered two swift blows with his right hand to the soldier. One to the chest and another to the neck. Then, gripping his opponent's head with both hands, he twisted it, snapping his neck.

The man fell lifeless to the ground. Without wasting time, John seized his weapon, which appeared not to have a laser sight like those of the men chasing him and slung it over his back. After searching him thoroughly, he found the man's dog tags.

They read Grisha Lokitnov. Possibly Russian, though the language he spoke was not Russian. He would have realized that, as he moderately understood the language, having been forced to learn it due to his job. He searched his pockets and found a photograph of Grisha with his family. He was a tall blond man with very short hair, blue-eyed with a square face. He had a beautiful blonde woman, and they were holding a baby in their arms.

For a moment, he felt bad, as he too was a parent, but at that precise moment, his paternal instincts returned, and he thought again that his own family and his daughter mattered more to him. He found a flask on him. To his great surprise, while he expected to open it and smell the distinctive scent of vodka invading his nostrils, a different smell came out, equally heavy but more familiar. Whiskey.

The other items on him, like a lighter and some cigarettes, were equally useless, although the cigarettes especially betrayed that the man had already been on American soil since the specific brand was American and wasn't exported to any other country. Having taken only his opponent's weapon, he continued onward, searching for Leah.

Where were the others? He didn't know if he would ever find them again. Looking up at the sky above him, he suddenly realized it was nighttime. Strange. Just moments ago, the sun was high in the sky, and now, suddenly, the sun had disappeared, and the moon made its presence known, with stars filling the black sky.

"No way, this can't be!" He murmured.

He turned behind him. The road he had come from was not the same as before. He ran to verify if what he had just seen was indeed true. It was! He couldn't recognize the landmarks he was passing by. He had never been there before.

Once again, he had gotten lost in the streets of the mysterious city, which seemed to change structure continually, trapping him within it. He felt his pulses racing. At the same time, the colors around him became vivid.

He felt strange. He shouldn't be happy or feel euphoria, yet at that moment he felt like he could easily start running and never stop. Neon signs, wild metal music from the last decade, and voices echoed from everywhere.

"Dad?"

He tried to turn toward the direction where he had heard the voice. He knew that voice very well. It was Leah's voice.

Fifteen

Once again, he didn't know what had happened before. He remembered very little. His memory was fragmented. One moment, he was wandering around the city, and as far as he could recall, it was noon; the next, it was evening, and he found himself in some sewer, running as if something was chasing him.

Now, he was there. He couldn't determine exactly where that was, but he realized he was inside a building from which he could see a tropical landscape outside, calm and serene. It was daytime. He wondered for a moment if he had slept at all, and after more images flashed in his mind, he concluded that the most likely answer was that he hadn't slept at all.

Yet, he didn't feel tired. It was as if he was caught in a current. He could easily run a marathon or go out to have fun. Have fun? Why would he have fun? He was in an unknown place where his life was in danger. There was no time for fun. And yet, a part of him struggled to urge him to start moving rhythmically.

In front of him, a few meters away, stood Leah, looking down at the ground in fear. Next to her, a young girl with red hair in a police uniform had her arms wrapped around her and was trying to calm her down.

"What's your name?" John asked her.

"I already introduced myself," she replied.

He really had started to develop memory gaps.

"Oh yes, right. Leah, are you okay?" John said while moving his eyes to face his daughter.

Leah didn't respond.

"I'll make sure we get out of here, okay?"

"I'm just glad you're here with me. I don't understand any of this!"

He wanted to answer her, *do you think I understand?* But he didn't say anything to help her calm down a bit.

"I can't understand why we went out for a walk after lunch earlier. We got lost and now, we're here."

"I have no idea," he managed to reply.

"And that hole? You saw it, right? A giant red dot spreading beneath my feet and suddenly, it sucked me in. I can't understand anything."

He didn't remember the event she was describing. He began to wonder how many hours they had spent together. And all those hours he had spent with the police looking for her? It was as if it had never happened, based on her account.

"Have either of you seen Palmer or any of the other officers? Joanne, I'm asking you too if you know anything."

The girl looked at him, perplexed.

"Eda; that's my name, Eda!" She corrected him. "I lost contact with your search party since noon, presumably from the day before."

"What search party?" Leah asked. "When was my father in a search party? Unless that happened when I lost consciousness after that flash appeared beneath my feet."

"And one more thing!" Eda added. "The flash you described, I didn't notice anything like that. Just red dots from laser sights. Someone or some people are in the woods. I was shot at." Eda stopped for a moment, as if she was trying to rephrase her words. "Me and my partner."

"We had the same from the same guys," John replied.

"Wait a second. Laser sights?" Leah asked, confused.

"Yes," John answered.

"I saw something like what you're describing. When we were reaching the city this afternoon and stopped in the woods. I thought they were hunters. They aimed at me and then at you, but then they stopped; they must have realized we were people and not prey."

"Today?" John asked, knowing that he had been searching for his daughter for at least one and a half days now.

"Those hunters are the ones who attacked my partner. But we started looking for you yesterday."

"And our team, both before and after we communicated on the radio," John replied. "Leah, what do you mean by today? At least a day has passed. Maybe two, judging by the sun outside."

"And what do you mean you were with a team and looking for me? We were together the whole time. Until I found Eda. By the way, Eda, how did you know me?"

Eda sighed. John could easily tell she had had a truly rough time in the woods. Her eyes could give away the pain and the tiredness, but there was something more about that girl that John could sense, although he couldn't find the words to describe it. Regret for being there? No. It was something else. Something that felt like Eda had probably wished her life was different from what it was now.

"You are the girl we've been looking for since yesterday," she managed to answer after a brief pause.

"What?"

"Really! You disappeared two nights ago, shortly after dinner. We've been looking for you ever since," John told her.

"I could swear, I could swear none of this ever happened."

"So, you don't remember, then?"

"No."

"What exactly do you remember?" He asked her.

"We were sitting down for dinner. I think I wasn't feeling well. I don't remember what happened in between, but we found ourselves in a city and were wandering around. It was night, and there was no one anywhere."

"Interesting," he replied, rubbing his chin.

"What are you thinking?" Eda asked him.

"There's a logical explanation for all of this, but we need to investigate."

"Meaning?"

"28 October 1943. That was the date the Philadelphia Experiment took place."

"Bullshit! That's pure conspiracy theory, Dad."

"I'm sorry, but it is real history. Certainly not as exciting as the movie your older cousins dragged you to see, and you brought me along to the cinema, but it's still reality. The ship was brand-new and literally a gem for its time. It was, however, given to the Greek government along with two other similarly new ships to cover any trace of suspicion."

"Parts of the ship were sealed, and the teleportation equipment was removed. Around the same time the ship was donated to Greece, the army began conducting top-secret research on the mountain of Penteli in Athens. Information about what was inside the cave on the top of the mountain was never officially documented anywhere; however, a massive amount of radiation equipment, as well as experimental teleportation devices were reported being transported from

Athens to another countries to end up in American army bases until their traces completely vanished."

"So, you want to say that the guys with the lasers transported us to another dimension?"

"I wouldn't say that," John began to explain. "You have a lake here in the area, right?" He asked Eda.

"Yes, quite a big one, actually."

"One hypothesis is that the Eldridge was teleported to the lake. After all, quite a few people reported seeing a ship appearing in several different places at the same time, although we don't know all the locations where it appeared since there weren't witnesses everywhere."

"So, this created some kind of field in which people are teleported?"

"Yes, that could explain why each of us has experienced different events at different times. Leah, for example, has experienced the passing of at least one day, according to her account, while I've been here for at least two days. One and a half, if we want to be more precise."

"And the second theory?" Leah asked skeptically.

"Perhaps the phenomenon caused by the Philadelphia Experiment can autonomously occur in nature, or maybe in the future, someone has invented a way for people to travel back to the past. It's very possible that the soldiers we see are coming from the future, perhaps trapped within their own experiment, and this experiment may have had several disastrous consequences, if one thinks that there's an entire city in the middle of nowhere."

"Furthermore, I tried to interrogate one of them, and he spoke a language I didn't understand. It wasn't Russian. I can't tell what language this was but it seemed ancient. Almost like a language from a forgotten civilization. On top of all that, the man didn't have the same weapons as the other soldiers, neither did he have a suit that made him invisible, nor a weapon with a laser sight."

"His weapons looked strange. Almost as if they came from the future. The city, moreover, looks in some parts destroyed, as if a war had taken place. It's likely that the experiment happened during a war or that some device was activated at that time."

He paused briefly, looking around. He recalled the events that had taken place inside the strange cabaret—the dead, the dance with the woman, the horror he had experienced.

"Logically, this field also creates many anomalies," he finally added. "I found myself in a place, where the people sitting inside were at least five decades back in time."

"So, you're trying to say we're now traveling through space-time," Leah replied.

"I can't find another logical explanation. The only thing I still don't understand is that the police dog, Lacey, like all animals, doesn't perceive the danger."

"Maybe it has to do with the monsters?" Eda asked.

"Monsters?"

"I saw a strange man with green hair running at high speed in a way that seemed like his bones were broken, right toward us, as Ronnie, my partner, and I were driving to get here. I haven't seen him since then, as he disappeared, but there may be other creatures like him."

"I don't know. Really. Do you remember anything else?"

"Yes, but I'd rather not remember it at all."

"Meaning?"

"I've been in this place for almost a week."

Sixteen

Eda was wandering through the forest. She cursed every now and then, irritated. She believed it was her fault that she was there. It was her fault that her life had taken such a turn. Earlier, after managing to climb the cliff and arm herself with a stick and a stone, she had attempted to head down to the jeep after first finding a narrow path leading down into the woods.

She had left her gun there. It was raining heavily, and she was soaked. She approached the jeep, and after finding her handgun, she quickly grabbed it and started walking toward the forest.

A loud bang echoed, and she found herself flying mid-air. She fell hard against a tree. When she turned her gaze back, she saw the jeep, which had been thrown into the air, just like in the action movies that played on Octane Channel, usually before midnight as an off-air message would appear on screen before the channel would change its top left sign into a music key, since there was an arranged broadcast takeover during nighttime by Cadenza TV until six in the morning and usually, the Baroque Hour would air two hours after midnight.

"Pierce would tell me that I'm too tough to die if he saw this," she said, thinking about her colleague's reaction if he had been there.

She always left her gun under the seat. Of course, she had never needed to use it and despite leaving it there was against regulations, Eda never felt comfortable carrying a weapon around, as she had joined the force to help people instead of intimidating them.

Finally, the moment had come when she would use it for the first time. A ten-shot SIG Sauer P226, quite convenient and easy to handle. She checked to see if the magazine was full. It was the first time she had done so, since until then, she had never needed to worry about whether her weapon was loaded, and she placed it back in the gun, satisfied by the sound of the magazine locking in place. Meanwhile, the rain had just stopped.

For quite some time, she continued wandering alone in the forest. She had now taken off her soaked uniform shirt, keeping her badge in her pocket, leaving on the gray sleeveless tank top she wore underneath. She was searching for Ronny, but in vain.

He was nowhere to be found. Not even a trace of his blood to determine approximately where her colleague might be. Night was approaching, and she was still alone. She found shelter in a wooden shed about three kilometers from where she had left the jeep.

There was a water jug, a radio setup, and a diesel generator there. She took the jug, and after unsuccessfully trying to communicate over the radio, she grabbed some blankets she found on a shelf in the makeshift shelter and fell onto one of the three mattresses she found to sleep.

It wasn't long before the dots appeared, spilling into the space and moving nervously, searching for her. She wrapped herself tightly in the blankets. She took all the blankets she found on the shelf and threw them over herself.

It wasn't the best camouflage she could have thought of, but it was enough to make her, combined with the darkness in the shelter, look like discarded rags on the floor. All night long, the dots danced. They searched to find her and finish her off.

She wondered why they didn't try to approach the shed, without being able to provide a logical explanation. Of course, this worked to her advantage. Early in the morning, the dots had disappeared. She had managed to sleep only half an hour, as from the tension and fear, she couldn't fall asleep until she finally lost consciousness.

After once again trying to use the radio, which she had left on all night, she continued searching for the others. She made a short stop at a small spring to fill the jug she had taken from the shelter and moved on. The dots hadn't appeared at all by then, and she wondered if those people, whoever they were, had grown tired of trying to kill her or if they were merely following her silently, having set up an ambush to kill her later.

Eda had begun to get used to the idea of holding her gun in her hands, and so she no longer felt strange as she had in the first hours. If she wanted to be honest with herself, she hadn't even realized she had been holding it all that time. She was hungry, but she didn't have anything edible with her.

On a tree trunk, she found some peanuts and approached to grab a few from the hole. A squirrel darted out, startling her, and disappeared into the forest.

Surely, a handful of peanuts wouldn't keep her alive for long, but she hoped to find something else to eat later.

She continued wandering through the woods for hours. She didn't know how many had passed, but she was sure time was moving on, estimating that she had walked quite a distance. Nevertheless, she couldn't find the others anywhere. Neither the sheriff and his team nor Ronny. It was hot.

Why did her first experience in the field have to be like this? She thought for a moment. Who knows who these guys are? I bet those sons of bitches are hiding somewhere behind some foliage, enjoying my desperate struggle for survival.

She tightened her grip on the gun in her hand, feeling the tension overtaking her body. The fact that the unknown assailants had shown no signs of being in the area for quite some time worried her more than knowing her opponents were close.

This, of course, was because it prevented her from somehow calculating her opponents' movements. She weighed her chances of coming out alive from this ordeal, and after a few minutes, decided that her odds were below zero. She laughed bitterly at the thought. When she opened her eyes again, she was no longer in the forest.

She was in the middle of an amusement park. It had gotten dark, and the moon shone in the sky. The abandoned amusement park, now a pile of ruins, was dark. No one was there except for her. No one to play on the rides, to grab hot dogs from one of the stalls, to go up on the Ferris wheel—which had now tilted—to see the magnificent view from above.

Papers and dried leaves were scattered around. Surely, the place had been abandoned for at least two decades. She looked toward the deserted bumper cars a little farther away. They had remained stopped in various places on the track. I wonder when was the last time someone saw them.

Suddenly, she jumped in fright. The lights of the amusement park turned on, and an eerie scream that resembled laughter began to echo.

"Come to the House of Horrors! This is where the fun begins. Hahaha!"

She pulled out her gun and started aiming around as cold sweat soaked her from head to toe. Her gaze turned to a colorful building with swirling painted colors. A clown was painted on the wall of the building.

"Come inside the building to have fun with you and your friends!" A voice said from the loudspeaker, tangled with amusement park music, which suddenly began to distort until it stopped, as if the power supply to the loudspeaker had been cut off. At the same time, the music echoing in the area continued to play.

"Get inside, you stupid little bitch!" She heard the voice scream with intensity, and she felt every inch of her body tense. "Once I get my hands on you, you'll wish you had died earlier in the forest!"

That was him! The man who had been chasing them in the woods. It was definitely him, since he had just mentioned the forest. She ran to hide. Laughter echoed. Slow, malicious laughter, as if mocking her.

"It's pointless to run, little girl. Wherever you hide, I will find you."

She moved into a narrow alleyway that ran between two amusement park buildings, a food stall and a mirror house. She walked slowly, holding her gun tightly with both hands. The sound of the still damp ground and sparse grass beneath her feet was very pronounced, as the beats of her heart had become just as intense, and every sound now seemed much louder than usual.

She was fully alert. She noticed something like a shadow in front of her. An unusual shadow that reminded her of the man they had seen in the forest, or the clown's figure drawn on the building wall.

"Behind you," the voice sounded melodiously.

She turned around instantly to see if he had spotted her. There was no one there.

"Or maybe someone wasn't behind you?"

She stepped into the middle of the amusement park promenade, which was now dark again. Even the music had stopped.

"Where are you, you bastard? What do you want from me?" Eda screamed.

No one answered. It was as if all of this had come straight out of her mind. As if it had never happened. She felt a rage inside her. Excessive and inexplicable rage. She could tear a person apart if she found one in front of her. Then she bent down, placing her hands on her head, as if instinctively wanting to protect herself.

Something pierced her. She felt nothing, except for a breeze. When she opened her eyes again, she was on a deserted two-way street with a lane in each direction. Vast fields of wheat stretched to her left and right. She was alone in the dark, without any traffic lights on the road.

The only light she had to see where she was going came from the moon, which loomed large and imposing, bigger than she remembered it to be before. In the distance, the lights of a city could be seen from where she was standing.

She tightened her right hand to make sure her gun was still there. So that's what it felt like to hold a weapon.

A light breeze blew, causing the plants to sway, making a chilling sound that reminded her she was completely alone and didn't know if any of her enemies were nearby. She heard a metal creaking sound and turned to her right. An old rusty sign was swaying in the wind. It was a sign displaying the name of the city that lay before her.

RN

The first two letters of the name were missing, making it hard to read the rest of the name, and she couldn't figure out where she might be. She hadn't been in Beaverstale long, but she had visited some of the nearby towns. None had an amusement park, and she didn't remember ever being on this road before.

Additionally, the fact that she was no longer in the forest and couldn't remember how she had gotten there seemed ridiculous. Something was definitely off, and she couldn't think of what it was. Ultimately, her first true experience in the field would be something she would never forget, if she survived.

Seventeen

She was walking toward the clinic. She felt scared. Mainly because of Etu's bizarre behavior. She had never seen her beloved act this way, and it made her anxious. What was happening to him after all? She was going to see Lazlo at the clinic and ask for help.

Maybe he could provide some answers, probably after someone at the clinic would examine him again. Of course, this depended on Etu being cooperative, but for now, she was trying to think positively.

When she arrived at the clinic, she walked quickly straight to the reception desk. A petite African-American woman was there, answering phone calls. Seeing Nancy approach, she gestured for her to wait until she finished the call and served her as soon as she had scheduled the patient's appointment she was speaking to on the other line.

"I'm looking for Doctor Lazlo, please."

"Hi, Nancy! Yes, of course, hold on a moment while I call to see where he is. He's literally working alone today."

"Why is that? Did the others take the day off?"

"Harold. He's acting a bit strange today."

"Strange!" Just then, both of them heard an angry scream, and instinctively turned their gaze toward the room from which it had come.

A slender, young woman of medium height with long blonde hair emerged from the room, struggling to unbutton her medical scrubs. She was one of the nurses.

"Olga, please, why are you shouting?" Lazlo asked, now stepping out of another room.

"Get that ridiculous piece of shit out of the clinic, or you'll be treating patients alone without anyone's help when your alchemy suggestions don't work on healing patients! I'm resigning," she replied with a thick Russian accent.

"But why, what did he do to you?"

"What did he do? What did he do?" She shouted. "He tried to kill me with a scalpel, screaming that I'm a Soviet spy. I didn't leave my country when I was twelve and sacrificed everything my peers did, for him to treat me this way, this maniac."

The woman walked past them, heading for the exit. Once she reached the front door, she took off her scrubs and was left in a pink tank top. She angrily turned back to the others who were in the waiting room at that moment and threw it on the floor.

"I'm leaving!" She shouted.

Nancy walked toward Lazlo, who had remained frozen, trying to process what had just happened. He hadn't even noticed her, and even when she approached, he didn't pay her any attention. He was lost in thought. Why was Harold acting like that? Especially to Olga who had been one of the most helpful nurses she had ever encountered in her entire life. No! Olga did not deserve that behavior from anyone at all.

"Doctor?" She said to him.

"Uh? Oh, Nancy, hi."

"I came to see you to talk about—"

"Yeah, look, I'm sorry I didn't stop by your place today, but I didn't find time. I'm practically alone here today, with no one to help me. You know the clinic has always had troubles regarding its personnel but today, things are getting out of hand. It's not just Harold's strange behavior and Olga leaving. Today, I literally feel as if I am alone in an empty clinic, hunted down by faceless mannequins disguised as patients."

"Etu is acting very strangely, Doctor," Nancy insisted. "He's become a different person. I really don't recognize him."

"Yeah, I heard that on the phone," he told her. "You said he suddenly stopped showing symptoms, right?"

"Exactly! I didn't get to finish talking to you because he grabbed the handset from my hands and hung up, then he was acting so, I don't know, weird?"

"Weird?"

"Yes. He's never been like that. It was as if he had switched personalities. I snuck out of the house and came here. I'm scared of him. I think that if I stayed a second more inside the house, he would not even hesitate to hurt me."

"Hmm," said Lazlo, deep in his thoughts.

"Do you suspect anything?" Nancy asked him.

"I don't know, and Harold, as I told you and you've probably figured out, is acting as if he's a different person."

"Doctor, you need to come see something," a short black-haired nurse said to him.

"Just a minute, Miranda."

"Now!" She insisted.

The three of them walked quickly, with Miranda leading them to one of the clinic's rooms. Once they saw the scene, Lazlo and Nancy froze. In front of them lay Harold, who was sprawled face down on one of the empty beds, moving inappropriately and having pulled down his pants.

"What the hell are you doing there?" Lazlo yelled, outraged.

"This is how Harold gets the job done! Oh hey, I'll be done in a few seconds if you want to use the room!"

"What the hell are you saying, you mother—"

"Nancy, please calm down! Harold, I'll be right there to talk to you, don't move from there!"

The two of them walked toward the exit. Nancy was furious and muttering curses.

"This has never happened before. He's never done this. He's been acting very strangely since this morning. I'll give him a sedative and have the nurses do toxicology tests on him."

"Do you suspect anything?"

"I don't know, but I intend to find out."

"Doctor, it's urgent!" Matilda shouted.

"What now?"

"It's Harold, sir."

"My God. What has that idiot done now?" He said, glancing at the woman who looked bewildered.

"Har—Harold."

"I'm going to check," he replied curtly and ran inside.

Nancy followed him. Screams echoed from the room where Harold had just been, and two nurses came running out. Lazlo tried to ask them what was happening, but they were terrified. As he reached the room, Lazlo paused for a second and then ran inside. The scene was horrific.

"Are you okay? Answer me, are you okay?" The doctor repeatedly asked, trying to help Harold, who lay on the ground, covered in blood.

Blood was everywhere in the room. Harold trembled, holding his stomach as his intestines had spilled out. At the far end of the room, the window was broken, as if someone had tried to escape.

"Bring me Alex now!" Lomaz shouted.

"Right away."

"Hurry, we're losing him! And bring a cart with tools as quickly as you can!"

Nancy glanced at the room. Various tools were scattered in different places in the room, soaked in Harold's blood. Surely, someone wanted to take him out. Could it be connected to his behavior? Doctors came in and asked her to leave the room.

"Who will take care of the others?" Miranda asked.

"Call Wilkinson and Lara; tell them it's urgent!"

Miranda left the room, muttering, "Damn it, she hasn't taken two months off! Wilkinson is going to skin us alive!" She saw her walk away cursing and started heading toward the exit. She thought for a moment that perhaps it wasn't a good idea to go home, but maybe she should face her fears and not be afraid to talk to her beloved, no matter how much his behavior had changed in the last few hours.

"Nancy, don't leave!" She heard the receptionist call out, hanging up the phone.

She turned to look at her.

"What's wrong?"

"It's about Etu," she said to her. "They're bringing him here."

Eighteen

He had received a phone call from the clinic. It was urgent, the woman on the other end of the line had told him. *Perfect!* He thought. His first day as a replacement for the chief was going splendid—if he wanted to be sarcastic.

He arrived as quickly as he could at the clinic and parked the patrol car in the parking lot, taking up two spaces. A man inside his car nearby, waiting for his wife to finish her shift, yelled at him to back up and park properly, but Jeffrey ignored him and continued walking.

"What do we have here?" He asked the woman at the reception as he entered the building.

"It's Harold, Jeff. Someone tried to kill him."

"What the hell? Are you sure? Harold is one of the most peaceful people in town; he has never harmed anyone!"

"Go to D-4 and check for yourself if you don't believe me," she told him, exasperated.

He walked down the hallway. Everywhere he looked, he saw staff running around in a panic. Several of these people were certainly supposed to be off or on leave that day; yet, they had shown up for work after all. Something was definitely wrong. He noticed two nurses whispering to each other.

"I can't right now. Tell him to go home. I have too much work."

"Okay, Jess. I'm going to the parking lot to find him."

That wasn't Miranda's husband after all, he thought dismissively, about the man that had yelled at him.

He reached the room the woman at the reception had mentioned. They had moved Harold, but he found police officers already investigating in the area.

"Pickens, thank God you're here! Palmer is nowhere to be found," a woman told him.

"What the hell are you all doing here, Audrey?"

"Someone tried to kill Harold. The same happened to firefighter Etu," the brown-skinned, young Latina woman answered, turning her head toward the others, causing her braid of jet-black hair to flick momentarily.

"Wait a minute, wait a minute!" He said. The cars! He remembered for a moment that he had seen other patrol cars outside the building when he arrived. "Who called you?"

"What do you mean? The nurses," she answered, indifferent.

"You should have gotten my permission first! Do you hear me? Since the chief is out of town, I'm the new chief!" He began shouting.

Everyone in the room stopped for a moment and stared at him. Then, they returned to their work. He was infuriated. It should have been him instead of Palmer running the department in Beaverstale.

Palmer was an old buffoon who kept reading newspapers, eating donuts and drinking black coffee while reminiscing of the old good days when he was a sheriff. Sure, he had his connections and it was no news to Pickens that Beaverstale was a corrupt town run by dinosaurs that refused to give up and make way for newer generations.

It should have been Jeffrey leading the police force in Beaverstale. He was younger than Palmer, obviously stronger and faster and he was intimidating instead of looking like a happy old grandpa ready to tell bedtime stories to kids. With Pickens as police chief, Beaverstale would be in fear of every police officer instead of disrespecting the badge, talking to officers as if they were best pals.

Should Pickens be in his rightful place, Beaverstale would know law and order instead of the state of anarchy it had fallen into long before the disappearances, ever since the 80s when every goddamn tourist would visit the town to get drunk by the lake.

"Let's get something straight, Pickens," Audrey told him. "You're not the sheriff. You never were, and you never will be. I don't care if I get transferred to another city for misbehavior in case you decide to lick the mayor's ass, but I prefer you know the truth. And besides, where were you when the call came to the office asking for us to come?"

Shit! He thought. *I sat in the bathroom with that magazine for two minutes, two fucking minutes!* He checked his watch. He was starting to lose track of time. He probably had sat there for more than the two minutes he was trying to convince himself had passed. But he couldn't even remember what else he had done all day.

The truth was he didn't remember much about yesterday either. His head felt ready to explode. He was irritated and in pain. But he tried to keep it together. He wouldn't show anyone what he was feeling. Not if he wanted to be looked at with respect.

"This isn't going to go down like this," he told her. "You'll see what happens to all of you!"

He left the room and asked one of the nurses where Harold was. He would ask him what had happened. At least that's what he intended to do until he reached the entrance, where one of the officers was outside.

"You can't go in."

"Seriously, you punk?"

"If you want him to get hurt, then go in. They're operating on him, Jeff. He might not make it."

"Perfect," he muttered, then shouted, "This is my day!"

"They brought Etu in too."

"Is he at least in better shape?"

"He fell from the first floor of his house. Glass and blood everywhere. He was literally crawling. The woman from the house across said she saw him crawling on the asphalt."

"Seriously, has everyone lost their minds?"

"She reported that Etu told her some men were targeting his house with laser scopes. He told her they were also in the woods when you went in."

"Get out of here!" He laughed. "We didn't find anyone with a laser scope."

"Etu said he couldn't see them, other than the scopes, they were literally invisible. They've trapped the others in the woods."

"Did the invisible killers also drip green phosphorescent blood after being shot?" Jeffrey scoffed. "Fuck all of you for trying to fool me."

"Fine, go ask him. Assuming he's able to talk at all, that is, he's in there," she told him, pointing to the room where he was located.

He walked until he reached the room where Etu was. He was lying on a bed, powerless to move. He looked just as they had described him. His body was covered in scratches from shattered glass. They had covered him from the waist down with a white sheet, probably to keep him warm, despite the high temperature. He approached and stood next to him.

"What happened, champ? Everything okay?"

"Tra—trap."

"What?"

"They are coming."

They? Who are they? So, the nurse wasn't kidding when he said some people were hunting Etu?

He left the room. As he walked toward the exit, he felt someone bump into him. He hadn't noticed her at all. It was Joanne, the journalist.

"Sorry," she said, flustered.

"Sweetheart!" He said to her. "What brings you here?"

"I came to see Harold."

"Oh right, of course! You two—"

"It's nothing official," she stated sharply. "Jeff. Surely, you saw enough in the woods, right?"

For a moment, he considered everything he had learned about Etu. Perhaps the sheriff had not succeeded after all if the theories about the mysterious men chasing them were true. Maybe it was time to solidify his position as chief. Palmer had his connections but Pickens had his way of influencing people even if that meant convincing them with any means possible.

"Of course! I'll tell you everything."

"Great, I'll be there in a minute!"

"Wait a second, sweetheart!" He said, grabbing her by the hand.

"What?"

"Come to my place at five. Okay? I'll tell you everything."

"Okay, okay, fine," she replied, pulling away.

He had about two hours. He would go home and get ready. He certainly needed to think up a good lie. A believable story about what they had seen in the woods. He hadn't seen anything. How could the others have seen something? He would call later some of the others who had left the woods before the mysterious visitor and Palmer decided to go back to the woods with a few more officers.

"Jeff!" He heard a surprised voice and turned to see the mayor.

"What are you doing, my friend?" He replied warmly.

"I'm afraid I'm not well at all, and soon, I'll have to personally make sure you're transferred if you don't take drastic measures," he responded, irritated. "Two people are in the hospital, news that someone or some people are murdering the residents of the town is about to leak, and you're nowhere to be found, even though you're filling in for Palmer, who I hear is in the woods, something I learned just half an hour ago. Where the hell were you when I called the department?"

"I was coming here," he managed to say.

"You were coming here, right. In addition to being useless at your job, you're also a terrible liar. This isn't going to go down like this!"

"Why didn't you go into the woods?" He muttered.

"What was that, Pickens?"

"I said, sorry, I'll make sure to find them."

"Way too late, Pickens! I've already spoken with all three governors. I don't care if they tell Washington to send the military, Arnold Schwarzenegger, Rambo, or the FBI's bald men in black, but this mess is about to end today."

"Do you seriously believe the words of the Apache?"

The mayor turned angrily toward him, grabbing him by the collar and shoving him against the wall. Everyone in the waiting room stared at them, bewildered. Then, he started to speak to him quietly.

"Etu is an exemplary man. Not just for the fire department but for the entire town. He ran into the woods to protect his cousin. And thanks to him, we know what happened in there."

Nancy was there. She had just walked close to them. Jeffrey hadn't seen her at all during that time. She approached and slapped him.

"You're really ridiculous," she said, then walked away.

"Pickens, do me a favor," said the mayor. "Get out of my sight before anyone believes I'm hanging out with you."

He walked toward the exit heading to his patrol car. Then, he drove home. He felt his head heavy and was irritated. Not so much for the way he had been treated at the hospital. He couldn't pinpoint why he was feeling this inexplicable irritation now.

He momentarily didn't notice that he was driving very recklessly and nervously until another officer passed him and signaled for him to pull over by playing with his lights.

"Jeff?" The officer said in surprise, getting out of his patrol car and approaching.

"No, it's Sylvester Stallone. Of course it's me, idiot!"

"I couldn't just leave it to chance. The way you were driving, I thought some maniac had stolen the car."

"Okay, give me a speeding ticket. And now, leave me alone; I want to go home."

"Alright, Jeff. Have you learned anything about Palmer and the others?"

"No, of course not!"

"I'll be at the office if you need anything!" He told him and took a step back.

Jeff left, revving up the engine and leaving tire marks from his patrol car. A few minutes later, he found himself at home, a single-story house with a gray roof and white wooden walls. The yard was simple, with grass and an old oak tree at the back of the house.

A metal fence separated the house from the others. He hadn't spent much money to buy it, nor was it anything special, but it was exactly what he needed. A comfortable and quiet place. And the decor inside the house was not much different. Cheap furniture made from very simple materials, among which was a very old bookshelf that he never used.

He walked over to the kitchen counter, made from medium-density fiberboard, where he had left a bottle of whiskey. He thought it might be a good idea to have a drink to relax before Joanne showed up. He pictured her arriving at his house on her impressive high-displacement motorcycle, a red, blue, and white Honda RC30, wearing her black leather jacket with red stripes on the sleeves and her shiny red helmet.

His thoughts were interrupted as the phone rang. On the other end was Audrey. She sounded quite upset.

"Pickens? You need to come to the hospital immediately!"

"Audrey, sweetheart, what's going on?"

"First of all, I'm not your sweetheart. Second, hurry up and get to the hospital!"

"How dare you speak to the police chief like that?" He yelled angrily.

"You're not the chief," she corrected him. "They've brought Pierce and Etu's cousin in here, that young guy, Quill."

"Are they okay?"

"Both bleeding profusely. They can barely talk. They mentioned something about an ambush. We found them by accident, hearing Lacey barking."

"Did she spot the attackers?"

"No. She was barking at Quill and Pierce for us to get them. Especially at Quill, who even now seems to have completely lost it."

"What the hell?"

"Pickens? What are you hiding? You saw something in there, didn't you?"

He hid nothing. That was the truth. He was probably the only one who hadn't seen anything. He could think of using everything the others had said to his advantage to pretend to be the hero, but in reality, he didn't know absolutely anything.

"Pickens?"

He slammed the phone down violently, almost mechanically. Coming out of the woods, he, Harold, and the officers with him, no one had complained about anything unusual. He picked up the phone again and nervously typed a number.

"Come on, damn it, answer me."

No answer. He decided to head to the bathroom. He turned on the water at the end and started singing as the hot water cascaded over him, relaxing every part of his body.

Please leave your message after the beep.

"Get up, get on up—get up, get on up—stay on the scene, get on up—like a sex machine, get on up!" Jeffrey started singing.

The answering machine started playing a message. Jeffrey couldn't hear it as he was in the bathroom, his mood having changed completely, as if it was the best day of his life.

"Pickens? Pickens! They just brought Philip and Andrew, who were with you in the woods. They're in terrible shape! Philip was found by his wife, bleeding. The firefighter you had with you, Jacob, is missing, and Gary was just found hanging by the ceiling in his living room."

"We checked preemptively after we heard about the others, but as you understood, we didn't make it. Pickens, don't be an idiot and tell us what you saw yesterday in the woods. Do you know something you shouldn't have learned or seen?"

"Psycho killer. Qu'est-ce que c'est?" Jeffrey continued singing.

"Pickens, if you're home, answer now! We need to find out what's going on finally! Lives are at risk."

He stepped out of the bathroom and immediately put on his brown bathrobe. He walked slowly toward the living room to drink a little more of the whiskey he had in the kitchen, which was separated from the living room by a cooking counter.

"Pickens? Damn, it!"

He had just heard the last part of the message and was walking toward the answering machine when he suddenly saw her. In her hands, she held her helmet and had opened her jacket.

"How did you get in?"

She gestured for him to come closer as she started disrobing. Joanne Atkinson had just entered his house and, despite her relationship with Harold, it seemed she was now trying to make Jeffrey hers.

This is it! He thought. *Finally, my luck is smiling at me!* It was time to pretend to be the hero and enjoy all the benefits.

He stepped toward her. She was now naked. She smiled at him. For a moment, Jeffrey lost himself completely. He awkwardly smiled back and continued to approach.

He hesitated. In front of him, he had just seen something that terrified him. He fell down in his attempt to take a step back. Joanne, who was still standing in the same spot, had just changed completely. As she smiled at him, a dog growl suddenly started echoing.

The next moment, her teeth opened wide, and her face started to rip apart as if she were wearing a mask, revealing a row of sharp teeth, surrounded by a hair-covered head without eyes or a nose and with pointed ears. Blood stained the furry head as Joan's torn face was now split in half and reached down to the creature's neck.

The large teeth closed, hiding the smaller teeth behind them. Joan's skin continued to tear away like thin fabric or as if the monster was wearing her as a disguise. Blood had begun to stain the floor as it dripped from the continuously tearing skin.

As the skin was completely removed, it revealed a body equally furry as the head, thin but hard and muscular. The monster's arms were long, with slender fingers that ended in serrated black claws.

"What the hell?"

Two large brown wolves without eyes or noses appeared in the living room, entering through the open door and stood to the left and right of her. He was afraid of the wolves. And dogs. His turn had finally come. So, this was why his colleagues and the other team members had gotten seriously injured or had met tragic ends.

Had Gary seen that creature and decided to end his life before the beast mutilated him? What would his own end be? He looked the monster in the eye as it prepared to lunge at him. His end had come.

Nineteen

They were getting ready to leave the building. Eda was right behind them as John and Leah moved forward. Leah stayed right in the middle, so they could cover her in case something happened. They started descending from the stairs carefully, keeping their weapons concealed.

"As soon as we exit the building, we'll act as normal as possible. If enemies show up, we confront them if we can; otherwise, we find cover and move on," John said. "Leah, stay between us. You don't have a weapon, so you're an easy target. Now, focus!"

They exited the building. People walked past them, not paying them any attention. John looked around for enemies. None. It was as if they had never existed. He scanned the buildings surrounding them. None of them resembled the ones he had seen before.

"Eda?"

"Yes?"

"You said you approached a European city or something that looked like a European city, right?" He asked her.

"Yes. Why?"

"Me and your colleagues did too. Look at the buildings."

Small two or three-story apartment buildings rose around them. In the distance before them, the buildings were built right next to each other on the right side of the street. To the left, the sea. A harbor and palm trees lined the sidewalk.

"We're not in the same place!" Eda exclaimed.

"I saw something from the window that gave me that impression, but I wanted to make sure," he explained to her.

Meanwhile, passersby continued on, without giving a damn about them whatsoever. They seemed as though they hadn't seen them standing among them.

"Excuse me!" Eda said to one of the people walking near them.

The man walked on without even turning to look at her.

"Maybe it's not a good idea," John told her. "We could get into a lot of trouble if we talk to them, and if those who are trying to kill us are watching."

"Strange though. He didn't even turn around."

John thought for a moment. He looked around. A seaside bar. Maybe if they went there, they could talk to someone. Perhaps they'd find a phone to call for help.

"Come with me," he told them.

The three of them headed toward the bar. They would pretend to be customers. John had some money in his pocket, so they could easily pass as patrons and blend in with the crowd. He grabbed the doorknob to open it and thought of something that momentarily puzzled him.

Even though they were right by the sea, he didn't smell it at all. Meanwhile, he still had the scent of the forest in his nose. He opened the door, and the bar room appeared before him. Everything followed a wooden theme, as the floor, the stairs, the bar counter, and all the furniture were wooden.

He took a step inside, and suddenly, his vision went black as a red flash blinded him, as if someone had thrown a red beam of light on them. He instinctively drew his gun and fell to the floor, where he remembered the nearest table being located.

"Take cover!" He shouted.

When he managed to regain his sight, he discovered he was in the forest. The bar, the harbor, and even the passersby had disappeared. The worst part was that both Leah and Enda were gone.

"Damn it! I can't believe this," he growled.

At that moment, he felt them approaching. He didn't know where they were, but they were close. The invisible enemies. A part of him was about to start screaming for explanations. It was the part of the innocent civilian he buried deep inside, or rather, had buried long ago.

He quickly buried that thought, back where he had buried the lost part of himself. It wasn't the right choice. His opponents were waiting for him to lose his composure and make a mistake. He might not have managed to spot them, but he could hide somehow. Trick them.

He ran and quickly dropped to the ground. Then, he hid behind the bushes he found nearby. That's when he remembered that he had previously taken a weapon from one of his enemies while in the ruins of the strange city.

Instinctively, he felt around his back and waist to find it hanging there, but it was gone.

Cold sweat trickled down from his forehead. The gun! He thought. He still had it. Alright, God really loves me after all. Calm down, John, you're getting anxious, and you're going to make mistakes. That's what they're waiting for too!

He felt a touch on his back. His heart raced so loudly that for a moment, he thought he might burst from the pressure. He hadn't heard anyone approach. It was as if his ears were completely deaf. Numb, perhaps. He wondered if he could even hear at all.

Maybe he was hearing, but not with the ability he would have in any other moment. He guessed it was from the stress. He focused on the shudder that ran through him at that moment as he had just felt the hand touching him. Cold and slender. Foreign to his body; he could feel it through his shirt.

His hand tightened around the grip of the gun. His finger, ready to pull the trigger instinctively, would soon pivot to attack the enemy. His legs tensed and took a position of readiness. His left hand was prepared to deflect any movement from his opponent.

He felt his eyes bulge as he saw blurry in his peripheral vision, having very clear visibility in his center, a sign that he was fully focused and ready to strike. If he had to take stock of how long it had taken him for all these instinctive movements to occur, he could confidently say it was something less than a fraction of a second. He had reacted mechanically, as he had been taught to act. He had acted like a soldier.

"Leah?"

Gunshot.

Twenty

She was stunned and without the ability to create any logical explanation she could give to anyone. He was being carried in front of her, battered, bloody, and mutilated. He was on a stretcher, with doctors rushing around in a panic. Another victim. No one seemed optimistic about whether he would survive, but the doctors and nurses had a duty to care for him even if he wasn't the most likable person in town.

"Monster!" He tried to say as the stretcher he was on passed in front of her before losing consciousness, as the medics' screamed orders at each other, unable to communicate.

"Adrenaline injection, now!"

"We're losing him, do something quickly!"

"Come on, move it! What have you been doing all this time? Get everything ready fast! We need to attend to him immediately!"

"Injection. Yes, injection, where's the injection?"

"You can't be serious, get it and bring it here. You all make space, get everyone out of the room, so we can operate!"

"But—"

"Now, do what I told you, or we'll lose him!"

"Joanne Atkinson?"

She turned toward the person who had addressed her as soon as she heard her name. Her long blonde hair followed the movement of her head, flowing with her brown-chocolate eyes looking at the woman who was now close to her.

"Audrey Sandoyo."

"I saw you a little while ago in the building when I was coming in."

"And how long ago exactly did this happen?"

"About one and a half? I'm not sure. Why?" Joan asked, trying to understand why the police officer had approached her. "Has the person who tried to kill Harold been found?"

The woman examined her for a moment with a scrutinizing look. Then, she told her to follow her. She led her outside the building where there were no people, so she could be as discreet as possible.

"Joan, I'll be as brief as possible. How well do you know Jeffrey Pickens?"

"Very little," she replied. "He's known to me and my colleagues for his sociability." Joanne was truly trying to find words to describe that disrespectful bastard in a polite way, even though everyone knew that nobody liked Pickens at all.

"Did you meet him today at all?"

"He asked me to visit him at home when I asked if he had seen anything strange in the woods when he and his colleagues were there. Why do you ask?"

"And you said you were here about an hour ago, I see."

"Is something going on?" She asked insistently.

"Joanne, I'm in the unfortunate position to tell you that you are currently considered a suspect in the injury of Harold Curtis, as well as Jeffrey Pickens," she replied.

Harold? How could she harm her beloved? She felt a knot in her stomach as she remembered that just after she had visited him, he had begun to tremble. What was the reason? And how was it possible for Harold to be afraid of her?

"I don't understand."

"You will need to come with me to the station, Joanne."

"There must have been a mistake. Also, Pickens was fine when he was at the hospital earlier."

"Jeffrey called for backup at his house, he reported that you visited him and that you attacked him."

"Me!" She responded indignantly. "Since when? Why?"

"We don't know, but Harold, whom we spoke to earlier, kept mumbling your name, breaking down into a panic. It took a sedative injection to get him back under control."

"That's ridiculous! Harold and I are a couple. I was at the office until I learned he was injured; the manager can confirm that."

She thought for a moment, looking around. Joanne was staring at her, confused, trying to understand if all this was part of some bad joke. Meanwhile, she was starting to lose her patience.

"Are you going to pin the injury of the other men who came out of the woods on me too?" She asked angrily.

"We have information that a group of snipers attacked them. You will need to come with me to the police department. In our haste, we haven't had time yet to call the Internal Affairs Office and the FBI to handle the matter, so you'll need to wait there while we contact them."

"This is unreasonable! You can't do this—"

"Sorry to interrupt!" A woman's voice came from the background.

Nancy, who had apparently stepped outside the hospital, had heard their conversation and was now approaching them near the two ambulances where they stood.

"I'm the fiancée of one of the men who are in the clinic," she began. "I arrived here earlier because I was worried about the health of my fiancé, who strangely exhibited flu-like symptoms yesterday and was acting oddly today. The woman is telling the truth as I saw her coming in much later and she hasn't left the building at all since she arrived because she's waiting to hear about the doctor's condition."

Audrey looked at them both with suspicion for a moment. It was understandable in such a state of panic. Then, she took a step back to leave.

"Joanne, I'd ask you to stay home today in case we need to contact you," she said. "For now, I apologize for the disturbance."

She left, leaving them alone. Joanne turned to Nancy.

"Thank you so much," she managed to say.

"I stepped out to get some air and happened to overhear your conversation. It would be unfair to accuse you of something you didn't do. I'm sure you're not responsible."

"Thank you."

"Between us, that jerk Pickens deserved what he got from whoever attacked him."

Joanne didn't respond. She was still shaken by the fact that she had almost found herself a prime suspect in a crime she had never committed. She walked for a bit in the parking lot and then rode her motorcycle to Jeffrey Pickens' house. She knew very well that she wasn't to blame for whatever had happened to him, but maybe she would find the answers she was looking for at his home.

It didn't take her long to arrive. The patrol cars had left, so she could search the house for anything that might lead her to understand what exactly had happened and why Pickens had called her a monster as soon as he was brought to the hospital.

The door was locked. Of course! She should have expected that. She wasn't the protagonist in some movie where she would magically find a way to get into the house, and that meant she might have to look for a less convenient or even legal way to get inside.

She looked around, searching for a solution. There were two possible ways to enter the house. The first was the classic option of the broken window, something that would automatically mark her as a prime suspect in the case the moment she considered it again.

The second option was to grab onto the old oak tree at the back of the house. Then, she would jump and grab onto the roof of the house, climb up, and approach the chimney. With a little luck, hoping she hadn't gained too much weight from her dinner with some famous chef three days prior, she would descend through the chimney and reach the interior of the house.

"It's a shame it can't be that someone left the keys under the doormat like in the movies," she murmured, panting as she attempted to climb to the edge of the roof.

She approached the chimney and looking at it, wished she wouldn't get stuck inside. Theoretically, she fit, and there was even extra space. After all, if one excluded her chest—which could not be considered too small but not enormous either—the rest of her was relatively petite.

"If my butt fits, then we're good."

She put her left leg inside. Then her right. She held on to the walls and began her descent. She had deliberately left her leather jacket on the bike, so she wouldn't sweat, and also, so she wouldn't get soiled or scratched as she would be in the chimney.

Of course, to her surprise, she discovered that the chimney had likely never been used, as apart from tiny particles of dust, she didn't feel the presence of smoke at all, something she confirmed as soon as she reached the base of the chimney, where the stone was pristine.

He wasn't the only one who had bought a house with a fireplace that he intended to never use. She emerged from the chimney and moved into the living room. Blood everywhere. She stopped.

One would say that whoever had attacked Jeffrey hadn't stopped at all, even when—logically—Jeffrey must have started begging for mercy. That image reminded her of something she had seen previously. Of course! In the clinic.

Naturally, she hadn't seen the complete crime scene like she was now, since the cops were in the area, not allowing anyone to enter, but it didn't differ much from the little she had managed to capture with her eyes. Someone had attacked Jeffrey.

The weapon used was nowhere to be found with a quick assessment, but logically, it should have been sharp. A knife? A cleaver? A chainsaw? It was certainly something capable of inflicting all those wounds she had seen on him when they brought him into the hospital, blood-soaked and crimson. Some items had fallen to the ground. Some had broken.

She looked around with complete focus. From the way the objects had fallen, it was clear that Pickens had tried to hold onto the various furniture in the space, having fallen to the floor, and had knocked various items off the furniture in his attempt to grip onto something.

Perhaps the killer or killers had continued to hit him. No one ruled out the possibility that he had managed to grab one of them and they had wrestled on the ground, crashing against the furniture, until the assailant immobilized him, continuing his torment. But what she couldn't find anywhere was the reason he had called her that word earlier.

"Can you believe that so many people have gone down?"

She turned her head toward the direction from which the male voice had been heard. Someone had entered the house through the back door of the yard and was making their way toward the living room. They hadn't seen her, but if she stayed in the house much longer, they would find her, and then, it would be difficult to explain anything.

"It's rather unprecedented that this time there were survivors. I personally thought no one would return."

"Search his room. I'll go to the living room, okay?"

In the meantime, Joan was already at the front door, turning the knob to open it.

"Did you hear that a journalist might be involved in all this?"

Her heart began to pound quickly.

"These are Audrey's theories. Don't listen to her too much! I agree that that's what her and Pickens' statements claimed, but people are in a state of delirium, and I wouldn't take a word of what they told me seriously. Who knows what their eyes saw?"

The door had opened. With quick steps, she rushed away from the house, tripping on the doormat and falling to the ground. The mat shifted slightly and the key to the door was revealed. For a moment, she thought of unleashing all the curses she knew and whatever else might come to her spontaneously at that moment, since she had never expected a police officer's key to be conveniently placed under the welcome mat. It was probably the spare key.

She turned back and froze for a brief moment. One of the two men would be approaching the living room and would see her. She needed to act composedly and quickly. She grabbed the doorknob and slowly closed the door without making a sound. Then, she moved as far away as possible from the house.

The answer lay in the woods. There was no other logical explanation. Someone was trying to silence them for something they had seen in the woods, or perhaps several people. She gathered in her mind all the information she had heard up to that moment. Some were in the woods. Everyone had stated this.

She had heard some of them say they had seen dots from laser scopes targeting them. Others, like Pickens, had reported monsters. If she wanted to be more specific about the latter, she was the supposed monster, but she was sure she had seen something in the woods and in his house, and that he had been in delirium at the time she had seen him in the hospital. Perhaps he had mistaken her for the murderer who had entered his house.

She had now made her decision, and there was nothing that could make her change her mind. She would visit the woods to learn the truth about everything happening in there, gathering evidence and information that she would present to the world waiting for her report to know the truth.

The main reason she would go to the woods was to clear her name from false accusations. She was a journalist, not a murderer. She had just arrived outside the house that the two tourists had rented upon arriving in town before the man's daughter disappeared and all these unfortunate events occurred in their city.

The Buick Regal was still parked outside the house, in the exact same spot where they had left it upon their arrival. For a moment, she thought that perhaps they were responsible for everything happening in the town, although she knew that the mysterious disappearances of people had been happening in the woods long before those two appeared. They could very well be members of the group of murderers, terrorists, or soldiers in the woods for whatever reason.

She opened the plastic visor of her helmet and drove her motorcycle to the back of the yard. She wanted to hide it, so that if someone passed by, they wouldn't see it. This way she would avoid any misunderstandings from malevolent mouths—and there were certainly plenty of them—that would spread false rumors.

Joanne Atkinson runs away into the woods after learning she is a prime suspect in the attempted murder of her lover and the deputy sheriff! Or *foreign tourists and the town's well-known journalist, accomplices in a plot to eliminate the town's police—Motives unknown!*

Though they sounded more like news headlines, they didn't differ much from the sensationalism with which the malicious people in this town would represent and embellish their false statements every time with more lies. After making sure the motorcycle was well hidden, she dismounted and removed her helmet, letting her blonde hair flow freely as she shook her head to untangle it.

Clouds had begun to appear over the town, which meant she would probably need her leather jacket and it wouldn't be a good idea to leave it on the bike. So, glancing once more at the street to ensure that no one was watching her, she started walking toward the woods.

Twenty-One

She was standing between two ambulances. She didn't want anyone to see her. That moment of weakness would be purely personal, something she would share only with herself. She was crying, her eyes were red and painful as they had swollen. Her life was just fine.

Everything was perfect, and she lacked nothing. They lacked nothing. In his arms, she had found a wonderful family. All of this felt very distant now as she thought about having just seen him in terrible condition on a stretcher, with IVs and tubes connected everywhere. And the blood. He was covered in his own blood.

They had told her there was a chance he wouldn't make it. He had lost a lot of blood, and they were doing everything they could to keep him alive. When they had announced that possibility to her, she felt her entire body go numb. She still hadn't processed the words she had heard.

Her head was buzzing, as if she had just woken up from a long sleep. She tried, in her indescribable sorrow, to think back and reconstruct all the events just as they had happened. Etu had disappeared for an entire night, looking for his cousin.

Hours later, he had shown up at the fast-food place where he worked and had taken her to go home together. There, he had started showing possible flu symptoms and then, as if by magic, had gotten better and was acting very curtly, almost as if he were a different person.

Then, he was in the hospital. So was his cousin, Quill, who had been brought in shortly before. She had tried to talk to Quill, but he hadn't made any sense in what he was saying. Both Quill and Etu were in a state of panic. Quill had been injured less seriously than Etu, but he seemed to be in shock and was trembling.

"They're in the woods!" He had told her. "They have weapons. No one will get away."

Jeff had been brought to the hospital too. Seeing him had made her feel an immense satisfaction for a brief moment. Maybe he deserved what had happened to him. Then, she thought of the others. All of them battered, covered in wounds, and among them was the man she loved. She shouldn't have thought that.

Now, she stood waiting for the slightest change. Maybe by the end of the day, she would hear some good news. Perhaps someone would come to tell her, "Hey! Everything's fine, Etu will be out soon and is in no danger."

In vain. The longer she waited there, the worse she felt. The clouds were thickening in the sky. A sign that it would rain. Everything around her was beginning to take on a dull color, but she felt that dullness within herself too. Ultimately, she might have lost everything after all.

She remembered when she had cried, as her beloved was in the woods. She cried because she believed she would never see him again. She felt the same now as she waited to find out what would ultimately happen to Etu.

She stood up to go back inside the hospital. She felt dehydrated and was getting very warm. After all, a lot of time had passed since she last drank water, and she needed a cold bottle. She approached the vending machine, and after putting a coin in the designated slot and typing in the product code from the label on the shelf, the bottle dropped down, and she quickly grabbed it to open. She drank greedily, not realizing that the water had finished.

Someone was approaching her from behind. She hadn't noticed at all. They were walking quickly, without stopping. She was lost in her thoughts. Once they came close enough, she felt a shiver. They hadn't touched her, but there was an instinct within her that something was about to happen. When they touched her, she jumped as if she had been hit by an electric shock.

"Sorry," she managed to say, seeing him startle. "Doctor? No, no. Is everything alright?"

Lazlo stood there for a moment, contemplative, making Nancy fear the worst. She felt her heart pounding violently as she waited to hear the bad news slap her in the face, shattering all her dreams and the previously peaceful life she had experienced next to Etu.

Come on, tell me; I think I'm ready now.

"Come with me for a minute," he told her.

So, this is what it must be like to be told that the person you love doesn't live anymore. This must be how it feels.

They walked for a while until they reached the backyard of the clinic. He probably wanted to make sure nobody would hear him. Nancy looked at him, confused. If he was going to tell her the bad news about Etu's death, then why hadn't he done it inside the clinic? What was with this melodramatic ceremony?

"Nancy, I have good news!" He started to tell her, making her calm down for a brief moment, only realizing then that her throat was dry again and numb. "Etu's been stabilized for the moment. I personally made sure of it."

"I don't understand, why didn't you tell me that inside the building?"

"Nancy, I want to ask you a few things, as I'm a bit confused myself. You see, I didn't waste any time after I made sure that Etu's and the others' health is in good condition, except for Jeff, of course."

"Except for Jeff?" She echoed.

"He didn't make it."

"I see," she replied as warmly as she could to pretend that she understood, "What exactly do you want to ask me?"

"What exactly were they looking for in the woods? I've definitely heard that story about the passerby's daughter who got lost in the woods, but I can't understand many parts of it. You see, this is the first time we're dealing with the woods since we lost the officers back in the incident with the resort."

"Everyone thinks we're crazy in this town, and no one does anything—not to mention the fact that technically, we might not even exist on the map as a town, considering that people like me who came here did so exactly because we wanted to have a quiet life away from urban centers and tourist attractions."

"I just want to know if he told you anything about the woods. If they were looking for something more than just that girl."

"He didn't tell me anything, no."

She saw him thinking, staring at the floor.

"Is something going on?"

"A lot, but I'm not sure."

"What about?"

"Has he ever mentioned anything about the woods?"

"The Apache of Beaverstale believe in spirits. And Etu partly does too. Beyond that, he mentioned something in the last hours about invisible men with weapons, they were targeting them."

"Yes, that's what they all say," the doctor agreed.

"Do you think we're in danger?"

"Please promise me that until I've confirmed my theory, you won't say anything to anyone, alright?"

"I swear!"

"I don't believe that all that happened was caused by humans in invisible suits."

"What do you mean?"

Twenty-Two

His memories played before his eyes like a film. He could now think calmly. Perhaps some of the memories had been altered. Some, particularly the recent ones, might have been completely lost. He had his eyes closed. He still hadn't realized it, but for now, he was dreaming.

Perhaps, in the end, what he saw before him were not memories at all. Perhaps some images were desires, fears, or even indifferent pictures that passed before his eyes without him being able to provide a logical explanation. He remembered as a child being puzzled about why people dream.

How it was possible for someone to spend hours, days, or months in a virtual world that their own brain created with the help of their imagination and memory, in just a matter of minutes or hours. He had never found an explanation for that question. Eventually, he had stopped caring. It was simply something that happened. Now, however, he was asking again like a child. *Why?*

He slightly opened his eyelids. Everything around him was blurry. He blinked his heavy eyelids to recover. He was no longer in the forest. Nor at the harbor. Not even in Beaverstale. The floor beneath him was smooth and metallic. He tried to lift himself, but he realized he was tied up.

In front of him was a woman he didn't recognize. She was also tied up on the opposite side of the room. A large mirror was behind her. To his left sat Leah, and to his right was Eda. Sheriff Palmer was sitting next to the woman. They were all bound to a table with state-of-the-art handcuffs, in his experience. Had they been captured by the men in invisible cloaks? He would find out very soon.

"Hey. Psst! Leah," he whispered. He still hadn't fully regained his senses.

"John!" He heard the sheriff whisper from the other side of the table. "I'm glad to see you again!"

"I'm glad to see you," he managed to say. "What about the others?"

"I have no idea. I've lost contact with them for," he thought for a moment, 'a month'.

"A month?"

"We got cut off on a mountain. We were chased by a huge reptile with many eyes. Two large ones, like all reptiles, and two smaller ones right beside the large ones, with the outermost ones smaller than the others. Thatcher had disappeared. As for the others, I saw them shooting in panic as we were climbing the mountain. They said someone was shooting at us, but I never saw anyone, nor did I hear gunfire other than our own. I only saw the monster. Then, I was alone."

"I see."

"You think I'm crazy, don't you?" Palmer asked him.

"After what I've seen, no! I will gladly believe anything you throw at me."

"Dad, are we getting close to Uncle?" Leah asked, dazed, as she was just regaining her senses.

"I'm sorry, sweetheart; we're not getting closer."

"Where are we?"

"I don't know."

He saw her starting to panic as she realized they weren't in the car anymore. Perhaps she was beginning to remember their wandering in the forest and all they had seen.

"What is this place? Why have they tied us up?" She began to speak loudly.

"Shh! Calm down," John told her. "Look across, discreetly."

"A mirror."

"Yes!"

"Oh my God, they're going to interrogate us!" She said as quietly as she could, trying not to scream from her terror.

"They might be observing us. I still don't know what's going on."

"Is Eda okay?"

"Yes, she's sitting next to me," he said, leaning slightly so she could see.

"She's asleep. Right?"

"We all must have fainted. She'll recover in a bit, don't worry."

"Where did you disappear to, John? One moment we were running through the ruins of the city, looking for a way to escape and return to Beaverstale, and the next I turned my head, and you were gone," the sheriff asked.

"I lost you too. I don't remember how. Who is the woman next to you?"

Palmer turned his head to look. He hadn't noticed her until then.

"Her name is Joanne Atkinson, a journalist by profession. I don't know what she's doing here."

"No, stop, get away from here, I'm telling you! Go away, I'm not afraid of you, you bastard, get away from me, old man!" Eda began to scream as she was coming to.

"Eda, it's us, calm down!" John said.

"Go away, leave me alone!" She continued shouting as she struggled against the chains while seated beside John, still with her eyes closed.

"Eda!"

"Leave me alone," she said, and suddenly opened her eyes wide, gasping sharply as she began to realize she was tied up in a room with the others. "Let me go. The clown," she tried to explain.

"The clown?" Palmer asked.

Meanwhile, Joanne had also begun to regain her senses and was now looking at them all, bewildered.

"Yes, the clown or whatever that thing is anyway; it has green hair, sharp teeth, and pale skin, like a vampire, it was chasing me. I saw it when I was coming with Ronnie to find you."

"Where are we?"

"Joanne, first of all, how did you end up here? We don't even know where we are, but it seems strange to me that they chose to bring you here as well," Palmer said.

"They tried to kill Jeffrey, Fred," she replied. "The same with Harold. They framed me."

"Framed you?"

"They said they heard Jeffrey telling them that I visited him, which is not true," she said, looking him in the eyes. "I'm a journalist, Fred; for the love of God, I decided to go into the forest to find out what was going on since some of your team ended up in bad shape and were brought to the hospital."

"My team? Who? Is Thatcher okay?"

"Thatcher is missing. I'm sorry. They brought Quill and Pierce."

"Ronnie?" Enda said. "Has anyone seen Ronnie?"

Joan shook her head negatively.

"It's my fault," she began to say. "I shouldn't have let him out of the car, they shot him, and that—" she paused, looking behind Palmer and Joan, widening her eyes, and then, after a brief pause, she screamed, "Behind you! It's behind you! Watch out, it's behind you!"

"I'm afraid no one is behind you," a male voice echoed as a suited man with gray hair entered the room.

He wasn't very tall, but he had a particularly imposing stance that made him appear tall, dressed in an expensive dark blue suit with thin white stripes, a white shirt, and a dark blue striped tie. The silver Rolex on his left wrist gleamed under the lamp's light as he raised his hand to straighten his tie.

"My name is Adam Foster," he said, looking each of them over one by one. "CIA," he said while simultaneously, John said the exact same thing. "Very well, Mr. Emerson! I see you can read people."

"It isn't hard, having seen countless like you over the years."

"I've read enough about you. It's a rather interesting résumé."

"Not exactly the best for someone looking to get a job at Wall Street, of course," John mocked.

"I believe Richard Marcinko would be quite jealous of your adventures, Mr. Emmerson. Didn't you operate under his commands in Operation Eagle Claw? I wonder why he didn't recruit you for his Red Cell unit."

"And you don't need to know."

Adam approached Eda and patted her to stop her trembling.

"There's no use," he said, looking at the sheriff. "Larry?"

A muscular man in a black and white suit entered the room. One might say that if he stretched, his jacket and shirt would rip, revealing his overly muscular body, which was easily discernible even through the suit, as his chest was huge, as well as his arms and legs.

"Yes, sir!" The tall, white, brown-haired man with very short hair responded.

"Watch these here for a moment. I'll take Mr. Emerson for a bit so we can talk."

Three armed men with bulletproof vests and powerful M-16 rifles entered the room and grabbed John, after first unlocking the mechanism with which he was tied to the table and chair. He struggled for a moment to be let free, but it was in vain. They had no intention of being nice to him.

The last thing he felt was a blow from the butt of a rifle, and he lost consciousness. Periodically, he saw fragmented images until he came around. Guards supporting him on their shoulders. Guards dragging him down the corridor. Someone tying him to a chair.

It was cold. He felt it everywhere as water poured down on him forcefully. Someone had emptied an entire bucket of water on him. He jolted himself awake and looked around.

"Ten minutes. Good score!" Adam told him, standing a little further away, admiring how fast it had taken for John to recover.

"Where is my daughter?"

"I'll tell you something, the quicker you understand this, the better it will be for you," he said as he approached him. "I ask the questions here."

John stared him in the eyes. He would have killed him if he weren't tied up.

"Do you know Area 51, John?"

"Did you set up a base here too? What do you call it? Area 69?" John mocked.

"Cute. No, the building is named after the experiment; Aeolus."

"The ancient God of winds?"

"The first experiment was conducted about a decade ago in a supermax prison in Santa Fe."

"Ha! If you're talking about the riot that happened on 2 February 1980, then it has nothing to do with the wind. The wind didn't kill the inmates or the guards, the inmates themselves acted violently due to—"

"Oppression and the abysmal conditions within the prisons, blah-blah-blah! Yes, you read that correctly. One day, such well-cooked truths will circulate freely through computers instead of relying on people who write books or newspapers, and everyone will add their own touch. Everyone will hear and see the exact same things!"

"Imagine a world in which we can convince citizens to follow guidelines for their own safety or for the sake of the environment, while we'll be the ones putting the environments or their own sakes at stake! Imagine millions of acres of trees burning to the ground for citizens to pay more taxes in order to protect the environment through money that will be spent in constructing wind turbines instead of reforestation."

"Imagine a world so obsessed with whatever will be considered as right that the meaning of the word itself will be lost. Well, John, no. I don't want to upset you, but it wasn't the oppression and the abysmal conditions that made the inmates start killing each other."

"The day before the experiment, we secretly administered a dose of psychedelic drugs in their food, and then, we brought them all to the main assembly hall, where they listened for hours to a recording instructing them to attack the guards and their fellow inmates as soon as the recording stopped."

"They were so brain-dead that they never realized we administered another dose at the end of the brainwashing process, and so, as soon as the recording finished, they began to kill each other. As for the guards, don't be fooled! No guard ever died."

"The inmates had been given a small dose of addictive substances for a month, and for about an hour each day, they gathered in the same room for us to brainwash them, so they would get familiar with the voice."

"Let me guess, the president never learned about the experiment."

"Exactly, John! I wasn't in charge of the experiment then, but due to some do-gooders from the Pentagon, the experiment was terminated, and our names almost went straight to the president's desk and we would be condemned."

"With the knowledge we had and the data from the first experiment, we began the same experiment a year ago, using new techniques and more advanced technology, here in the forest of this small town that hardly anyone knows. We simply used inmates who signed to reduce their sentence if they participated in the experiment."

"I'm not a prisoner, as far as I know, nor have I ever signed any paper agreeing to participate in any experiment."

"Passersby, as well as tourists from a resort, unfortunately, became sacrifices for the experiment, as they happened to be too close," Adam confessed.

"So," John hesitated. "There are no invisible men."

"You're a sharp one! There are no Russian soldiers either," Adam said, staring at John with mockery. "Oh, yes John, I heard you mentioning that too many times. In fact, we were able to witness everything you people did. Perhaps you saw what you wanted to see."

"So, if you are thinking that I am a bad person, you should probably take a hard look in the mirror and ask yourself whether prejudice is actually something that makes you a better man."

Prejudice? Maybe. Maybe John had suspected everyone else except the very people that were actually too close to him to ignore. People he had seen deploying in the field with him. People he had helped escape from prisons in Afghanistan. People he had worked for at times.

"This time, we improved the composition," Adam continued. "We used ketamine as a base and also cocaine and LSD; basically, screw the rest of the details. There's a list of drugs and sedatives used in the mix and I'm not here to bore you to death; you've primarily received ketamine, but don't worry!"

"We wanted you sober, especially you, as we have much to discuss, so we administered an injection to neutralize the effect of the mixture. The difference this time in the experiment is that the mixture is administered through the air. Over two hundred devices with motion sensors are placed in the forest, spraying gas on anyone who passes by them."

"Meanwhile, with cameras, we can see what each test subject is doing and how they react. Through speakers, we instruct them on what to do. Of course, the mixture is designed to affect only humans, not animals, so as not to cause any damage to nature."

"Look at you, turning out to be an animal lover. Just like a certain Austrian painter."

"The speakers are connected to us, here," Adam continued, ignoring him. "Through messages with calm and clear speech, we achieve complete control over each subject. The calm speech method, according to the lead scientist working on this project, will be called Autonomous Sensory Meridian Response."

"If it were a name for shoes, though, you wouldn't sell a single pair. Bad marketing."

"You can mock as much as you want, but this method will someday become widespread, resulting in one of the next generations using it as a form of entertainment."

"And I thought the drugs you gave us were entertaining enough to last through the day."

"And now, Mr. Emerson, after I've explained what's happening here, I expect you to tell me who sent you to sabotage the experiment. Which jerk from the Pentagon gave you the mission? I just learned that the mayor of the city called the governors of the three neighboring states because some of your team came out of the forest."

"I don't want to have to destroy the entire town to preserve the safety of the facilities and the continuation of the experiment, so tell me! Who sent you?"

"Nobody!" John replied tersely. "I'm on leave. You took my daughter into the forest."

"Indeed, the little one was found alone in the forest long before you assembled an entire troop to make an incursion. I'm puzzled why you don't seem like someone who would use close ones as bait," Adam replied pensively.

Silence followed for a moment, which seemed to last much longer than the few fractions of a second it really took. Then, Adam abruptly turned to John, pointing at him with his finger.

"Who sent you?"

"Nobody! I didn't even know this damn city existed."

"You were sent for the disappearances, I'm sure, it can't be a coincidence! Your daughter was merely a pretext, but it didn't go as you expected, and she happened to end up in the forest too!"

"You're insane," John replied.

"I'm a patriot!" Adam protested.

"By killing innocent citizens? That's not patriotism. Your people in Langley would be ashamed of people like you."

"I explained to you that this was merely a necessary sacrifice. Besides, they entered the forest. And you, Emerson, you also killed several innocents today, bringing them into the forest," he said, activating a screen that was on the wall in front of John.

The cameras had recorded him along with the others. There were no enemies anywhere, no monsters, nor the big, strange city that they had all seen. They were running through the forest. The deaths were caused by themselves. Some committed suicide, others killed their companions. None of them ever realized their actions. For them, the invisible men would always be to blame.

"Your hands are stained with blood," he told him, showing him a snapshot from one of the cameras, as John shot Colby fatally.

"But—how? Why?"

"This gas will strategically serve our victory against any enemy," Adam began to explain. "Although the first attempt ended with people chasing us to excommunicate us and leave us jobless; this time they will agree, as the threat is closer than ever!"

"Please, shut up."

"The United States of America cannot accept defeat from a bunch of savages who were nomads until yesterday, nor can it fear any country; this weapon will lead us to victory!"

"Victory against what? Against the invisible men and you?" John asked sarcastically, shaking his head.

"Against Saddam and the threats he spews, idiot!" Adam shouted, outraged. "We have known for a long time that Saddam is building a powerful army to be able to threaten any nation on earth to recognize his sovereignty. Do you know what weapon he possesses? Nuclear warheads! Do you know what else he possesses? Chemical weapons capable of killing tens of thousands of people. He will create a new superpower and maybe he will decide to expand!"

"And you intend to go visit Iraq, deploy your devices and cameras on the streets of Baghdad, and get the residents hooked on drugs."

"That would happen if I decided to write a script for a movie or a book. Very creative thinking, but no! We will bomb their camps, their convoys, and every area we believe could be hiding those bears who decided to pretend they live in civilization and not in the medieval times to which they belong!"

"Within a few hours, and with simultaneous brainwashing from speakers placed on vehicles approaching their convoys, they will become disoriented and kill each other, searching for the invisible enemy."

"So stupid that it almost sounds brilliant."

"The best part is that those who are sprayed and return to their cities and homes will suffer from obsession and certainly withdrawal symptoms, as you should have started to feel if you hadn't received substances to neutralize it. They will start to have hallucinations until they eventually end up self-harming after going into a manic episode."

"So far, only a few haven't harmed themselves and just went through that stage screaming. We have made the substance strong and effective! Without the antidote, they're done for," Adam triumphantly announced.

"I think you've convinced me; very good plan."

"It's the only way to achieve victory, Emerson. I'm sure."

"I'm sure too."

"I'm glad we agree!"

"I'm sure, after what I just heard that you're a psychopath planning to create a monstrosity!"

Adam approached him and hit John hard in the stomach with his left fist. John groaned.

"Are you going to keep barking all day, little puppy, or will you bite?" He asked, leaning forward to look him in the eyes while John struggled to recover.

"Anyway, I have work to do. Whether they sent you to stop the experiment or not, you and your friends will receive such a large dose of antidepressants that you'll all end up as pot plants in some clinic. No one will ever believe you or anything!"

"Before you go," John said.

"A little quickly, though!"

"You said you administered substances to counteract the gas. The officer, that Eda, why does she still have hallucinations?"

"I'm not a scientist, although I plan to ask the scientists here at the facilities. I suspect she has some mental illness unbeknownst to her; bipolar disorder, schizophrenia, or something like that and certainly, as you've understood, there's not a single c...c...c...clown anywhere," he said, mimicking Enda's stutter caused by the excessive fear that had overwhelmed her.

He opened the door to leave, and John turned his head slightly to look outside. A guard was standing at the door.

"Please watch *Mister Blonde*, will you? If he dares to act smart, kill him."

"Yes sir!"

The door closed, leaving him alone. Alone in his thoughts. This was not how they solved problems. His entire country was threatened. The very freedom it proudly shouted. The very freedom he was fighting for. And while what Adam had just told him about the external threats was not entirely wrong, Adam himself was an internal threat to the foundation of the nation people like John defended every single day.

Because at the end of the day, Adam would not hesitate to kill that very foundation of America, being its citizens, should any information leak about the existence of his secret facility. And he wouldn't hesitate to kill even more people, even within the CIA itself to maintain his place within it.

Adam was no hero. He was someone that needed to be stopped. Because that very gas could easily turn against the citizens, should Adam one day begin developing fears such as Americans becoming too patriotic for his vision of balance.

One day, that very gas could be used to turn every single citizen into brainwashed robots destroying whole cities and performing terrorist activities. Adam was not an American. He was another lunatic that wanted to shape future history.

John needed to find the others and they needed to get out of that building, but he couldn't find any way out. He was trapped in a tight square space where escape was impossible. Perhaps this time, the great John Emerson from the Special Forces would not manage to escape danger. Perhaps he should finally come to terms with the fact that he was too old for this.

Twenty-Three

No one could tell her where she was going. They certainly took her with them when they needed her and asked her to do things for them or to follow them, but there was a small but essential difference between them. They were humans, and Lacey was a four-legged creature.

She missed him ever since she had returned to the city. She had searched for him everywhere, but it was in vain. She couldn't understand why all of this had happened. At first, they had given her an item of clothing to smell, and she followed the scent trails until, for some strange reason, they had started shooting and running.

Some of her colleagues had been killed. Then, they had scattered, ultimately making her lose Bob, as the others pulled her along to follow them. So, when she finally reached the hospital after finding Quill and Pierce, she waited for a while and then returned to the woods to find him. Bob was still out there, and she was sure of it.

Back in the city, they were looking for her. From the moment she had left the clinic and had started walking through the city to reach the forest and find Bob, everyone in the force had been trying to locate her because, for a moment, they thought that whoever had done so much harm to the other men in the unit might have found her and injured her, or worse, killed her.

Of course, she didn't know that as she hadn't realized what had happened to her injured colleagues (although she remembered seeing some of them fighting each other at one point), nor did she care. The fact that they were worried about whether she was okay left her completely indifferent.

It was Bob who mattered to her, and she had to bring him back safe and sound. He was the one who took care of her, fed her, and many times, took her home with him. Essentially, he was her master.

The forest was quiet. After all, it was afternoon, so many of the animals were now seeking shelter or returning to their nests, while at the same time, nocturnal animals were coming out to look for food. Squirrels, hedgehogs, a deer, and even an old wolf were the animals she encountered on her way. She had been born and raised in the city, so seeing other animals was something new every time it happened.

Not that she had never seen a squirrel before, especially beavers, which gave the city its name. She had seen plenty of them bouncing from tree to tree in backyards, but being in the middle of a forest and seeing so many animals piqued her curiosity, especially for the animals she had never seen before.

She searched for a long time, sniffing the trails. Unfortunately, there were quite a few obstacles in her path, not just branches and fallen trunks but also steep slopes, and to get through, she often had to look around to find a path that would help her continue her way to Bob.

For a moment, she remembered a time when she had hurt her leg one day while being trained at the department. She was still young and clumsy. Bob had run over to help her and had spent several days bringing her treats, in addition to the food the other colleagues gave her, to make her feel better.

That was certainly one reason they had gotten close. Someone had cared for her and treated her well. The others had treated her well too, but he treated her better than anyone. He was a good man. She hoped that once she found him, they would go back, so he could treat her to a hot dog and play with her. Maybe he would watch her chase her tail, which made him laugh heartily.

Suddenly, she felt something that made her stop running abruptly. Instinct. If she didn't want to get soaked, she had to hurry. She ran even faster, trying to reach the spot to which the trails were leading her when suddenly, she heard a sound she knew all too well and had already anticipated earlier.

Thunder. The rain was coming from afar, but it would soon be near, and she would be soaked entirely. She was bored with the need to shake herself to get most of the water off.

Bob's scent trails were now becoming stronger, indicating that he was nearby, and the distance was narrowing. What condition would she find him in? She continued running, now feeling the first raindrops falling on her. It was still drizzling.

That gave her a little more time before she found Bob and they returned to the department. Eventually, it started to rain much faster than she had anticipated, soaking her just as she feared it would. The rain would also make it difficult to locate him, as many of the trails could be lost, but she had no intention of stopping until she found him.

She heard a groan. That was him! He was about fifty meters away, so if she ran just a bit faster, she would be able to get closer and finally see him again. She felt quite tired, but she convinced herself to run as fast as she could. She had aged, and that meant she tired more quickly, but she was so stubborn that she wouldn't let her age get in the way, especially not at that moment.

She let out a whimper as soon as she saw him, wrapping her body around him while he sat on the ground. He had wounds and seemed to have wandered alone in the forest for hours. He was dirty and smelled of dirt and blood.

"Lacey," Bob managed to say.

She nudged him with her head to convince him to rise. He was so weak that all he could do was blow out a breath.

"I can't. Just leave me here and go! Everything's gone to hell."

She didn't understand what he was saying, but she could tell he was unhappy about something. Maybe he felt that way because he could no longer walk. She barked, wagging her tail.

"Okay, okay. I hope they don't find us," he said, searching for his gun. "Oh, darn it. Alright, girl, I need you to listen very carefully! There are some very bad people in the woods. Do you understand? We need to be very careful and not let them find us. If you catch the scent of even one of them, bark, so we can run, okay?"

She barked once more, wagging her tail playfully. Bob laughed. "You're the best!" He said, smiling at her while petting her fur.

They moved on for a while. She was now following the trails that would take them back to the city. After all, she knew the route, and although it was raining, she could find her way, even if it took her a few extra minutes. They would definitely find their way back.

Occasionally, she would see Bob looking nervously around to see if anyone was following them, but seeing her not react, he felt relieved and kept walking alongside her.

"Did you see them? That's them!" He suddenly said, pointing toward the trees.

She didn't understand. What exactly was he showing her? Whatever it was, she couldn't smell it.

"Can't you feel them? They're here!" He said, bending down and trying to pull her behind a tree to take cover.

She still wouldn't react. She nudged him with her head and began licking his face.

"Now's not the time for playing, Lacey. Those guys have us in their sights, for God's sake, can't you smell them?"

She started wagging her tail and as gently as she could, bit his shirt to pull him, forcing him to rise and move.

"You can't smell them. They're gone? That's it! They've left!"

She agreed, bouncing around, barking once and starting to wag her tail playfully again.

"Alright, let's go!" He told her.

They walked a little more until they found themselves near the highway. They would logically walk along it toward the city. Lacey led the way, with Bob following behind.

"You know, if you were human, I'd suggest we celebrate the fact that we're still alive by grabbing a few beers tonight, if we can make it to the city."

Suddenly, they both heard the sound of an engine. A car stopped beside them, and the window rolled down. Bob seemed to recognize both the vehicle and the driver.

"Bob, what's going on?" He heard a man's voice from the car.

"Morris! Good to see you here."

"You look like hell. What the hell did you do in the woods?"

"Long story. I'll explain on the way."

"You're lucky I was passing by! I went to visit my sister. Get in, I'll take you to town."

"You heard him, Lacey. Get in!"

The two of them climbed into the truck, with Lacey sitting right in the middle, as there was no way Bob would let her sit in the back. To him, Lacey was a true friend. He treated her as if she were a person. They had made it. Finally, they would return to the city.

She watched him lose consciousness as he fell forward. His heart was still beating. He was sleeping. She rested her head on him, feeling his warmth. He needed this sleep after everything he had been through.

Twenty-Four

John was still locked in the room where Adam had interrogated him earlier. He was still thinking about what Adam had told him—the gas, the experiments, even the thought of using it as a weapon.

He couldn't stop blaming himself for not considering the possibility that they might have been given some narcotic that caused them to hallucinate, and he replayed every guess he had made until then, such as that there might be soldiers in invisible suits, or that perhaps they were in some magnetic field that could teleport them.

He had thought in an immature and foolish way; after all, he knew that someone might consider creating such a gas, even though he didn't know if it would ever be possible to implement this idea.

But he should have expected it. He had heard rumors of various absurd ideas, such as unleashing a virus with political and economic motives, like paralyzing a country's economy. He had heard plenty of such theories, so it shouldn't have seemed strange to him that someone had thought to act independently against the government by constructing such a diabolical weapon.

But the worst thing was that he knew how much the agency had been trying to get rid of such radical figures within their structure, as such radical minds had more than once put the nation's safety at risk through their actions.

Adam was dangerous. Not only because of what he was planning to do in order to eliminate any threat, but about what John knew Adam was capable of doing in case he felt that his actions were not appreciated by the people of the country that had given him the right to be Adam in the first place. He was sure about this.

If Adam became suddenly an enemy of the state officially, he would not hesitate to sell his demonic creation to the highest bidder. That man and his plan to do experiments without the government's approval clearly showed one thing:

For each Adam, it was never about patriotism but rather about making a point and acting as self-proclaimed heroes.

What every Adam wanted was power and recognition by all means. Should Adam escape from all this, it wouldn't be strange to John to find out that Adam would become the next president of the United States, covering up every dark secret of his actions by unleashing wars around the globe instead of defending the very borders of the nation.

For a moment, he recalled when he had been imprisoned for two whole days in a Turkish jail while participating in a top-secret mission with Greek Special Forces soldiers. He had managed to escape by making the guards believe they had to get closer to him. He had apparently tricked them, and that was what he intended to do now.

He still remembered the snapshot of an inmate who had been isolated after being absent from the gas for at least seven hours, as the footage shown by Adam had shown John. The man had fallen to the floor and was rolling around, hitting himself until in the end, he had sunk his nails into his neck and cut himself open, ending up dead on the floor.

So, going without the gas drives you completely insane, huh, Adam? Now I'll show you what madness really means! He thought, checking if there were cameras in the room. To his great surprise, there were none, even though he was sure that behind the mirror on his left, there was at least one recording his every move.

He had to be convincing, and he didn't know if he would achieve anything. Maybe he was just going to end up being another VHS video tape archive in their collection of experiment archives, and a poorly shot one at that, since after a while, the show should stop, but he had to try.

He forcefully pushed the chair with his legs so that it fell to the floor. From there, he had to act quickly. He was handcuffed, but he could do a lot with them. After threading his feet through the handcuffs on his hands, he now had his hands in front of him and could move with greater freedom.

He turned toward the wall and, looking at the mirror that rose half a meter above him, began to scream after first giving himself a hard hit below the belt.

I haven't felt this kind of pain since I brought up with Jessica in high school, he thought as he doubled over from the pain. He had to be as convincing as possible. He started pretending that he was having seizures. Someone would come sooner or later.

"Shut up!" He heard someone say from outside the door.

The pain was passing, and he needed to do something to stay convincing. He hit himself again in the same spot.

"Damn it!" He screamed frantically.

He hit himself a few more times in the same spot, screaming as loudly as he could. Ultimately, maybe he wasn't such a good actor after all, although he didn't care about that. After all, he was good at the job he did.

"I said shut up! Didn't you hear me?"

More screams echoed.

"If I come in there, I'll beat your sorry ass, you hear me?"

Time for the grand finale, he thought, grabbing the waistband of his pants and squeezing his testicles with all his strength to scream as loud as he could.

"Alright, buddy, you asked for it!" The guard who entered said, shaking his arms to appear intimidating to John, who observed his every move from the corner of his eye through the two-way mirror.

"Help," John managed to say.

"And now you'll shut up for good," the man said, before John turned toward him, putting his hands between his opponent's legs and pulling him down to the floor.

The guard fell, and John seized the opportunity to climb on top of him and place the handcuffs around his opponent's neck, trying to choke him. The guard began pulling the handcuffs, trying to escape. His already bulging arms were now close to tearing the black short-sleeve shirt he wore under his bulletproof vest, as every vein in his body was bulging as if ready to burst.

He had to act quickly without thinking. If he kept this up, it was quite likely that the guard would decide to hit him. Perhaps their roles would be reversed. He brought his right hand under the guard's chin and his left hand to his forehead.

"You're going to die!" The guard growled, trying to get loose while saliva dripped from his teeth as he fought furiously.

"I'm old," John said as he prepared to turn the guard's head with all his strength, "and the only thing that can kill an old man is retirement."

A hollow sound of a cracking bone echoed, and the enemy was now lying face down on the floor with John sprawled over him, breathing heavily.

"It's really thrilling to do this job even when you're on leave," he said, laughing hoarsely.

He quickly searched the guard's pockets and holsters, trying to forget that he was still in pain. He had never attempted anything like this before, as the last time he escaped, he had simply provoked the guard to enter the room to start beating him to death, but this trick he would remember forever, recounting it to his colleagues as a true story that would sound like a joke.

The guard didn't have keys for John's handcuffs, but he did have a knife, which John quickly seized and began to calmly try to unlock the cuffs. It wasn't difficult after all.

As soon as he heard the relieving sound of the handcuffs opening, he grabbed the guard's gun and automatic weapon and put on the vest as quickly as he could. He grabbed the knife, the guard's radio, and a dagger and started running toward the exit, stumbling from the pain.

"Damn it! So, this is what it's like to beat yourself up to escape from a cell," he said while continuing to laugh nervously.

As he exited, he saw a guard passing by on his left. Without wasting any time, he aimed the gun he had snatched at the guard and shot him in the head.

"I hope you didn't take this job to feed your wife and kids."

He had to decide whether to start searching to the left or the right. The hallway led in those two directions, and he didn't know where his daughter was. He tried to remember the route the guards had taken when they dragged him to the room where Adam had interrogated him earlier.

The doors were on the right side, except for a few exceptions. From where he was, the only way to check the doors to the right, heading toward the room he had been in, was if he followed the hallway to the left. He began to walk carefully, checking for any cameras or guards. He needed to open several doors very carefully. No one was supposed to realize he had escaped.

Of course, at some point, they would discover the body in the hallway, and that wouldn't take long, considering that, first, it was the main hallway, and second, he had shot him with a gun that didn't have a silencer, but he had a few seconds before someone found the dead guard in the hallway and the other inside the room where he had been interrogated and sounded the alarm, making every armed man appear, chasing him.

He was about to open the first door from a hallway he had just reached, having already left the previous hallway behind him, turning into another and having already reached the end of it. He opened it slowly and very carefully.

If someone was behind the door, they would quickly finish him off, but he hadn't anticipated that behind this door would be Larry, the muscular giant who was violently beating Palmer to interrogate him. So, Adam hadn't been completely convinced that John's appearance in the woods was merely a coincidence after all.

Larry turned toward John and managed, with a grip, to seize John's hand and slam it against the wall forcefully, making the gun fall from his hands. He was tall, and John would have a hard time hitting him without his opponent parrying him in time.

He took a blow to the face from Larry and then another one. John punched Larry in the stomach to see his opponent laugh, as the blow hadn't hurt him. Meanwhile, Palmer had approached, bouncing on his chair and opening his legs between Larry's, causing him to lose his balance.

In that moment, John stabbed Larry with his knife in his left shoulder. He screamed in pain and forcefully grabbed John by the vest to pull him close. John started falling to the floor. Meanwhile, Larry had turned his head to land a powerful kick in Palmer's face, knocking him on his back along with the chair.

"You little bastards are going to die!" Larry laughed.

"First you!" John said, pulling the knife along the shoulder, wounding his enemy fatally.

Larry grimaced, revealing the pain he felt as blood poured from his suit. He grabbed John's hand and, with his left hand, hit him once more in the face. Then, after he managed to pull John's hand with the knife, he grabbed him around the neck with both hands and, with slow movements, pushed him against the wall, managing to rise himself while lifting John.

As the oxygen diminished in him, John couldn't think of anything and thrashed around, trying to find a way to free himself. He tried to press the wound of his enemy, but Larry, despite the pain he felt and despite buckling, did not stop squeezing his hands around John's neck. Soon, he would die, as everything around him became blurry.

This is it! He thought, fumbling for the strap of the automatic weapon slung over his shoulder. Larry hadn't had time to take it away from John, in the panic and confusion, leaving John with a small but significant escape margin.

He grabbed the gun with his left hand to aim it at Larry as quickly as he could, and with his right, he pulled the trigger instantly, filling Larry with holes as he began to convulse while the bullets pierced him one after another.

Both fell to the ground, Larry on his back and John with his arms protecting himself, so as not to fall face-first onto the floor. He quickly propped himself up, grabbing Larry's gun from the holster in his suit and approached Palmer.

"Are you okay?" He asked.

"Tell me the truth, John. Was your visit to our town a coincidence?" Palmer asked, coughing.

"I swear to you, yes, it was! Now, where are the others?"

"They decided to interrogate us one by one and put us in separate rooms. They kept asking me how I knew you and why we were in the woods until they left me alone with this maniac. What the hell is this place, anyway?"

"They're making some kind of psychedelic gas," John said to Palmer, who was looking at him with confusion etched on his face. "Long story, I'll explain it to you as soon as we get out of here, I promise!" He said and handed him Larry's gun after he had freed Palmer from the handcuffs with the help of the knife.

He grabbed the gun that had fallen to the floor and snatched Larry's radio, handing it to Palmer.

"For now, we'll stick together, but once we find Eda, we'll split up to find an exit together after locating the others and destroy this place," John suggested.

Palmer nodded. Affirmatively.

"Just in time!" John exclaimed as the alarm began to echo throughout the building.

"Great! Now, everyone will be looking for us."

"Don't worry!" John told him. "If we stick together, we have a shot at making it; I just want you to stay focused."

"Count on me!"

The two men left the room and continued down the corridor. They heard voices at the end of it. They weren't guards' voices. The guards' voices were heard from behind them as they ran in panic.

"Head down to the lower level! It's heading for the girl!" They heard one of the guards say.

"Remember to thank them for giving you directions without you having to ask," Palmer said sarcastically.

They continued straight. They wouldn't go down the stairs yet. The screams of anguish they heard made both of them wonder what might be happening. They opened the door slowly and stood still, frozen by the sight.

She was lying on a medical bed. Tied up. Her clothes were placed on a chair further away. A young man in a lab coat with straight blonde hair styled in a way that looked almost airy and light was about to get closer to the bed while she lay tied, screaming for help.

"Calm down, junkie! Soon, you'll be given a large dose of antidepressants and sedatives, and it will all come to an end! Just let the needle do its work."

The man received a hard blow from the handle of the gun that Palmer was holding, and he fell unconscious to the floor. Meanwhile, John rushed to free Edna, who was trembling in panic.

"Are you alright?"

"Please, please let me go, please."

"Eda, calm down! Hey! It's us!" John said, trying to bring her back from her delirium.

"Mr. John?"

"Here!" said Palmer, giving her his hand to help her raise herself from the bed.

"I heard them talking among themselves while they thought I was drugged from a substance they gave me after taking me from the room I was in with you. They said they wanted to study me further because they think I'm mentally ill and they want to see how I react."

"Slow down, Eda!" Palmer told her, looking confused and trying to keep up with the pace at which she was speaking. "Calm down and explain to us what's happening."

"Mr. Palmer, I swear I had no idea that I suffered! I'm not crazy, or even if I am, I love my job, and I like being in this body with the colleagues I have; I don't want that to be a reason for me to have my right to this profession taken away by the state."

Palmer looked at her for a moment. So did John, who felt bad for Eda. He still felt grateful that she was watching over his daughter while he was completely lost in the woods under the influence of the gas. Eda hadn't let anything bad happen to Leah, and as he saw it in her eyes, Edna wasn't about to let anything happen to John's daughter because she was a kind person with morals and values.

Even under these difficult circumstances, under which she had needed to perform her duty, she hadn't stopped trying to carry it out until the last moment and now stood before them, tearful.

"I don't care what they said about you," Palmer finally replied. "As long as you're in the unit, you give your best every day, and that's enough for me. As for those bastards, it would be better if they all went together to a psychiatrist to have their twisted minds examined instead of trying to see if you have a problem or not."

A smile began to form on Eda's face. Her cheeks flushed so much that her bright red hair appeared less red than her cheeks.

"Thank you so much, Sheriff!"

"Don't thank me! The town needs you. Beaverstale needs people who do their duty with dedication. The country needs people who put duty first."

"Besides, you were watching over my daughter," John added. "That alone proves that you do your job right!"

"Thank you both."

"We have to hurry," John said. "Eda, did you see where they took the woman who was sitting with us?"

"Joanne? No, I have no idea."

"Okay, it doesn't matter! We'll go down to find Leah, and maybe we can find her too."

They exited the room, starting to head downstairs.

"Do you think she's still there?" Palmer asked, reminding John that the guards had headed there a little earlier in their attempt to locate John and Palmer.

"I guess if they had come to the floor we were on, then the room with the crazy doctor would be one of the first places they would search."

They continued down the stairs very carefully as John and Palmer went in front, as they were armed, leaving Eda to follow until she found a weapon in case they neutralized a guard.

John had thought to give her the gun he was holding and use the automatic one he had found earlier, but seeing the shock she had just undergone when the doctor had nearly raped her if he and Palmer hadn't arrived in time, he preferred to wait a bit to be sure that she could think like a police officer and that she wouldn't put herself or them in danger.

His thoughts scattered as soon as they reached the bottom of the stairs, as three guards were in the corridor they had just reached; one on the right and two on their left. All three were heading for the stairs, probably to check the situation on the upper floor, but unfortunately for them, they hadn't made it.

Palmer shot the first of the two men on the left in the head, with the bullet piercing his right eye as blood splattered while he screamed before falling to the ground lifeless, just as another bullet hit the other man in the jaw before another one hit him between the eyes, causing him to jolt backward.

At the same time, John had thrown the knife swiftly, making it spin until it embedded in the guard's carotid artery on the right. He exhaled, turning to Palmer to see if they had both succeeded. Palmer nodded at him.

Eda approached the guard on their right and grabbed his gun. Ultimately, John intended to let her use it. She might have thought it would be better for her own good to leave the fighting to the others and try to calm down, but maybe she could handle it.

After all, for her to take the initiative to fight them herself meant she wasn't going to let this tragic event that had nearly occurred, stop her from continuing to do what she knew best—being a good police officer who would never give up her job for any obstacle.

"Take his radio too," he told her.

Now, all three of them had a radio, so they could communicate at any time.

"In case we find the gas, what do we do?" Palmer asked as they moved forward.

"We destroy it, along with the lab," John said.

"Wait a minute."

"What's going on?"

"I think I know this place!" Palmer said, looking out a window on the left side of the hallway they were now crossing. "Of course! I know where we are!"

"Some building near the town?"

"A factory. We had several residents in the city who worked here in the 70s making parts for a car company until the company went bankrupt and the factory closed."

"So logically, we're in what used to be the factory's office department, right?"

"Yes, and just so you know, the factory is huge, which means we haven't covered even one-fifth of it. At least I'm sure they'll keep your daughter and Joanne here since the building doesn't have any other office rooms, so they couldn't keep them anywhere else."

"I hope you're right. They may have already decided to move them since the alarm went off."

"I have a question," Eda said. "I remember we sent a helicopter a few months ago to find out what was happening in the woods, which eventually returned with the pilots reporting that they hadn't found anything. Also, if I recall correctly, Mr. Emerson, you told me that you tried to contact with an emergency frequency. How come no one has dealt with these facilities?"

"It's a covert operation by a corrupt CIA agent," John explained to her.

"And what of it?"

"No one knows about this place. Foster, the man behind this operation, told me himself about it. The very man who ordered them to move me into another room. He definitely found a way to rescind any orders issued for an investigation in the woods, at least at the level of a military operation or service operations like his or the FBI."

"Bastard."

"Eda, just so you know, we tried to call, as John told you, but we had to cut off our conversation with the Pentagon."

"That's it!" John said.

"What are you thinking?"

"We're going to contact them again," he told them.

After grabbing the radio in his hands, he turned the lever to the frequency he had used previously. He hoped they would hear him, no matter how absurd everything he would tell them might be.

Twenty-Five

He was driving without paying attention to the other cars or even any pedestrians trying to cross the road. He was speeding in his sleek black BMW Alpina B10 Bi-Turbo, which he had ordered from a tuning house in Germany a few months ago.

Under different circumstances, he would never drive anything but American, but he was a speed enthusiast, and this wild four-door sedan with its three hundred thirty-five horsepower and a grille with four headlights that looked crazed as if the car were ready to leap and devour anything in its path was a vehicle he couldn't resist, just a few days after reading about it in a magazine.

He had even requested an installed navigation system, directly sourced from a used Mitsubishi Eunos Cosmo, as well as a built-in phone device. He never wanted to be out of touch, as his job didn't allow him to disappear.

He was driving from Huntingdon, Pennsylvania, in the direction of Washington. It was about a three-hour trip, and he had already covered half the distance in fifty minutes.

They had called him shortly after he had arrived at his vacation home with his wife and kids, located just outside the city near Raystown Lake, at the precise moment they were getting ready to grill some salmon that their neighbor had caught alongside him and his family, forcing him to pull away from the festivities, dress as quickly as he could in his neatly pressed suit, cursing and swearing, get in the car, and start driving like crazy while swearing and cursing throughout the journey.

He received several phone calls while driving, and although it was dangerous, he didn't seem to care; he was nervously typing in numbers, contacting various people who needed to report to him.

"Yes! Yes, I'm on my way! Get the B-35 ready and bring me Bill Summers to take over technical support. What? I don't care where he is and what he's doing! Make sure he's there immediately or you'll regret it!"

Then he hung up the phone to call another number.

"Yes? Lambert, do you hear me? I need a huge favor, I'm arriving in Washington shortly, I want to meet with you because it seems my leave just got canceled. Yes, yes! I need you to keep me updated and to check on everyone, and of course, contact the Secretary of Defense to come as soon as possible!"

"What? What do you mean why they called me to take charge? Let me give you a name that might help you understand. John Emerson. Yes, from Task Force Scorpion. What? Damn it! No! They don't officially exist anymore, but it seems as if the re-activation of the entire task force and not just John will be necessary should this situation here go south."

He had almost arrived at the Pentagon. After entering the city, he had committed more than twenty traffic violations, ignoring stoplights, signs, and priority vehicles, constantly flirting with death, as there were many times he nearly caused a serious accident.

The car was roaring, its engine trembling furiously as he pushed it to its limits, constantly shifting gears and flooring the gas pedal. Upon arriving, he pulled out his badge, opened the window, and the guard immediately opened the door for him.

"Good evening, Colonel!" The soldier said cheerfully.

"What good do you see?" He replied irritably.

John, you owe me a huge favor! He thought as he parked his car. He got out and started walking toward the building. He had been partially informed about the situation. He looked at his watch and realized that it had only taken him an hour and a half to arrive.

It was almost seven in the evening. It hadn't gotten dark yet since it was summer. For a moment, he considered suggesting to a screenwriter who was a friend of his, the idea of writing a screenplay about the life of a soldier within twenty-four hours since his life could literally serve as inspiration for his friend, as he had often found himself needing to stay up all night or having to travel a great distance in a short time to resolve some issue of national importance.

Of course, his thoughts went up in smoke once he realized he was approaching the main entrance. He knew only the absolute essentials and would soon learn the rest.

John Emerson, his close friend and once under his command, was in a forest outside a very small town and claimed that a CIA agent was acting independently of the president, attempting to conduct some kind of experiment. That information had been provided to him, but the medium-built blond man with the perpetually fierce face that made everyone believe he was glaring at them was not convinced things were that simple.

"Colonel Morgan?" He heard a woman say to him as soon as he stepped into the building. "Please follow me!"

"What exactly is happening, Sandra? And how come they brought you here?" He asked the short young woman, showing that he knew her.

"Didn't they inform you?" She asked, her brown ponytail moving along with her head as she was speaking.

It had been a long time since Sandra had managed to get that sweet transfer to the NSA, working as an analyst. But as long as she had been in the CIA, Sandra had been one of the people Colonel Peter Morgan could trust with his eyes closed.

While Peter Morgan was not a colonel within the CIA ranks, Sandra would always call him that out of pure respect for his successful career and out of admiration toward his sense of duty.

"Only the basics. That a corrupt CIA agent is running an operation in a town in—everywhere, that no one knew about it until now and that I'm in charge of the operation, upon the order of the Secretary of Defense, shortly after he learned of the incident."

"Exactly! How do you know the man who called us?"

"I'm afraid I can't discuss that with you," he replied. "To be honest, I'm glad he happened to be there."

"Peter!"

The colonel turned his head and saw a tall gray-haired man approaching him. The two knew each other very well, as they had been forced to work together under similar circumstances in the past. That's how they met, Peter Morgan having worked for a very long time as a CIA operative and later officer and now being Task Force Scorpion's commanding officer even after the unit had been disbanded officially.

Peter Morgan hadn't seen action in quite a while, being ordered to work as an advisor for covert operations unit establishment programs by the CIA, however, he knew that once Task Force Scorpion would be reactivated, he would have to get back to doing what he knew best; commanding.

"Bill, good to see you."

"NSA has done a check on CIA documents, Peter. Things are starting to get complicated," the man said.

"Not that they weren't already."

"Adam Foster is connected to an experiment that took place in the Santa Fe region about ten years ago. The CIA wanted his head, even though he wasn't in charge back then. Since then, he has been under the agency's radar, and theoretically, they don't trust him."

"I'm almost moved to tears. They should have captured him back then, or when he helped Edwin Wilson in 1982 and managed to convince everyone he had an alibi to prove he wasn't involved with that case."

"They arrested the head of the operation at the time, and he is serving life in prison. Foster was demoted along with his other partners as a disciplinary action."

"So, he's acting outside the agency's orders. Again."

"Unfortunately, yes, Peter. Moreover, I must inform you that the secretary has approved the use of the defense satellite if deemed necessary."

"It won't be needed!" Peter replied confidently. "I have complete faith in John."

"Is he really that good, Colonel?" Sandra asked.

"He's the best," he replied without looking at her.

They arrived in a large hall with a very high ceiling and a giant screen at the far end. Desks with computers were set up in the center of the hall. He counted ten, with one operator at each. The screen displayed real-time satellite images. What struck him was the time displayed on the screen. He looked at his watch to be sure.

"Welcome, Colonel! We hope everything is in perfect order," Sandra said as they entered the hall. "Over here is Max, a genius with computers."

"Yo, dude!" The young red-haired man with the backward cap said, straightening his fringe that had fallen over his left eye with his hand, so he could see better.

"Max!" Sandra scolded him.

Peter looked closely at him. This was the best they had? A kid in skate clothes with an earring in his left ear? *Wonderful,* he thought, *if I don't slap him, then he'll be very lucky.*

"It's fine, it's all good!" Peter said. "Kid, I have a question. Is the time on the screen correct?"

"Of course!" The young man answered cheerfully. "I mean. Yes, sir!" He said after Sandra stepped on his foot to make him realize he was being rude.

"Strange. My watch never makes mistakes."

"About that, the satellite displays everything with a ten-minute delay. Unfortunately, it's the best we have at the moment, but you can see whatever happens where the satellite focuses."

"Alright! I want you to check everywhere for soldiers and if possible, mark them, so I know where they are."

"Right away!"

"Sandra?"

"Yes, Colonel?"

"Is there a way to communicate with John?"

"Of course, Colonel. Connect him with the sergeant immediately!" The short, brown-haired woman said with her ponytail flying behind her head as she walked toward the center of the hall.

"John? This is Colonel Peter Morgan; do you receive me?"

"Colonel! I'm glad to hear from you despite the circumstances," John replied.

"I'm glad too. Update me on the situation there."

"I'm inside a forest in Beaverstale. There are devices with motion sensors inside the forest that emit some kind of gas containing psychedelic substances. A team of rogue CIA agents, led by a man named Adam Foster, is conducting experiments."

"I know that man. I should feel lucky that you have managed to find him and that our suspicions toward him were more than correct. Have you managed to find the place where they are making the substance?"

"Unfortunately not, Colonel!" John replied. "My daughter happened to be exposed to this substance, and I followed her into the woods along with some police officers. They managed to capture us, and just a little while ago, I managed to find and free my daughter."

"We are five people in total. Four since a reporter who was captured along with us decided to help us by getting back into her cell, hiding a radio inside her pockets in order to have Adam spit information about his plans."

"Excuse me, John," the Colonel stopped for a moment. "You said your daughter is with you?"

"Yes."

"How? I mean—"

"It's a long story, Sir. However, I want you to know that I had no knowledge of this place prior to me and my daughter ending up here."

"Do you know where that reporter is?" Peter asked. He knew he had no reason to not believe John. If there was any person that was loyal to his country more than anyone else, it was him after all.

"With Foster, Sir. We freed her a moment ago, and she decided to help us learn more information about the substance. We've given her frequency to the staff, so you should definitely be able to hear whatever conversation she has with Foster."

"Hold on a second, John," he said, turning to the staff. "I want to hear her frequency immediately!"

"Yes, Colonel!" Everyone shouted in unison.

"So, the gas cannot pose a danger to animals due to those microorganisms you've placed?" Joan's voice started echoing in the room.

"That's her voice?"

"Yes, Sir!" Sandra replied, who was standing beside him.

"John and the three others he has with him are hiding for now, upon our orders," Bill began to tell him. "We thought that until the gas is found, it would be good for them not to move and become easy targets."

"Well done!" Peter replied abstractly as he tried to concentrate on the woman's conversation with Foster.

"I tried to explain to your friend. I truly did," Adam said.

"Don't worry! I didn't come to the woods for him anyway."
"Right! An ambitious journalist. But I can't give you news for any article."

"Has she said anything so far about where the gas could be?" Peter asked insistently.

"No, since they gave her the radio, she hasn't made any effort at all," replied a bald, stocky man sitting in front of one of the computers.

"Business class view of the spectacle?" They heard Adam say.

"Exactly! So, what are you intending on doing with this gas anyway? You have the means to start a new world war with this tool in your hands anytime you wish."

"It's simple. I am planning to recreate Woodstock, only this time, America and Europe will be brought into total chaos before I save America as its new leader. Imagine protestors and justice warriors without a voice of their own. Imagine everyone's voice being dictated by subliminal thoughts. Imagine a nation so weak to its knees by the decadence that it would only take a miracle to recover. And imagine a nation falling into darkness while envisioning they're heading toward the light!" Foster was explaining with a tone of arrogance, as if he had already managed to make his plans turn into reality.

"That sounds like a corrupt nation."

"My dear, your own town is corrupt. Look at Palmer. He should be home collecting fish in a bowl or better yet, he should be in a nursing home. Yet, he's still wearing a uniform. Or what about Lazlo? Did you know he is not a real doctor but instead a cartel member who left Miami to avoid being assassinated and found shelter in your village? Don't tell me you have ever believed that old, bald, fat with his silk Hawaiian shirts could actually be a doctor?"

"I'll give you John and the others, if you promise that I'll be inside the cloud of the gas, covering the events so vividly that all my colleagues will surely want to rip their hair out."

"And how exactly are you going to bring them to me?"

"Your agents and the guards haven't found them yet. Why not wait for them to come to us in a certain place that they will consider being of importance? Oh, what's back there, by the way?"

"Oh, of course! Follow me."

"Center," she muttered as quietly as she could. *"Ground floor."*

"Do we know the building's layout?"

"No, but with a very good design simulation program and based on the outside structure, I can reconstruct the building's layout with a twenty percent deviation!" Max replied, opening the program on the computer without getting Peter's approval.

"Good idea, dude," Peter responded thoughtfully, mimicking Max's way of speaking.

"Here's where the gas is produced, my dear! As you can see, the staff is very careful with what they do, because with one wrong move—"

"Ouch!"

"It's a concentrated dose of ketamine and heroin."

"Damn it! He caught on," Peter growled.
"I'm almost done with the layout, guys!" Max said.
"Why?" Joan asked.

"Because of this! You thought I wouldn't figure out that you and your friends were setting me up?"

"He must have found the radio, Peter!"
"I know, Bill. Connect me with John! John? Did you hear what happened?"
"Unfortunately, yes."
"Ready!"
"Thanks, Max!" Peter replied, looking at the layout. "Where exactly are you?"
"Colonel?" Palmer said. "My name is Fred Palmer; I'm Beaverstale's chief of police and former sheriff. I happen to have been to this place a long time ago, so I might be able to help."
"The woman mentioned something before communication was lost with her. Center and ground floor."
"Of course! She's referring to the main hall of the—once—car parts factory of Oiseau Automobiles. They've probably remodeled the space."
"Excellent! John, I want the gas to be completely destroyed and to find out who supplies them with the substances, we may need to take another trip to Colombia or wherever they produce the raw materials that Adam uses. The drug trade, especially by agents who are supposedly working for the good of this people, is unacceptable, and personally, I will do everything to put a stop to it!"
"Yes, Sir!"
"And John?"
"Colonel?"
"I have orders to use a satellite defense system in case you don't succeed. I hope it won't come to that."
"You have my word!"
"Uh. Yo! Colonel?"

Peter turned his head to look at him with his left eyebrow raised, obviously annoyed by his inappropriate behavior.

"Um. I can basically maybe find the source for the drugs."

"I'm not surprised," he mocked.

"Well, now. I'm not exactly the best hacker in the world, but thanks!"

"Oh, you were talking about computers. Of course!"

"Why, what were you talking about?"

"Forget it! What exactly were you saying?"

"We'll do just like with Hop-o'-my-Thumb, of course! Only instead of dropping crumbs ourselves, we'll search for crumbs, specifically the crumbs that were accidentally dropped during one of their transactions! All I'll need is Foster's file, a list of his close associates from the past, places he has visited, missions and—"

"Alright, do whatever you think is right! Sandra, can I speak to you for a minute?"

"Yes, Colonel!"

"Until we receive notice from John, I want us to have a small assault team prepared and ready to engage. Even if we have to use the system, they may manage to escape, and I can't allow that!"

"Yes, Sir!" The woman replied and started to walk away from him.

"And keep an eye on this kid here. Does he really know what he's doing?"

"Do you remember what you told me about John?" She asked him.

"Yes?"

"Max is the best when it comes to computers!"

Twenty-Six

He was standing a few steps away from her. Her lifeless body was abandoned on a hospital bed in a room filled with such beds. According to the information Palmer had given him, it was not far from the area where they were preparing the substance, a large, long room with a high ceiling, which connected the second and third floors, as the ceilings of the first and second floors were missing, so the second and third floors functioned as bridges.

This was designed to allow oversight of the production process in the factory when it was built; however, now it served no purpose whatsoever and instead created additional problems for the staff, as there was not enough space, despite the building being excessively large.

They had deliberately separated. He would look for the gas and think of some way to destroy it, while Palmer, Leah, and Eda would find some exit and hide outside the building, so they would be safe once John completely destroyed the building.

Of course, the initial plan also included the possibility of rescuing Joanne, but none of them knew if she was alive. Now, he was looking at her dead body before him. He had heard their conversation on the radio.

Adam had administered a pure dose of heroin and a large dose of ketamine. Ultimately, he was not much different from the typical criminal, as he had gone through the trouble of buying all these illegal substances and did not hesitate to use them on innocent citizens.

She had died of a cardiac arrest. Her eyes were still wide open as she stared into nothingness with her lifeless and motionless gaze. For a moment, he felt guilt. He had let her pretend she had betrayed them. If she hadn't accepted that idea, she would still be alive.

And now she was there before him, and the more he looked at her face, the more it seemed as if she was trying to say, *I'm sorry; I couldn't make it,* without him being able to tell her something like, *I'm to blame.*

The plan remained the same. John would find a way to destroy the building while Fred, Leah, and Eda would find a safe place to hide outside the building. Due to the fact that they did not have masks, they could not move far from the building from which they had just escaped.

The colonel had ordered former SEAL Team Six and Delta Force members that belonged to the Scorpion Task Force, stationed close to the area to remain hidden in strategic points surrounding the city and the forest, outside the borders deemed dangerous, about two miles away from the central circle marked on the map where the city and that part of the forest were located. They had deployed rapidly, on choppers, four, six-member squads in total.

Once John would confirm he had successfully exited the building, the strike teams would advance and bombard the building with utmost secrecy, as part of the strike teams would locate and disable all the mechanisms that released the gas. They had already devised the perfect story to cover the incident regarding the factory.

Obviously, the residents had been quite alarmed by the disappearances, but they could never be allowed to learn the exact truth about everything that was happening there. The scenario provided as a cover-up story was the action of a Bolivian drug dealer who used the abandoned factory as a front, kidnapping and subsequently killing anyone who got too close.

For the people who had ended up in the hospital, it had been decided they would learn the truth under the condition that they would never speak of what they had learned to anyone. No one was ever to learn of this incident, other than those who had experienced it firsthand.

He moved toward the end of the room, always keeping his gun ready to spring on anyone who appeared before him. He needed to think of a way to destroy that place completely, and there were, of course, not many options. He had gathered three grenades from a guard at the gate, who was the only one who had something like that, hiding them well, so that no one would suspect anything and decide to take even stricter security measures.

Meanwhile, the alarm had stopped ringing, even though they were still searching for them. It was evident. He estimated it was seven-twenty, something confirmed by a watch embedded in some device within the room he was crossing.

"Fred, have you made it outside?"

"Yes!" Palmer replied. "Have you thought of anything?"

"Nothing! Do you know if there's an office, maybe a director's office on that side of the building?"

"No, absolutely none, as I told you before."

"Damn it," he said.

"Why?"

"I'll need to provide them with information regarding Foster's potential collaboration with drug dealers, as they asked me. Wait a second!" He said and changed the frequency. "Colonel, I have not yet found any document confirming the theory about Foster's collaboration with drug dealers."

"Never mind, John! We are investigating in parallel. Have you found any—?"

"Hey, yo! Is there possibly a desktop computer, a palm computer, a laptop, or something like that?"

"Many, and in various corridors," John replied. "Who are you?"

"It's the genius they sent to handle the computer department, John. For now, do whatever he says."

"Kids in the Pentagon. Now that's beyond me," John muttered.

"Open one of the computers and follow the steps I tell you exactly!"

"Okay, kid."

"It's still in the experimental stage. Some buddies of mine are experimenting with it and say it will soon be the biggest revolution in the world!"

"Back to the matter, Max!" Peter told him. "Tell John what to do."

"Ah, yeah, excuse me!"

Max guided John in the simplest way possible to operate the computer in the room with the beds. As Max had predicted, they were connected to a supercomputer inside the building and not only that, Max now had full control of the files on every computer.

"Max. Is that supercomputer you mentioned flammable?" John asked.

"It has quite a few circuits and could cause a pretty big boom."

"How big?"

"The computer would be blown to pieces."

"The building?"

The young man burst out laughing.

"No, no! You can't blow up the building with the computer."

"Great! Change of plans for the second time," he replied. "We will communicate later!"

He ran as fast as he could, trying at the same time not to make noise. A few steps away was a guard. He did not intend to let this opportunity slip by, so he quickly approached him, grabbing him with his left hand, bringing his arm around his neck, and with the gun he held in his right hand, he began aiming at his right carotid artery, pressing it with the tip of the gun.

"If you scream, I will pull the trigger!" He warned him. "Where does the building get its power?"

"Ground floor. The west wing."

"Great!"

"Even if you disable the generator, they can turn it back on from a computer. Why don't you just surrender?"

"I don't like surrendering," he replied, pushing the man's head against the wall to neutralize him with a solid blow to the heavy industrial concrete.

"Fred, I think I found a solution to the problem."

"What exactly are you thinking?" He answered.

"The building is powered by generators. Maybe I can get a little creative."

"That could definitely do some damage to the building."

"The only thing that worries me is how much damage we can do. The building has an automatic fire system. In the generator room, they likely use substances like heptafluoropropane in case of fire. I don't know about the other rooms. I'm also not sure how easily the fire can spread and destroy the rest of the building."

"Can we do anything to help?"

"You better not do anything for now. Keep your eyes open in case you see any of the devices, and don't approach them! Do you have breathing masks in your department?"

"No, but they definitely have some in the fire department. Meanwhile, I must inform you that the perimeter is better guarded than before! We saw guards returning to the facilities from the forest. I guess everyone is looking for us."

"Call for reinforcements and tell them to wear masks! Tell them to bring some for us too."

"Alright, John. Good luck!"

He had thought of a plan. After finding a place to hide, he changed the frequency on the radio to communicate with the Pentagon.

"This is John, can you hear me?"

"Of course, John!" The colonel replied. "What's going on?"

"Does the satellite you mentioned clearly display the area around the factory?"

"As far as I can see, yes. It shows everything with a ten-minute delay on our screen."

"Can it trace back to previous days?"

"Sir, I can do that on my screen!" He heard Max say from the background.

"Of course he can!" The colonel confidently replied. "But why?"

"The building is powered by generators. They surely get their fuel from somewhere, and the fuel surely arrives in some vehicle or vehicles. If they want to remain hidden, I'm guessing they are not making trips with these trucks very often and probably keep the trucks in an area within the factory, filled with fuel, so that they can feed the generators whenever needed."

"Max, can you search for what he requested?"

"Right away!" Max replied.

He waited for a little while. He had begun to lose his patience. He wanted this adventure to end as quickly as possible and to leave this cursed forest with his daughter.

"According to the satellite, tankers come and go every week. I've counted at least six, two of which seem to have left the facilities."

This means I can do quite a bit of damage before the strike team arrives, John thought.

"John, if possible, I would like you to check their defenses," the colonel told him. "I want to know if they have vehicles that could repel the forces we will send."

"The perimeter is well guarded as long as they think we are still all inside. I've also asked the sheriff to call for police reinforcements to get us out of the forest before the strike team arrives. Inform all teams!"

"John, I hope you understand how important what you are doing is!" The colonel pointed out, wanting to thank him for the courage he had shown up to that point.

"Yes, Sir!"

It took him some time to reach the west wing of the building, but he finally arrived. He had to hide several times from guards who were searching all the corridors, speaking on the radio and constantly reporting that John and the others had not been found.

At least that relieved him somewhat, as it meant Leah was not in danger. He might sound a bit selfish for thinking of her first, but deep down, he was also worried about Palmer and Enda. After all, they had spent quite a few hours together trying to escape that forest, which made him feel quite close to them. Not as close as he felt toward Leah and his wife, but close enough to respect them.

He carefully opened the large double doors leading to the generator area. One wrong move and he would end up blowing himself and the factory to pieces.

Twenty-Seven

"Have you found their frequency yet?"

"No, not yet, Sir. I will need a little more time," said the slender man to Adam, who was nervously standing behind him, waiting to hear that some results had been made.

He had just found out from his men that three radios had been stolen, and he was certain that John intended to leave the building. It was quite clear. What was not clear, and what he wanted to know, was whether John planned to cause damage and possibly sabotage his work before leaving the building, although Adam could bet John was a man that would rather burn the factory to the ground than just leave and never come back.

The first measures he had taken were to order tighter security for the building, with all the guards returning to the premises, as well as to check if any of the other prisoners had escaped. Shortly before Joanne was found by Agent Angel Hayes, he had learned that three more weapons had been stolen, along with two more radios.

Once they had moved Joanne, about whom he had read enough to know she was a journalist and quite dedicated to her dream of becoming one of the best, he had decided to interrogate her. When she would pretend, upon seeing him, that she wanted to help him, he wouldn't believe for a second that such a thing could be true.

When he would finally get the radio from Joanne, it would already too late. Just before she would die from the injection he would administer to her, she would manage to change the frequency by quickly turning the dial.

The man sitting in the chair in front of him, using a tabletop wireless communication device, was one of the engineers working in the facilities, and he had to find a way to intercept the frequency momentarily, so he could learn John's next moves. He had to admit it; he was good enough and had managed to cause him quite a bit of trouble up to that point.

"Are you finally going to find it, for Christ's sake?"

"I'm an engineer. I have no idea about radios," complained the man.

"Listen to me. If you don't want me to blow your brains out, then find me a solution right away! I will count to three. One. Two."

"Stop!" He begged. "I think I found it."

"Let's hear it then. See? You can do miracles when you're focused," he said, putting the weapon back inside the holster of his suit's jacket.

An annoying sound interrupted his thoughts. The satellite phone on the table rang throughout the room. Who could it be, and what could they want? He thought it wouldn't hurt to answer.

"Yes, who is it?"

"Bastard, you sold me out!" An annoyed man on the other end shouted.

"Carlos, Carlos. Why would I do something like that?"

"The cops have surrounded the whole port, you old bastard! They just entered the warehouse and are arresting my men one by one."

"In that case. Good for you!"

"How did you say that?"

"As soon as the data from the experiment is given to the president, and he understands the danger the country is in, he will have no choice but to resign and the office will be mine. Insects like you only exist to benefit my plans whenever needed. Thank you, by the way, for your help so far and for our sweet cooperation, of course."

"I'll fuck you up!"

"Goodbye."

The engineer looked at him, stunned and sweating. Just moments ago, Adam had nearly shot him, killing him. He adjusted his glasses, which had slipped a bit, to see better, and continued to stare at him through his large square lenses.

"Is this the frequency?" He asked.

"Yes, Sir!"

"Good. Let's hear what our friend is up to."

A loud bang was heard, shaking the entire building. A few seconds later, the alarm began to ring.

"That bastard. He is trying to blow us up!" He shouted. "Find him and kill him, you idiots!" He bellowed into the radio.

He rushed out of the room with quick and nervous movements. John had just revealed his intentions, and from what it seemed, what he was truly afraid of was about to happen. Over the radio, he could hear the guards reporting a significant explosion that had occurred in the area where the generators were located.

This meant that the entire west wing was about to collapse. The fire wouldn't be long in reaching the central part of the building, destroying the lab where the gas was being produced. He pulled his gun from its holster and began to run.

"John, me and you have unfinished business."

Twenty-Eight

He stood for a moment, taking in the surroundings. A few large wooden crates provided him with decent cover, allowing him to decide the best way to cause as much damage as possible. The large generators stood side by side, humming as they operated incessantly. Three guards were walking around the space, and one lingered by one of the trucks, reluctant to look for John, Palmer, Leah, and Edna.

The trucks were likely still filled with fuel, which meant that if he could get even one close to the wall bordering the central part of the building, he could cause significant damage, potentially bringing the building down at least on one side.

Moreover, by blowing up the generators, he would create a power outage since they were all concentrated in the same spot. Obviously, when the factory was constructed, no one had foreseen that one day, it would become a base for military experiments.

The two trucks remained near the generators where they were parked. The explosion would be sufficiently large, based on his calculations. Additionally, there were three black SUVs parked next to each other in the area.

"Drop your weapons to the floor!"

He turned to see a woman in a suit with jacket and tie, aiming her gun at him.

"I won't say it again!" She warned, her green eyes flashing with hatred. "Drop them on the floor now!"

"Okay, okay! Why are you getting so worked up?" He replied.

"Start walking slowly toward the center."

"Did you dye your hair with bleach? My daughter would definitely love to have such bright platinum hair like yours."

"Shut up and move!"

He took a few steps, simultaneously checking to see if the guards had noticed him. No one seemed to realize that he was there. How had this young woman figured it out? Just before he left the covered spot, John dropped flat on the floor, kicking her legs hard.

He saw her gun fall to the ground. He quickly got up and tried to grab his own gun, which was a little farther away, but she used her legs like a vise and started to squeeze his waist, while holding onto one of the crates to keep him from moving. After pulling him toward her, she climbed on top of him and began to choke him with both hands.

They both fell onto the crates, causing one to tumble down from the top to the ground and break, making the guards turn toward them.

"Look what you've done now!" He said, struggling to breathe as he quickly dropped flat on the ground, grabbing the automatic weapon and aiming it at the guards who were heading their way.

Even though he could hardly breathe and was struggling to use the weapon, he tried his best to aim at them. The gun began to jerk in his hands as he squeezed the trigger, aiming at the guards. He shot all four of them, managing to kill them. He realized that all the enemies had fallen to the floor, and the weapon was empty.

He struggled to free himself, but the girl was strong. With his left thumb, he hit her on the left side a few times, making her scream in pain. She continued to choke him, but now with her left hand, while with her right, she was digging her nails into his face, attempting to get to his eyes. He quickly shook his head to stop her.

He felt a blow to his side. She had delivered a hard hit with her left knee, and now, she was trying to rise. He saw her move toward one of the two guns on the floor and immediately got up and charged at her, throwing her to the ground. They both fell, one on top of the other.

He grabbed her head and banged it twice against the floor to incapacitate her. Once he got up, he heard Adam's voice screaming into her radio.

"Angel? Angel, do you read me? Angel?"

"She's sleeping like a baby," he muttered as he walked away from her, approaching the tank trucks after grabbing his gun from the floor and emptying hers, taking the magazine to use later.

He cut the side of the tank of the truck closest to him with his knife and immediately, breaking the glass, opened the door and cut the wires with his knife, trying to get it started. As soon as the engine ignited, he started driving quickly toward the wall.

Suddenly, he felt a hard hit on his right cheek, just after he had turned the vehicle and was heading toward the wall. Angel had jumped into the cab of the truck and kicked him in the face while holding onto the roof of the truck to enter quickly. Her face was bloody. He retaliated with a strong punch to her chest, only to receive a series of hits from the enraged woman in the face.

"You don't know when to give up, do you?" He said, trying to deflect her blows.

They were approaching the wall at high speed. Meanwhile, she continued to strike him.

"One thing I always told my daughter was this," he said, and pulled the handbrake sharply, turning the steering wheel abruptly.

The truck spun several times around itself, approaching the wall like a top. John seized the opportunity and kicked her with both legs, pushing her out of the truck and watching her fly into the wall as the truck spun out of control.

It made a few more spins before slamming into the wall, with its right side crushing into the cement, squashing Angel's legs with its front end as she had attempted to jump. She screamed with all her might.

"Always wear a seatbelt in the car," he said, getting out of the truck.

He looked toward the generators. He would throw all three grenades and then run out of the room as fast as he could. The explosion would be strong and dangerous for him. And so he did.

He had seen vehicles and machinery explode plenty of times, so he had no intention of staying inside and watching the generators erupt into flames, as parts of them would be thrown into every corner of the room at the same moment the two tank trucks would explode, causing a shockwave powerful enough to send every crate and barrel nearby flying away and igniting the oil line formed by the truck he had slammed against the wall, ultimately catching fire and turning it into a bomb that would demolish the wall.

He knew very well that's how it would happen, and as soon as the building shook and collapsed to the ground, he only turned his head and saw the damage that had been done.

He was far enough away. At least outside the room. The fire suppression system had activated, but it was no match for the blaze caused by the explosion in the west wing. He got up and started running toward the center of the building. He had found himself in a factory again, so he could imagine where Max had told him that large central hall was located.

"Colonel, I just blew up the generators! There were also three SUVs, which have been completely destroyed!" He shouted into the radio as he ran.

"Good job, John! The assault team is approaching. Where are you?"

"I'm nearing the room where the gas is made. I might be able to do something to ensure it gets destroyed."

"No! Get out immediately! The assault team will take care of it."

"The assault team might arrive too late, and Adam could manage to escape with a sample of the gas to continue his experiments!" John insisted.

"Damn it, John! I don't want you inside when the building comes down."

"I promise you," he said, "I'll get out of here alive, and we'll all meet for a barbecue in my backyard one afternoon. Me, you, Leah, Kim, and our wives."

"John, stop! Can you hear me?"

He shut off the radio as he approached. The main gate was open, so he immediately walked in. Meanwhile, he saw men in full protective suits running in a panic as guards shouted at them to evacuate the building. John temporarily hid behind a workbench and waited until they all got outside.

Once he was sure he was alone, he began walking toward the center of the hall, looking left and right to find a way to destroy the laboratory completely. He felt something pierce him, but it didn't cause pain at first. In fact, the pain took a moment to register, as he didn't have time to realize what had just happened.

He had heard a bang from behind him, and the next moment, his right arm rattled as if someone had shoved him with great force. It felt weak to the point that his gun fell to the ground. That's when he felt the pain in his triceps. If he had to describe to someone exactly how he felt, he would say he felt a strong burning sensation.

It was as if someone had pressed a hot seal against his arm. A sharp sting as the bullet had penetrated him. Fortunately, going by a rough estimate, the wound wasn't serious. After all, if he could reach his gun without taking another shot, he could use his left hand for now.

"I should have killed you earlier instead of deciding to show mercy and send you to a psychiatric hospital where at least you could breathe," he heard Adam say, almost growling behind him.

John turned to look at him, holding his painful hand with his left. In the end, he might not be able to use his left hand as he initially hoped.

"You think you can just escape without consequences?" John asked, looking at him.

"Escape?" Adam replied, annoyed. "Do you have any idea what you're about to destroy?"

"An abomination."

Adam sighed. Then, he approached John and aimed at him.

"I'll ask one last time. Who sent you?"

Gunfire echoed inside the building. Adam turned his head momentarily and then looked back at John.

"It doesn't matter. Soon, you and your friends will be dead. Did you hear that? The sound an MP5 makes is sweet. Listen to how beautiful and melodic the M16 sounds! I can't wait to see your daughter disemboweled by bullets."

He closed in on John and kicked him with all his might, knocking him to the ground. Then, he began to unleash continuous violent kicks, shouting and cursing at him.

Suddenly, Adam stopped shouting. He was no longer kicking. He had gone still. For a moment, John wondered if he had gone numb from the pain. After all, he had taken blow after blow to his ribs and face, so it seemed very reasonable for him to have lost consciousness, not feeling Adam's kicks anymore or even seeing Adam at all but instead hallucinating. But he had not lost consciousness.

He heard Adam trying to speak and then found himself on the floor with blood streaming down his chest. He supported himself on the floor with his left hand, which was now clasped into a fist, trying to turn his head and aim at whoever had shot him.

John tried to move slightly to see behind Adam. At that moment, he realized that the bang he had heard amid the blows was not a bullet meant for him but rather a bullet that had pierced Adam.

He walked slowly toward him as if strutting down some runway. He seemed to relish every second and take pleasure in watching Adam writhe in pain, resting his right hand, in which he held his gun, against Adam's chest.

He got close enough to use the tip of his gun to push against Adam's head, forcing him to lie down flat on the ground. Then, he emptied the entire magazine into Adam's head, blood spraying out and splattering onto John.

"Who's laughing now, asshole?"

"Eda!" John exclaimed, surprised.

"I thought you'd need some help, and besides, I owed you one from before."

"Thank you!"

"If we want to be realistic for once, after everything that happened today, they're probably going to kick me off the force."

"If we want to be realistic at all!" He told her, looking at her. "You did your best. You're one of the good cops. One of those cops who enter the force to protect people and bring justice, rather than just wearing the uniform to intimidate people."

"Thank you!"

John grabbed the radio in his hands.

"Fred, is everything okay?"

"People from the department have arrived, John! We're waiting for you at the SUV," he replied.

"We're coming right away."

He glanced at Adam's lifeless body, now still on the floor. Then, he signaled to Eda to leave. There was nothing left for them to do in that space. As they exited, they heard the sound of vehicles. The assault team was approaching. He looked at the sky for a moment and then looked back at the building he was leaving behind as he got into one of the two SUVs. They had survived.

Twenty-Nine

He was walking alone in the forest without any weapons. He had previously emptied his gun, trying to shoot for cover. His colleague was nowhere to be found. He had searched everywhere for her, yet nothing. His legs were wounded from gunfire, and so was his large left bicep.

Several times, Ronny had to grab onto a tree, even crawl to keep moving forward. He didn't know who the men that had opened fire with the intent to kill them were, but he was sure they were still nearby, and that he was in danger.

He heard footsteps and hid behind a tree. Someone was approaching, and as it was raining, their footsteps sounded wet on the soaked ground. The person grabbed him and threw him to the ground with their strong hands.

"Thatcher?"

"Ronny? Thank God, I found you!"

Ronny helped his colleague up. He noticed that he too had wounds from gunfire. The two of them leaned against each other, their arms cross-locked behind their shoulders as they tried to walk.

"The bastards attacked us. I don't know where the others from my team are."

"I don't know where Eda is either. They attacked us as soon as we got into the forest. I tried to reach you on the radio, but nothing."

"We drove them off."

"Why?"

"The guy who was looking for his daughter said they can track us through radio waves even when we're hiding very well."

"Who are they anyway? I couldn't even see them," Ronny asked, annoyed that he couldn't do his job correctly.

"They wear invisible suits. At least, that's what he told us."

"Great. Now I've seen and heard it all!"

They heard the sound of a vehicle that was far from them but moving parallel to the path they were crossing. It might be the ones trying to kill them.

"Did you hear that too?" Thatcher asked.

"Yeah. They might be moving on the road."

"Are you thinking what I'm thinking?" Thatcher said to Ronny, who was now looking at him, puzzled. "If we get to the road, we have a chance to find our way back to the city."

"I heard the sound again! Let's go see."

They started to walk slowly toward the direction where they had heard the sound, each helping the other to move as quickly as they could. They were both exhausted and wanted nothing more than to get back to the city and visit the hospital. They had run out of strength and patience. Their guns were empty, and they needed to find a way to survive if they encountered any of their enemies.

A black silhouette appeared several meters away. A tall, muscular man wearing all black, along with a beanie and a gas mask, was holding a small semi-automatic weapon. Without wasting time, they rushed at him, holding onto each other, and threw their weight against him, knocking him to the ground and starting to beat him.

"Where are the others? Tell us, you bastard!" Thatcher began shouting.

"Who are you?" The man asked, confused.

"Do you see the badges?" Thatcher said, puffing out his chest. "We're the police! Now, tell us why you tried to kill us earlier."

"Enough! Both of you, let him go!" Someone said from behind them in a deep voice.

"And who are you?" Ronny asked.

"Sergeant Major Luis O'Brien, Task Force Scorpion, and that's all you need to know. Do you have masks with you?"

"No. Why?" Thatcher said, starting to notice other men hiding behind the trees.

"Follow my men and put them on right now!" He said, signaling to his men to come out of their hiding spots and hand them two small reserve masks they had. "Which of you is the guy they keep calling Sheriff?"

"Neither," Ronny answered. "Why do you ask?"

"Stranded," the sergeant major muttered. "Alright! Follow us. The police chief, along with Corporal John Emerson, found a factory deep within the forest where hallucinogenic gas is being produced. The information I'm giving you is classified, and you're not allowed to speak to anyone about it once we get you back to the city."

"Gas?" Ronnie asked in shock and disbelief.

"So, the invisible men didn't exist," Thatcher muttered, stunned.

A loud noise echoed as they climbed a slope, and they immediately turned their heads toward the direction they had heard the explosion.

"The old factory of Oiseau Automobiles!" Thatcher shouted, recognizing the building from afar, as now one side of it was engulfed in flames, laughing as he witnessed the spectacle. "The bastards have been burned alive!"

Thirty

Peter was standing in front of the enormous screen, which was now displaying the factory engulfed in flames and the assault teams closing in. Although the footage was ten minutes delayed, it no longer bothered him. John had managed it.

"Sir?"

He turned his head and looked at Sandra, still smiling from the spectacle he had just seen on the screen.

"The DEA confirm that everyone who was in the warehouse with Carlos Ramirez has been arrested. Additionally, footage has been obtained inside the warehouse to make the cover story more convincing when we'll have to explain why the old Oiseau Automobiles factory in Beaverstale was destroyed."

"That's very good news!" Peter exclaimed.

"Sir," she said hesitantly. "Are you sure we're making the right decision to cover up this incident? I accept that it's the order of the Secretary of Defense, but I believe we have a duty to our fellow citizens."

"Unfortunately, the truth can sometimes be difficult to capture. I don't agree with it either, but believe me, for now, it's the best way. One day, the truth will come out, but for now, it will need to stay buried along with this factory."

She shook her head and left. Everyone in the room was celebrating as the mission had been completed. The only thing left was to find out if the strike team had finished destroying the factory.

"Colonel, do you hear me?"

"Yes, John!" Peter replied, relieved that he was still alive.

"Adam is dead."

"I see the assault teams approaching from my monitor."

"They are already destroying the factory, Sir."

"I can't wait for that barbecue and the beer, then!"

"That will take a while, Colonel. We have been exposed to the gas, and even though we were given substances to neutralize it, I'm sure we'll need to stay under medical observation for some time."

"I understand! John," he said, looking at the screen, feeling a lump in his throat as he tried to hold back a tear that never fell despite being quite emotional. "Thank you for everything!"

"And thank you, Colonel!"

"Listen to me, everyone!" He said, looking at them one by one. "If you have something to do, now is the time to do it. You can leave! Congratulations to you all!"

Everyone in the room started to applaud, relieved that this nightmare was finally over. He felt a strong pat on his back, as if someone were trying to hit him in a friendly way. He hadn't felt that kind of pat since he was on the high school football team.

He turned around, annoyed and saw Max looking at him with a smile. He was so excited about their success that he momentarily behaved inappropriately.

"Dude!" Peter said, hugging Max in a friendly manner, who was frozen and didn't react, wondering if the colonel had finally gotten annoyed and was planning to hit him in retaliation.

He started walking toward the exit of the room. Finally, he could enjoy his leave and was looking forward to being back behind the wheel of his car and returning to his cabin to find his wife and kids.

He turned the key in the ignition, hearing the sound of the engine roar to life. The car pulled away from the parking lot, driving under the golden sky. *What a day*, he thought to himself.

Epilogue

Two whole years had passed since then. The inability to share with anyone what had happened in that cursed forest was certainly something that bothered her. Someone had to eventually learn about that place.

It was summer, and Leah had visited the nearest department store in her town to browse the windows. There would surely be something to catch her eye. Her hair, now straight, fell to her nape. She had kept the clothes she once wore when she felt punk in her closet.

She still enjoyed listening to the bands that had expressed her thoughts in their lyrics, but now, Leah preferred to dress in Puma shorts and short-sleeved, solid-colored shirts.

However, her father hadn't changed at all, and although he had been away for three months without giving her and her mother any information about where he was, Leah knew that her father's taste in clothes was timeless and would never change.

The department store was bustling with life. People everywhere were looking at the displays, walking, talking loudly, and laughing. She went there fairly often. As strange as it might sound, Leah felt good about having moved to Beaverstale to study Information Science at the University of Tennessee.

The choice had been hers. She couldn't explain to anyone, not even to herself, how she had decided to return to the place she had sworn never to set eyes on again, the moment she finally boarded the vehicles that would take them back home and then spend considerable time in special detox facilities. But she had returned nonetheless.

During the semesters, Leah stayed in the university dorm, and in the summers, she stayed at the house that Felix had rented for her and her father, so she could work within Beaverstale.

Only five days remained before summer vacation began, and Leah spent her free time finding something to do instead of being cooped up in the student dorm.

So, the mall was the best solution, and having obtained her driver's license (yes, she never expected such a thing would happen) and her first car, a 1989 Ford Taurus station wagon, Leah could easily go wherever she wanted.

A few days earlier, she had found a store with video games in a corridor of the mall. As soon as she saw the Game Boy in front of her, she smiled. It was the first thing she had found on her bed when she had officially returned home after the odyssey she had been on, with a welcome card from her mother and a note from her father, apologizing for the worst vacation they had ever had.

It wasn't his fault. It was entirely due to the tornado that had caused that plane crash, forcing them to change course. Odd, though. Strange that in photographs she had found from the site of the accident, there wasn't a single injured person or body.

Five days later, Leah had already placed the key in the ignition as her classmates were busy with hugs, tears, and farewells, and she drove toward Beaverstale. She hadn't even called her mother on the phone.

When she had first arrived in Beaverstale at the beginning of the academic year, already enrolled and having rented the house, Eda had become her friend. In fact, all the victims of the forest had developed friendly bonds and often met for barbecues or other activities, but Eda and Nancy were the two people with whom she felt most comfortable spending her time, given that they visited her on campus often.

For Christmas, she had asked her father, who would visit her with her mother, for a very specific gift—a typewriter.

And so, she had spent an entire academic year away from her parents' home. Reading, going to the mall, playing basketball on Saturdays, and drinking hot chocolate with Eda and Nancy whenever there was time to visit Beaverstale on a cold day, traveling many miles to spend time with them. But for the weeks she would stay there, she didn't have her mind on hot chocolate and chats with the forest survivors.

She parked in front of the garage entrance. Inside, the house was clean and tidy. She walked quickly to her room, making sure to lock the front door. On her desk sat her shiny, imposing typewriter, waiting for Leah to start typing. In the attic, a mountain of video tapes.

It wasn't easy to find these kinds of tapes, filmed in such a terrible way that they almost looked as if someone had been drunk while holding the camera.

Among them, the tape with an episode of *Family Matters* that Leah had asked one of her classmates to give her.

But that wasn't the reason she had requested that tape; it was because the airing of the show had been interrupted to broadcast the breaking news report she was looking for.

Having spent a considerable time in the clinic with her father, with nothing particularly to do in her free time, Leah read newspapers or whatever else she could find available from the doctors. That's how she had found that pamphlet from *Eagle Eye News* that had sparked a battle within her, a battle she had decided to win. The battle for the truth.

An empty airplane on fire. A tornado changing their course. A forest at the mercy of a dangerous drug. No, the coincidences weren't connected, even though they were very convenient, but Aeolus was the God of the wind. She had learned his name and program from her father while discussing what had happened during the time they hadn't been together.

She would keep her promise not to let anyone know about the forest. But she wasn't obligated to remain silent about the plane crash and the tornado. Looking out the window toward the forest, she smiled and then turned her gaze to her typewriter, starting to type:

THE LIGHTS OF THE SHADOWS. ENTRY 1

Behind the Shadows

About the Film

The *Lights of the Shadows* was written and directed by Caleb Goldberg. Caleb had already been known for his controversial work on films such as *Furious Rex* and *Aquatic*, making the world puzzled as to how he had managed to apply such realistic visual effects, making his films almost as if they were real footage.

In 1995, Caleb decided he wanted to make an 80s action movie, only with horror elements mixed to the equation. When he approached Independence Entertainment, pitching his idea, the company refused to produce his film; however, film producer, Tom Burkley, from Dexter Studios Inc. happened to find out about said pitch and proposed Caleb to make the film together.

Filming began in early September 1998. Despite the fact that some well-known actors had agreed to play a role in the film, most of the cast consisted of names that were new to the industry and expectations were extremely low, regarding the way people would react to the film.

Since the budget was extremely low, the crew would have to invent ways to make the movie as immersive and entertaining as possible without sacrificing quality and from the very first moment, this was exactly what they had all agreed to, starting with the setting they would use for filming.

To find a suitable location, actors and to make the story's premise fit the budget, Caleb would spend three years until 1998, proposing draft after draft, watching them all be sent back for changes.

The original draft revolved around a completely different premise. In that, John, the main protagonist (23 years old in the original draft) would wake up in his apartment by the sea and exit the room to find himself into a liminal nightclub that would soon be filled with people dancing, only their faces would be gone, making them look like faceless mannequins.

Originally, Caleb was planning for a much bigger premise that would involve the concept of dreaming and waking up in the same dream in an endless loop, but Dexter Studios demanded Caleb should change the entire premise and make the dream fit a single area to limit the budget. Eventually, Caleb managed to convince Dexter Studios work on the final draft that would turn into *The Lights of the Shadows*.

The Setting

The town of Beaverstale, also known as Beaverstale Village is a place known for its controversial location, as it exists within three states, as well as the Wild Beaver whiskey. In 1974 and later in 1979, two films would take place in Beaverstale, one being *Warstruck,* starring 80s action idol, Stan Kurtz, and the other one being the classic horror movie, *Feast of the Dead*.

Caleb, having helped his friend, Alan Gardener, in filming *Feast of the Dead*, had been enthralled with how magical Beaverstale looked with its fog, the continuous rains all year round, the wet asphalt and the forest which he fell in love with.

Despite the fact the residents and Mayor Oliver Price of Beaverstale did not want another movie to take place in their town, due to the turbulence the town suffered from visitors that had come to see every major location filmed in *Feast of the Dead*, ending up in breaking in and looting from the Montgomerys' house, an abandoned furnished 50s home that had been bought for the film and later, left abandoned once more.

Eventually, Caleb Goldberg managed to convince the residents that the town would benefit from the film, being allowed to film in it. The town would be visited by Smilefilm Productions twice during the 2000s, as *Cinderella Case* would take place in the town and its unconnected sequel, *Beauty in the Beasts* would make a throwback to both the prequel and *Lights of the Shadows* in 2022 by filming a scene inside the forest.

2011's soft reboot of the *Secret Asset* spy film series would not only include Beaverstale as a location, but also the clown appearing in *The Lights of the Shadows* would be featured as a villain in the film, after British filming company, Leaf Green Entertainment and Hindi-Chinese Tiger Entertainment would acquire the rights to use the character.

In 2008, the township of Beaverstale would replace the *Welcome to Beaverstale!* sign with a new one, adding the phrase *Home of Wild Beaver Whiskey and Hollywood Horror Films*.

Due to budget limitations, most of the scenes were shot in Beaverstale, even scenes such as the pre-titles scene where John, the protagonist and his squad were sabotaging a factory, where parts of the old Oiseau Automobiles factory were used and Seagull Beach in California was selected as the most suitable for being used as the beach in the intro scene.

For every scene taking place in a fictional abandoned Eastern European city, Caleb used scenes from a documentary he had released just a year ago, regarding the destruction Russia withstood after the fall of the Soviet Union and the discrimination Russians were subjected to, titled *The Other Side of the Coin*.

For the interior of the buildings, the filming crew used scenes filmed in Body State Historic Park, Pinetree County Sanatorium and a rehauled interior of the Texas filming set inside Dexter Studios.

Film Reception and the Trial of 2006

The film would not hit box office, but would become a cult classic in 2020, when scenes would be released online on Contact Touchscreen, owned by social media company Contact, immediately raising a cult following who would ask whether 2005's plane crash incident in the state of Arizona was not a real incident but a movie stunt for a sequel to the *Lights of the Shadows*, also asking whether there would ever be a sequel to the film. In 2027, Dexter Studios published a post on Contact Connect, announcing that there might or might not be plans for a sequel to the film.

In 3 October 2005, Flight LA205 had departed from Los Angeles LAX Airport to arrive at New Smyrna Beach NSB Airport in the Bahamas. After being hit by a sudden tornado, the aircraft was forced to crash land in Arizona, causing an explosion in the farms of Yuma County's Welton.

Following the incident of Flight LA205, Caleb Goldberg was led to trial by the US government, believed to be involved with the emergency crash landing, after officials stated that there had not been any dead bodies or injured people apart from the piloting crew members on the plane or anywhere near the crash site.

Caleb was accused of conspiring against the United States, plotting the crash landing and the tornado that hit the aircraft. Owner of Eagle Eye Media Network, Casey Monroe would also be led to trial, as footage of a fictional airplane crash with the EEN channel logo appeared in the movie, further raising questions.

After Feather Airlines, the company owning the airplane, distanced themselves from the event completely, suspicions began rising, especially after the flight's documents seemed to have been altered.

Caleb Goldberg would be a primary suspect to this case until the airplane's black box was found and recovered, immediately exposing the truth to the public. CEO of American company, Feather Airlines, Alexis Mitsotakis had signed an illegal deal with a logistics company in Miami, Florida, agreeing to deliver 40 tons of Quadrosilvanium, a highly flammable solid substance with liquefaction capabilities, used in engineering for its shapeshifting properties.

In order not to raise any suspicions, the company had not used any of their transport aircrafts and instead, they had given flight attendants traveling bags to carry onboard, leaving only the crew of the three pilots to fly the plane, and the company informing them that the Boiler P-95 was to be decommissioned for scrap in the Bahamas, after reaching its destination.

Caleb Goldberg and Casey Monroe were freed of all charges, immediately suing the company for not revealing the truth after the incident, letting the two of them be turned into scapegoats. The CEO of Feather Airlines was arrested and sentenced to lifetime imprisonment, and the company was obliged to pay 50.000.000$ to the American nation, later filing for bankruptcy in 2009.

The Cast

Budd Cipriani (as John): Born and raised in Chicago, Budd Cipriani has been a top actor since his first role in gangster film, *The Crew of Eight* in 1979. Often portraying villains, mafiosos or contract killers, Budd was not easily digested as a hero in films, but in 1999's *The Lights of the Shadows*, the audience loved his performance as John Emerson, kick-starting a new era in his career, as during the 2000s, Hollywood would often choose Budd for the role of FBI investigator in films and even the role of head of the CIA.

In 2008, the audience would be reintroduced to Budd playing the role of a villain in George Valentine's *Three Dimensions* movie franchise, as he played the role of contract assassin and mafia boss, *Uncle Vinnie*, being praised for his performance and reminding the world that anyone can play any role great, as long as they have passion for what they do.

Andrew Kimble (as Palmer): Known for his role in the *Destroyer* movie franchise and his successful career as an athlete in the Olympic Games, the bodybuilding community and the wrestling society, Andrew Kimble became one of the most iconic and well-recognized 80s action movie idols, immediately being selected to play in the film.

While originally, Caleb Goldberg wanted Andrew to portray John Emerson, Andrew's involvement as secretary of education left him little to no time to achieve his massive muscular status of the 80s, making Caleb decide to give him the role of Palmer. Andrew and Caleb had been friends for quite a long time, allowing for Andrew to influence Caleb's decisions during production of the movie.

Mathew Gilbert (as Adam Foster): Mathew Gilbert's role as consiglieri of the Lorenzo family in 1972's *Saint Man* was a career-defining moment for him as he would continue receiving proposals for such roles until the late 80s. During the 90s, Mathew portrayed various fictional government officials in films and even played the president of the United States twice.

His calm posture was what made him suitable for portraying Adam Foster in *The Lights of the Shadows* as Caleb wanted **someone that would look intimidating without moving an eyebrow**, according to his own statement in an interview.

Having Gilbert appear mostly on the left side of the screen in each scene was intentional, according to Caleb Goldberg, who wanted to portray Foster as a figure of dominance and authority.

Foster was calm and almost expressionless during these scenes, indicating that he was indeed very dangerous and scary, as well as unpredictable. His body language was what made Adam Foster a truly intimidating villain, rather than the fact he had developed the gas mentioned in the film.

To this day, Mathew recalls his role as Adam Foster, often joking about how mechanical and inhuman he was told to act and often being interrupted by Caleb who would continuously ask Mathew to play colder.

Emma Tyler: Greatly known for her role as Regina in TV series *The Nightwatch* (2004-today), Emma Tyler began her career in 1997 during her late teens, participating in comedy TV series and movies in minor roles. In 1998, she was selected to portray Leah Emerson after appearing in a gothic outfit and spikey punk hairstyle for Four Times Rock band's video clip of their song *Reply*, which she was a member of until 2005 when the girl band was disbanded.

Caleb Goldberg mentioned in an interview that his, then, sixteen-year-old daughter had shown him the video clip and he had immediately changed his mind about having a more traditional teenager appearance for Leah, creating a greater contrast between her and her father that would show the struggle of John to get closer to his teenage kid despite the fact his job and the way he was raised, do not allow him the liberty of being able to understand newer generations that easily.

Emma would play a significant role in *Three Dimensions* film franchise and later, she would appear in spy film series, *Secret Asset*.

Sarah Jordan (as Eda): Sarah Jordan is an American actress from Traverse City, beginning her career as an action movie star in 1992, playing minor roles in movies until her big break in the mid-2000s when she was chosen to play as villain Densley Corleone in both Tiger Entertainment's spinoff movies of the *Secret Asset* movie franchise, as well as the official videogames.

In 1998, Sarah Jordan was casted to play rookie police officer Eda, due to her excellent performance as a soldier suffering from PTSD in *Bagdad—Zero Hour*, the film adaptation of Derek Mahoney's novel by the same name.

Sarah almost never talks about *The Lights of the Shadows* in interviews as she considers it one of the worst films she has ever participated in.

Daffy Silverton (as Jeffry Pickens): The film would not be what *The Lights of the Shadows* was and still is as a film for its fans without the iconic performance by Daffy Silverton. Daffy had originally accepted the proposal happily, but after the film, he decided to sue Caleb Goldberg and Dexter Studios for the role they had given him, feeling that him portraying an unhinged, immoral and corrupt police officer had led to backlash from his fans.

Daffy even testified against Caleb Goldberg, Dexter Studios and even EEN channel during the trial of 2006, in hopes of his own case being brought back in the surface and finally receiving compensation by the company and Caleb.

Eventually, Daffy's testimony for feeling the movie had secret messages hidden inside it were dismissed by the court. To this day, Daffy seems to have settled in for a smaller role in TV series *The Nightwatch*, portraying Regina's caring father.

Andrew Locklear (as Etu): Born and raised in Beaverstale, Andrew Locklear helped the filming crew in more than just one way, as he would often show them locations within the forest that they had no knowledge of.

Upon being casted to play as Etu, his only demand was that the true story of the events occurring during the war between the tribes and the incompetence of the settlers to assist the Apache would be mentioned in the film. Being half Mexican, Andrew Locklear has played roles in many Mexican TV series since his teenage years in 1992.

Henry Rodriguez (as Quill): Henry is a Spanish actor, appearing mostly in American, British, French and Spanish comedy TV series. In 1998, he was cast by Tom Burkley to play Quill. While refusing the proposal at first, as Henry did not want to act in anything other than comedy TV series, he eventually decided to take part in the movie.

Him acting fearful during the film made his appearance notable to the Korean film industry, landing him a contract to play in *Bewitched Romance* in 2002, along Korean actress Byeol Choi. In 2009, Henry was cast to play in TV series *Babel A.D.*

Chris Pinewood (as Bob): Chris's career would see a rise during the 2000s, especially during his participation in sci-fi, police thriller TV series, *Babel A.D.*

in which he was a leading character from Season 2 onward. However, Chris has appeared in many 90s films as a secondary character.

Adrian Morgan (as Thatcher): Adrian Morgan is an inactive actor who portrayed Thatcher in *The Lights of the Shadows*. He decided to give up acting after film production was over.

Ronnie Buddy (as Ronnie): Having dominated the bodybuilding scene during the 90s, Buddy was invited by none other than Kimble himself, who convinced everyone they had to include his friend on set. It is said that more scenes with him acting had been filmed, however, due to his extremely brutal nature, any fighting or action scene he played in made him look more like a villain than one of the heroes and victims.

These scenes were removed, creating a huge gap between them, which was filled with filler scenes. Buddy's performance was good enough and in the next year, he would be casted to play the role of the president of the United States in TV series *Countdown*, before Dean Collin would replace him days before production of the series would begin and then, he would be recast to voice a character in tactical shooter videogame series *Cerberus*.

Lomaz Black (as Lazlo): Known as *Hollywood's Psychiatrist* for playing that role in almost every film since 1971, Lomaz Black was cast to play Doctor Lazlo in *The Lights of the Shadows* in 1998. Black and Goldberg had worked together many times in the past and they are even cousins.

Mike Alfonso (as Harold): Mike Alfonso is an Italian-American actor. In 1998, he was cast to play a doctor in *The Lights of the Shadows* film, proving that despite being still new to the industry, he could act well, leading to him being recast by Caleb Goldberg in future projects.

Victoria Simonova (as Olga): Being Caleb's wife and a truly successful 80s actress, Victoria immediately accepted Caleb's invitation for her to play a minor role in his film. It was Victoria's idea for Caleb to make changes to the script and instead of an ending that would show Leah and her father spending time together a few weeks after the events of the story, she told Caleb to write the ending that was shown in the film.

It was also Victoria's idea to show the contrast and the ongoing prejudice against post-Cold War Russia in the film, especially between older people, wanting to add more realism to the story and making John truly act like a soldier, loyal to his nation, rather than another person losing themselves in the woods of Beaverstale.

Victoria had previously helped her husband to create his documentary and she even lent him camera footage of locations she had filmed as a teenager for Caleb to use in *The Lights of the Shadows*. These scenes are notable as they seem different from the rest of the film and while most of the footage for the documentary looks like it has been shot by a different camera, these few scenes make an even greater contrast.

Alexandra Vice (as Nancy): Alexandra Vice has not made many appearances in movies as she is mainly a pop singer, however, in 1998, she was asked to take part in *The Lights of the Shadows* as well as perform a few guitar instrumental tracks for Dexter Studios to use in the film.

Kary Finch (as Joanne): More notable for her voice acting in dubbed anime and videogames, Kary Finch was cast to play the role of Joanne in the film. She fondly recalls the time spent in Beaverstale, mentioning how participating in this film made her close friends with many of the actors.

James Heuer (as Peter Morgan): more notable for his roles as the protagonist of TV series *Countdown* and later *Babel A.D.* James is an American-Canadian actor with a truly impressive career. In 1998, he was asked to participate as a guest star in *The Lights of the Shadows* and he agreed, after reading the premise of the film.

In 2007, during an interview, Heuer recalled how difficult it was for him not to laugh during the scenes his character would interact with Max.

Stan Kurtz (as Alex): Originally, Caleb wanted actor and scriptwriter, George Valentine, who was then playing the role of agent Leo in *Secret Asset*, having just replaced Marvin Fisher, who played Agent Tom Brown in the same franchise, eight years prior.

Dexter Studios' Tom Burkley insisted Valentine was not extremely muscular, making him less convincing for the role, despite Caleb Goldberg's vision of the film moving more toward the horror genre territory.

Eventually, they invited Stan Kurtz, notably known for his role as Alexander Irons in movie franchise *Unkillable*, who agreed to play as a guest star provided he'd keep his alias, Alex during the scene and that they would make a reference to the franchise he'd been starring in.

The fact that many viewers had begun mentioning that George Valentine looked like a younger lookalike of Kurtz, ever since Valentine had appeared on TV and cinemas in the late 80s to early 90s, led to the former asking the company to apologize for the ridicule they had caused him.

Eventually, Dexter Studios agreed to make an effort to apologize by renting one of his five Valkyrie mansions for the film. In 2008, Valentine would be asked to provide the script for film series *Three Dimensions*, while also working on another sequel of *Secret Asset*.

After finding out they were about to cast Kurtz to play the role of Chase Irons in the film, George Valentine undertook special training to convince New

Dimension Films to give him the role instead. Due to trademark issues with the Irons surname, both Nuclear Entertainment and New Dimension Films agreed on the latter present Chase Irons as a relative of Alexander Irons, making a reference to their franchise, *Unkillable*.

Samuel Garcia: Despite being a skateboarding star of the 90s, extreme sports champion Samuel Garcia was cast to play the role of Max as a guest star. Acting as comic relief during the final scenes of the movie, Samuel Garcia, who had no acting skills, managed to play his role in a convincing way, being later asked to play in comedies during early to mid-2000s.

Sarah Doherty: Texas born and raised, Sarah Doherty is of Japanese, Azeri, Texan and Mexican lineage. While fans of Sarah know that her first role on the big screen was in 2004's movie *PrErase*, when she was 16 years old at the time of filming in 2003, she had also played minor roles in kids TV series during the late 90s.

Sarah was ideal for the role of Victoria, due to her confident nature as an actress, despite her young age, being younger even than Emma Tyler at the time. While Victoria is presented as a short teenager girl in the movie, in contrast to Leah who even appears tall during the scenes, the reality is much different, as Sarah is considered tall, at 172 while Emma is short at 162.

In order to convince audiences that—then 158—actress Emma Tyler was tall, they would often film her from lower angles, or zoom closer to her upper body to hide the fact that she was wearing boots to make her taller.

Caleb Goldberg would also rewrite the scene where Victoria and Leah chat with each other, making them talk on the phone rather than having to be in the same room.

The contrast between the two would become even more apparent while filming *Three Dimensions*, where Sarah, playing the role of Grace Norton, would show her true height in the scenes of the sequels to the original movie, when the two actresses would appear together on screen.

For the very same reason, George Valentine would have to wear special boots to hide the fact he was taller than Sarah only by a point, otherwise the role would be given back to Stan Kurtz whose height is 1,80.

Sarah has had quite a successful career ever since *The Lights of the Shadows* and *PrErase*, having played in TV series *Babel A.D.* from the second season onwards, as well as *The Nightwatch*, and having taken part in voice acting various anime dubbed and videogame characters, such as Christine in future warfare videogame *Line of Glory*, Nallary in RPG videogame *Lords of War* and Eva Yarova in tactical shooter videogame *Cerberus*.

Trivia

Valkyrie Mansion was actually one of the five mansions owned by George Valentine. This one in particular exists in Budapest, while the other four Valkyrie mansions exist in France, London, Tianducheng city suburbs and Texas.

EEN channel had lent footage from an airplane crash incident in Panama, as well as footage from a tornado in Florida and a huge traffic jam in California. Caleb Goldberg managed to wrap the footage into a scene, adding footage he had obtained by filming an airplane flying toward an airport with a Canon 518 SV Super 8 Camera. The result was stunning, making viewers believe that Dexter

Studios had used props to film it, despite the entire movie showing its low budget nature.

Sports car company, Oiseau Automobiles, owner Sebastien Beaufort had completely forgotten the company had a factory in Beaverstale, as operations had seized in said factory since 1974. Upon hearing about the film, he agreed on giving the factory to Dexter Studios for free.

After turning all of their vehicles hydrogen powered, Oiseau Automobiles hosted a 10-day event in that factory to celebrate the new models introduced to the market.